To Felicia

Outside the Lines

A REBEL HEARTS NOVEL

EMILY GOODWIN

Outside the Lines
Book One in The Rebel Hearts Series
Copyright © 2015 by Emily Goodwin
Edited by Kristina Circelli of Red Rose Editing

To Madelyn, my littlest princess

Other books by Emily Goodwin:

Contagious
Deathly Contagious
Contagious Chaos
The Truth is Contagious

Unbound
Reaper
Moonlight

Beyond the Sea

Stay
All I Need

Never Say Never

Outside the Lines
First Comes Love
Not Safe for Work

ACKNOWLEDGMENTS

It takes a village to write a book, right? Or maybe that's to raise a child. In my case, it's both. I need to say a big "thank you" to my husband, parents, grandma, and in laws for helping me with the tot so I could have the much needed quiet time to write this book. And another huge "thank you" to Christine Stanley, Erin Hayes, Lori Parker, the gals in the BIC group, and the wonderful ladies on my street team for believing in my work, giving me encouragement, and getting excited right along with me for this release.

Chapter One

Should I be ashamed I'm walking into a sex toy store with a wallet full of cash my grandmother sent me for my twenty-fifth birthday? And that I plan to spend said cash on a new vibrator since mine shorted out in the tub? I adjust my purse and pull my dark-blonde hair over my face, surreptitiously concealing my identity in case of major crisis number one happening: seeing someone I know.

I inhale, swallow down any lingering ounce of prude I have in me, and step into the shop. Normally I'd one click this sucker from Amazon, but after two weeks of no B.O.B.—and a year of no-real life boyfriend—I'm desperate. And why pay for next-day shipping when the sex toy shop was on my way home from work?

Someone moans and I freeze. What the fuck? Are people actually trying out the toys? No, that makes no sense. It's porn. It has to be porn. The same moan fills the store again. And again. It's rhythmic, like it's stuck on repeat.

"Come on in, honey, and she'll stop," someone calls from the counter, hidden behind a display of glow-in-the-dark condoms. Oh, and a few flavored ones too.

She'll stop? I blink, my legs still frozen, and then it hits me that instead of a motion-censored bell ringing, a lady in the throes of ecstasy moans. Fitting. Very fitting.

I step inside and look around. I've never been inside a sex shop before, though it's not because I have anything against them. With the lack of real peen in my life, I've come to rely on this sort of thing. But I always order online. What's the anonymity of the internet for, anyway?

"Can I help you find anything?" the woman at the counter asks. Her name tag lets me know she goes by "Vixen." That has to be a fake sex store worker name, right? She's short and plump with shoulder-length hair that's dyed in various shades of red. I stare at it a little too long before diverting my eyes. I like it. But my boss would have a bitch fit if I showed up to work with colorful hair.

"I'm just looking," I say and remind myself not to feel embarrassed. The woman works at the Adult Toybox, after all. She's seen it all and then some. Still, there's something about a single woman walking alone into one of these places that makes you feel like society is pointing their finger at you.

Well, fuck you and your social norms, society.

I walk forward and turn to the left, going down an aisle of games for lovers. Games that require two people. Or three … or four or more, as the front of that box says. I peruse down the aisle, curiosity replacing embarrassment, and whimsically think of a day when I can come in here with a boyfriend and buy something kinky for the night.

Edible undies?

Nah, too predictable and probably too sticky.

Butt plugs?

My cheeks clench at the thought. Nope. Definite no.

Handcuff, blindfolds, and a flogger?

Still predicable, but something I'm willing to try.

I pass through a display of lingerie, stifling a laugh at a male thong with an elephant truck to hold the shaft, and find what I am looking for. I actually smile when I see the shelves full of dildos and vibrators. I pick them up, looking at the boxes for … I really don't know. Details? I just need something waterproof.

"That's a good one," Vixen says, startling me. The woman is like a cat. I didn't hear her coming. "I have it and love it."

"Oh, that's good to know," I mumble.

"My husband likes to use it on me too. You can charge it on the wall and it's super quiet, so the kids won't hear even if they're in the next room."

I know my eyes are as big as saucers right now. I can't turn and look at her just yet. I blink, having to say something to break the tension.

"Is it waterproof?" I blurt.

"You betcha. And it has multiple settings. Want

me to show you how it works?"

She takes the demo off the shelf and for one horrified second I think she's going to hike her skirt and literally show me. My heart settles back into my chest when she holds it out and pushes a button, then turns up a dial.

"Hear that? Barely anything."

"That is nice," I say. "I'll take it."

She smiles. "I'll put it by the register so you can keep looking."

"Nah, I'm good with just that today."

"All right." She turns and we walk to the counter together in awkward silence. She slips behind the register and I dig my hand into my purse, feeling for my wallet. I have a moment of panic when I realize I didn't look at the price tag of the Silent Knight vibrator and hope I have enough cash to cover it. I could use the cash I had then put the rest on my card, but I'm close to maxing out that card—as well as my other one—and need to minimize expenses until payday at the end of the week.

"This," Vixen says and grabs a small white bottle covered in red Xs and Os. "This stuff is great. Just put a little on your clit before the action and it'll enhance the pleasure."

I will myself not to blush. Hearing someone talk so openly was refreshing, but a little unexpected.

"After three kids," she goes on and scans the vibrator. I watch with wide eyes as the total pops up

6

on the little screen. Thank God. I have enough cash to pay for it and pick up food on the way home. "I need a little pick-me-up before the hubs and I get down and dirty, ya know?"

"Yeah," I say and unzip my wallet. I considered myself an open book, but hearing Vixen talk about every detail of her sex life makes me feel like I had a lot more opening up to do. I pay and take my bag.

"Have fun tonight!" Vixen says as I turn to go.

"I will, thanks," I say automatically before I realize she's referring to me having some solo time with this neon-pink new best friend. Whatever. I smile and shake my head. "Have a good rest of your day."

"I get off in an hour," she says. "I can manage."

I hike my purse back up on my shoulder, not exactly sure what's accumulated in it make it so heavy, and push open the door, signaling a moan from the censor. I get one foot through the threshold when two women come up, stopping and stepping to the side to let me through.

"Felicity?" one of them asks.

On its own accord, my head turns to the source of my name. Then my brain kicks in a millisecond too late, reminding me that getting noticed was major crisis number one. But as soon as I see the angelic face of Mindy fucking Abraham, I'm in major crisis number two, which is seeing Mindy fucking Abraham anytime, anywhere, let alone here, several towns over from where we grew up.

It's amazing how just one glance at a person can make you feel so much.

And right now I'm feeling like we're back in high school and she's sitting at the popular table after being the new girl for two days while I've been trying for two years to get those kids to even know my name. I'm feeling like I just saw her making out with Todd Overman, my crush since seventh grade who I was sure would eventually fall for my nerd-girl charm and make lots of babies with me. Just looking at her flawless skin and perfect hair reminds me of everything I wasn't back then, of everything I'm still not now, and how unfair it is that people like Mindy fucking Abraham get ahead in life just by being pretty.

From the day we met nearly ten years ago, that woman has made it her personal mission to one up me in any and everything. Except, not really. She's just naturally better than me, and her lack of trying only made me hate her even more when we were teens.

Just one glance at her and the self-esteem I've spent years building comes crashing down and I'm shaken to my core. It took me until I became an adult to finally accept myself—to an extent. I still have a ways to go, I know—and embrace my flaws and fly my freak flag high with pride. And yet standing here, feeling like a sixteen-year-old girl hugging my X-Men notebook to my chest as I blink back tears and feel the burn of embarrassment in my cheeks, questioning everything.

Fuck.

After a mishap at MIT, I ended up graduating from our local college, and low and behold, a few classes with Mindy fucking Abraham. She never said anything to me, never acted like she had once mocked me to the point of tears over my Harry Potter obsession.

"Nope," I say and reach into my purse, fingers catching on the straps as I madly wrestle the contents for my sunglasses. I stab myself in the face in my haste to put them on. "You must have gotten me confused with someone else."

"Oh, sorry," Mindy says and walks past. "You have a familiar face."

"I get that a lot," I say with a nod and keep walking.

"I swear that's her," Mindy whispers to the woman next to her. I keep walking, not stopping until I'm next to my Malibu. I press the button on the door handle and plop into the driver's seat, exhaling. I'm a bit ashamed for letting myself come undone so easily. I shake my head, put my parcels in the seat next to me, and start the car. I'm calmed when Taylor Swift comes on, reminding me to shake all this off.

I grab Taco Bell on the way, thinking more and more about trying out the new vibrator the closer I get to home. I pull into the narrow, one-car garage attached to my town house, sliding sideways out of the car to avoid hitting my bike.

"Hey, Ser Pounce," I say to a fat orange and white cat that slinks around my ankles when I walk into the house. I kick off my black kitten heels and pad through the laundry room into the kitchen, sitting at the small island counter. I dig into my food as I unpackage the vibrator, more excited than I should be to discover it's fully charged. I toss it on my bed for later, do a bit of much-needed housework, and then log onto my computer.

I'm tempted to look up Mindy on Facebook, but eventually resist. Nothing good comes from online stalking, and I don't want to deal with the ill feelings I know I'll get when I see how perfect her life is.

But hey, it's not like my life is bad. I'm new to this town, having moved here six months ago for work. I hadn't made any good friends yet, besides my boss and his boyfriend. I wasn't particularly worried. I knew I'd make friends eventually. I still talked to my best friend, Erin, pretty much daily online or via text message, and I had a large group of online gamer friends. I couldn't complain about being lonely, that was for sure.

I text Erin, telling her about my awkward sex shop experience (her hatred of all things Mindy is almost as deep as mine), then settle in at my computer to play League of Legends for just an hour or so. Ser Pounce curls up in my lap, not bothered by my talking and angry muttering during the game.

At two AM I realize I need to get my ass in bed or I'm going to be dragging in the morning. Figuring if I skip the new workout routine I'm trying to stick to—it's not like I do much anyway—I can sleep in another forty-five minutes and be okay. I change into my PJs and collapse into bed, finding the neon-pink vibrator tangled in the sheets. I pick it up, wrapping my fingers around its rubber tip, and bite my lip.

Well, I do sleep better after a good orgasm, after all.

Chapter Two

"What are your plans for the weekend?" Mariah asks me the next day at work. I yawn and down my second cup of coffee. One good orgasm wasn't enough, and I ended up staying up way past my already late bedtime seeing if I could outdo the last until I eventually passed out. Not my proudest moment. And now my wrist hurt. Cue all the shame.

"I'm going home for my brother's bridal shower. Well, not his, I guess, but his fiancé's. My future sister-in-law," I added, raising my eyebrows.

Mariah laughed, her strawberry-blonde hair moving around her face. "I take it you don't like her?"

I turn away from my computer, swiveling the chair around with a creak. "I don't really know her, that's all. It's weird to think my little brother is spending the rest of his life—give or take a divorce or two—with this girl that I've only met a few times. And she's going to be part of my family and I'll have to spend Christmas and Easter and Thanksgiving and … and other holidays that I can't think of right now with her. Forever."

Mariah, who's been married for over ten years with two kids, laughs again. "I hate my brother's wife," she says softly. "She's a total gold-digging bitch. Joke's on her because my brother squanders all his money and can't put anything away to save his life.

We're all waiting on that divorce to happen. Hopefully before he knocks her up."

"What about you?" I ask. "Any fun plans?"

Mariah puts her hands back on her keyboard, quickly typing as she talks. "We're taking the kids to the beach and then the children's museum. It should be fun and they will be exhausted by the time we come home. That's horrible, isn't it? I look forward to my kids being worn out and quiet."

I smile. "The boys are eight now?"

"Nine. And so hyper." Her steel-blue eyes widen. "They never stop."

I press enter and wait for the page on the website I'm building to save.

"I should feel bad that I look forward to bedtime, right?" Mariah says. "I love those kids."

"Nah, I get exhausted cleaning the litter box and cleaning cat dishes. You're fine."

Mariah gives me another smile then goes back to work. I look at the clock, see I still have two hours until lunch, and get back to work. I'm building a custom website from scratch for a gardening company, and they've given me pretty loose reins to run with the project. Setting up sites is a cakewalk for me and gets boring day after day. But this job has minimal stress, it pays well, and I don't have to deal with people face to face, which is the biggest win of all.

I design a few graphics just because I can, email

them to the art director for approval, then spend the rest of the morning customizing HTML for the client. I take my lunch into the break room, sitting at a large wooden table that's under an air-conditioning vent, and shiver. The room is by far the best break room I've had at a job, with a snack bar, fridge full of free drinks, and donuts and bagels every morning. It's clean and well decorated, like the break room of a big company should be.

I dig into my food while texting Erin about designing our costumes for Wizard World in Chicago later this summer. She wants to go a Sailor Jupiter—again.

I text her: *Let's do Batman and Superman instead. You get first pick.*

She replies with: *You mean Catwoman and Wonder Woman, right?*

I shake my head as I bite into my turkey sandwich. *No, femme versions of the guys.*

She takes a minute to reply, and I know she's considering it. Finally she agrees, and we plan to come up with costume ideas while I'm in town for the weekend.

"Hey, Felicity," Cameron says.

I turn and smile. "Hey," I say once I finish chewing. "What's up, boss man?"

Cameron waves his hand in the air. "Nothing, nothing. How are you? Your hair looks super cute today."

I raise an eyebrow and set my sandwich down. My hair is in a messy French braid. "What do you want?"

He never compliments my hair. Just yesterday he was bitching about my split ends and lack of volume. Cameron walks through the break room and sits on the edge of the table across from me. He's dressed like he walked off a Ralph Lauren photoshoot for business casual wear, and smells like one of those fold-over cologne pages from a magazine. He's always so put together.

"Well, as you know, Marissa is due soon."

"Doesn't she have like a month left?"

"Three weeks," he says and puts a hand on the table leaning in toward me. "But she had an appointment today and it's looking like she's going to have to go on bedrest until she pops out that baby. Blood pressure issues or whatever. So, she's done at the end of the week until she comes back from maternity leave. Which leads me to asking … can you do me a favor?"

I hike an eyebrow. "Does it require a substantial amount of time or energy?"

"Not at all."

"Then maybe. Tell me what it is before I agree to anything."

"She's has a customer service appointment scheduled for next week. Can you go instead? The office is just across town. I'll even buy you lunch that day."

I purse my lips together. Customer service? Face to face? Helping people with computer problems common sense could figure out. Yuck. "Aren't I a little overqualified for this?" I ask. Hell, I'm overqualified for my job of designing sites, but this job pays well and offers twice the benefits as my old one.

Cameron narrows his eyes. "Do you want those free passes and day off for Comic Con?"

"You're evil."

"Not quite as evil as pairing that shirt with those pants."

"Hey!" I say and look down at the blue dress pants I'm wearing. My shirt is blue too. "It matches."

"No, it doesn't. At all." He laughs and shakes his head, going back to boss mode. "Seriously though, Lissy. It would save me so much trouble if you could do this. I know you're ahead on the garden site and don't have another client lined up until the middle of next week. I have a temp coming in for her, but not until *next* Monday. Please do this for me." He put his hands together. "Please, Lissy!"

"Fine. But just the one?"

"It should be just the one."

"Why don't I like the sound of that?"

"Because I can't be sure there won't be calls that need coverage until the temp gets in."

I huff and take a bite of my food. "It's fine. I can handle it. But you know how I feel about having to

16

talk to people. And lunch better be good."

Cameron laughs, the smile pulling up his full lips. He's a good-looking man and he knows it. "You're so easy to bribe when it comes to food."

I shrug. "Yeah, I do like to eat."

He raises an eyebrow. "It's not fair you eat like shit and never gain weight. I take one bite of a muffin and it's on my hips the next day." He smacks his own ass.

I run my eyes over him. "You look pretty damn good yourself."

"Only because I work my ass off in the gym. You wouldn't be saying that three years ago before I met Adam. He's whipped my butt into shape in more ways than one."

I let out a snort of laugher. "Maybe I'll have him be my personal trainer. Someday."

Cameron crosses his arms. "Let's be honest. You don't work out. Remember how running club went for you?"

I make a face and sigh. The only running I did was run late for club. Everyone was gone by the time I got there, which worked out fine since the donut store across the street opened only a half hour later. I wanted to get in shape in case of an apocalypse, but let's be real: no one really likes jogging. It's a lie they tell themselves and other people.

"Just enjoy that fast metabolism while you can, honey."

"I plan to. My mom says the same thing. She had hers until she had kids, so I'm good for, oh, the rest of my life."

"Lissy," Cameron says, seeing past my joke. "You are not going to be alone forever."

"I know," I say, and honestly believe it. I'll find someone eventually. I'm only twenty-five, after all. I have five more years until my biological clock turns into a ticking time bomb and I sob uncontrollably at my thirtieth birthday as I sit alone in my living room over not finding a husband. I'm not there yet, thank God. I keep busy. I'm happy. It took fucking years, but I like myself, my life.

Call me a nerd, geek, loser ... whatever, I didn't care—though I do prefer *intellectual badass* over all those—I've accepted myself and don't feel ashamed and the need to hide my love over, well, anything.

"Are we still shopping after work?" Cameron asks.

"Yeah, I don't have a dress for the shower this weekend."

"Great, because Adam's got a late session today and canceled dinner plans. Shopping then drinks?"

"Sounds good to me."

"Damn, girl," Cameron says when I step out of

the dressing room. "Where the hell have you been hiding those?" His eyes widen as he takes in the large amount of cleavage the dress shows off.

"Under work-appropriate attire," I say, feeling a bit self-conscious in the dress. It's a halter top, white with blue polka dots and belted around the waist. It's cute, I can't deny that, but I'm unsure of how it looks on me. I'm of average build, but I'm far from *in shape*. "Does it look okay?" I ask, wrinkling my nose at my reflection.

"Yes. Way okay. And it's on sale. You're getting it and wearing it."

I nod. At least this was painless. "Fine." I step closer to the three-way mirror, making a mental note to spend some time outside and get a tan before the wedding. "You don't think it's too short?"

Cameron shakes his head. "No, it's perfect for a bridal shower. Why are you worried? I've seen some of the costumes you've worn to Comic Con."

I shrug. "I'm playing a character, it's different." It's hard to explain to some people. Taking on a role lets you channel whoever you're dressed as. I'll be going to this shower as me, as the older sister of Jake Hills not as Ahri, the nine-tailed fox.

"Do you have Spanx at home?" he asks.

I raise an eyebrow. I did, but they are horribly uncomfortable so I tossed them in the trash the same day I threw away the expensive anti-wrinkle cream I'd recently bought. My body jiggles in certain places. I am going to age and get wrinkle eventually. Why agonize over it?

"Not wearing them." I look at myself again, eyes instantly going to my hips. Maybe I should get more. Double up on the Spanx, actually. It'll take a few inches off my middle.

Fuck. No. I'm not doing that. I am who I am, and I don't look that bad considering I eat like crap and don't work out. I never wear Spanx or other body-slimming witchery at Comic Con, and I feel like a fucking rockstar when I'm dressed up as one of my favorite characters.

I want to feel like that when I'm just me.

Why is it so hard?

"Get changed," Cameron says. "And then we'll talk shoes."

We leave the mall a half hour later. Cameron convinced me not to wear my Tardis shoes with the dress despite the fact the color was perfect. I got a pair of lower white heels instead, something practical yet stylish that I could easily move around in while decorating the venue for the shower. We grab dinner and drinks and it's late by the time I get home.

Like usually, I stay up too late watching TV, sleep in, and have to rush around like a mad woman to get all my shit done before packing an overnight bag and driving the hour and a half to my mom and dad's. I sing along with Rachel Platten on the way, and time passes quickly. A little guilt rises inside of me when I stop by the bakery Erin runs with her sisters before stopping home to see my mom, but I know if I go home first I'll never get out. Mom's a talker.

There's a parking spot right in front of the pink storefront, which stands out next to the red brick fronts that surround it. Located on the main street and right in the middle of this town, Sweet Treats sticks out and is always busy. I grab my purse and get out, locking the Malibu as I hurry out of the misting rain and into the store. A little bell dings above me and I snicker as I remember the moaning lady at the sex shop.

I'm so mature sometimes.

"Hey!" I call over the small crowd gathered in front of a display of colorful cupcakes. Erin's sister, Andrea, smiles and waves.

"She's in the back," she tells me and boxes up a cupcake for a little girl. I pass by and duck behind the counter. Erin is frosting a cake when I step through double doors into the back room. She looks up and beams.

"About time! I was wondering if I was going to have to call out a search party."

I laugh and shake my head. We've been friends since middle school, and though we've gone a while without seeing each other since I took this job, nothing is ever awkward around this girl. "I run on my own time."

"I've noticed. How was the drive?"

"Not bad, actually. Traffic flowed, which means I'll get stuck when I go home for sure."

"I'm almost done," she says. "I'm just doing the first layer now."

"Have anything to taste test?" I ask.

"Actually yes," she replies and carefully spins the cake. "Not really to test, but there's a batch of cupcakes that didn't turn out the right shade of green. Over there." She uses a spatula to point. I shuffle over and grab one. The green is kind of a puke color, but the cupcake tastes delicious.

Erin is washing pink frosting off her hands by the time I'm done eating. We go into the tiny break room to catch up for a few.

"I like the blonde," Erin says, eyeing my hair.

"Thanks. I figured I'll leave it for a while before going back to my original color. It's kind of a pain to keep up with."

A natural blonde herself, Erin laughs. "Yeah, but aren't dark roots showing trendy now? Or was that last season? Er, maybe last year?"

"Your guess is as good as mine."

We chat about work, our Comic Con costumes again, and how annoying Erin's husband David is. Really, he's a good guy and is good to Erin. She married him rather young while they were still both in college and I couldn't think of anyone better for my best friend.

"What kind of wedding duties do you have to do

tonight?" she asks as we walk to the front of the store.

"I'm not really sure. I think just dinner at my parents, house then get to the country club a few hours before the shower to decorate." I roll my eyes. "Is it really going to take that long to decorate for a shower? I get going all out for a wedding, but for a shower ... come on."

Erin laughs. "I'll be there like half an hour before with the cake. And your new sister-in-law *is* going all out. The cake she ordered cost as much as a wedding cake. You don't even want to know what the actual cake for the wedding looks like. It's gorgeous and big, and I'm excited to make it, but damn, her parents must have some money."

"They do," I say and feel bad that I don't know what they do. I should know this girl better, right? I pull my sweater closed, the mist had turned into rain, and give Erin a one-armed hug. "See you tomorrow."

"See ya. Have fun tonight."

I force a smile. "I'm sure it will be loads."

I tip the glass of wine, getting the last bit of red moscato. Waste not, right? I set the empty glass down on the coffee table next to me and listen to my brother tell what I assume is a funny story about work. Everyone is laughing, but I've zoned out a bit, thinking of who I could take as a date to the wedding. It was still a while away. I had time to find someone. Maybe even a boyfriend.

And if not, there's always Cameron. He'd at least be well dressed.

I look at the clock, wondering how much longer it will be before my dad orders pizza. My eyes wander around the living room. I know Mom's nervous about what Danielle and her parents think of the house.

I'm fond of my childhood home, of course, but it really is nice. Mom and Dad kept it that way, with upgrades every few years, redecorating, and obsessive cleaning. I didn't realize how much work went into it all until I moved out and had my own house to take care of. Along with the house, they have the cabins by the lake, renting out to vacationers who come to the serene town of Mistwood, Michigan. Between managing the dock and the rental boats, maintaining the Pinterest-worthy cabins, and keeping their own house clean, I don't know how Mom and Dad do it.

My brother and Danielle are sitting on the love seat, arms linked and looking so in love. Jake is tall like Dad, but has dark-brown hair like Mom and me. We both have green eyes, much unlike our parents, who have brown and hazel eyes. People say they can tell we are siblings, but I've never seen it. He's three years younger than me and has been a pain in the ass his whole life, but he is my baby brother and I love

24

him. I want him to be happy. He's a good guy and deserves it.

Danielle, on the other hand ... well, I don't know. I hope she's worthy of my brother. I try not to obviously scrutinize her. She teaches sixth grade history here in Mistwood, so I assume the woman has patience to deal with pre-pubescent teens day in and day out. She is petite and pretty, with auburn hair and freckles dotted across her cheeks. They've been dating about a year and a half, and got engaged a few months before I took the job in Grand Rapids, making it hard for me to actually get to know her. She's polite, excitedly talking wedding plans and details with the moms while the guys talked sports.

"Well," Jake says and stands, giving Danielle a hand up. "You two better get going so you don't miss your reservation." His eyes fall on me.

"Where am I going?" I ask, pushing my hair back.

"Dinner," Jake says, eyebrows raising, giving me a look that says I'm supposed to know this.

"Why me?" I blurt. He did say the two of us, meaning me and Danielle.

"All the bridesmaids are going," Danielle says with a smile. "And you're a bridesmaid."

"Oh," I say and shake my head. "Okay. Uh, when are we going?" I glance down at my Star Wars leggings and oversized black shirt. My hair had been up and down in a twisted bun all day and was currently hanging in a tangled mess around my makeup-free face.

"We should leave in no more than ten minutes," Danielle says, voice edging on annoyance.

"I'll get changed," I say and stand, hurrying up to my old room. Great. How was I going to get ready in time? I unzip my bag and throw out all the clothes I brought. I hadn't packed much, since I anticipated lounging around the house, the bridal shower, then going home.

I trade my leggings for dark jeans and the baggy T-shirt for a white tank top. I pull a gray button-up cardigan on, buttoning it halfway as I rush into the bathroom. I splash cold water on my face, dry it, then apply eyeliner, foundation, and mascara as fast as I can. I speed brush my teeth and comb my fingers through my hair. The natural waves are out in full force thanks to the rain and humidity. There's no hope, so I rake it to the side and braid it. I'm halfway down the stairs before I remember I don't have shoes, turn around, trip, and scramble to get them.

I make it back down in eight-and-a-half minutes.

"Thanks for going," Jake says quietly to me and hands me the keys to my Malibu. Apparently, I'm the DD tonight too. "I really want Danny to feel like part of the family."

I smile. "Of course. I want her to as well. And I don't know her, so it would be a great way to get to know her."

Jake beams, his eyes glazing over. Shit, he's in

deep. I broaden my smile, hating that a tiny bit of jealousy rolls around inside me. I want to be in love too. I want to plan a shower and a wedding and have everyone tell me how beautiful I will look in my dress.

Someday.

Maybe.

No.

It will happen.

Ugh.

I grab my purse and lead the way through the garage, unlocking the car. Danielle holds a pink Coach umbrella in one hand, the other on her head to keep her hair from blowing wild. The rain has picked up, and so has the wind.

"Hopefully your wedding day won't be like this," I say and get into the car. Danielle closes her umbrella, tucking it down by her feet, and gives me a horrified look. How dare I even mention rain and her wedding day?

"It's usually nice here in July." I smile. "So don't worry." I mentally curse at myself. Way to start a convo. "So," I begin. "Do you have pretty much everything done?"

Danielle relaxes against the seat. "Pretty much. I have one final fitting for the dress, but that's not until a month before the wedding. I'm trying to lose a few more pounds of course."

I raise my eyebrows and cast a glance at her. She is thin enough already. Why brides always think they

27

had to be model thin … I'll never know. "I think you look great," I tell her honestly.

"Thanks," she says and lets out a breath. "I don't look like the girl wearing my dress in the magazine ad."

If possible, my eyebrow hikes even higher. I turn onto the main road and head into town. "You do know those ads are Photoshopped as fuck, right?"

She twists, giving me that same startled look. "Yeah, I'm sure they are a bit."

I laugh. "Not just a bit. They are a lot. I worked a graphic design job for two whole weeks and was given photos to manipulate the hell out of. I felt evil to all womankind for doing that, hence the quitting. And it didn't pay well. At all."

Danielle just nods. "Well, whatever. I still want to look good."

This isn't going so well. "I'm sure you will. You're really pretty. And Jake has always been super picky. So knowing he chose you means he thinks you're really pretty too."

"Thanks." She smiles. "So, you program software, right?"

"I used to. I took a new job in Grand Rapids like half a year ago. I build websites."

She nods. "I'm so bad with computers. I can use Word and log onto Facebook and that's pretty much it. I couldn't even think about making a website."

"It's really easy," I say. "Well, for me. But I like

that stuff."

"It sounds complicated to me. Sometimes I have to have my students help me hook up my printer."

I laugh. "It surprises me how difficult it is for some people. But I guess that's normal, ya know? It's my thing. I like taking shit apart and adding new gadgets to my electronics at home."

"Makes sense. Why'd you change jobs?"

I shrug. "The new job pays twice as much and it was a chance to get out of this town for a while."

"Hmmm," she says and messes with her hair, which managed to stay stick straight and smooth despite the weather. "I have too many friends to leave here."

I know a backhanded insult when I hear one. "I stay in touch with mine."

"The bakery is owned by your best friend, right?"

"Yep, Erin. She's great."

Danielle smiles again. "I was impressed with everything she showed me."

"Yeah, Erin is super talented. She's been into baking since we were kids. That's how we met, actually. We were paired together in seventh grade Home Economics class."

"You guys have been friends for a long time."

"Yeah. She likes the same stuff I do." I drum my fingers on the steering wheel. A few more minutes tick by.

"So, uh, what do you like to do for fun?" I ask,

trying to keep a conversation going.

"I work out and have the girls over for wine night at least once a week."

"Wine night sounds fun." I like wine, and I like the night. "You guys just sit around and drink?"

"Kind of," she says and laughs like it's something super naughty. "We take turns bringing a bottle and some sort of dessert. We watch a show, like *Keeping up with the Kardashians* or *The Bachelor*, and drink and gossip. It's a lot of fun. If you lived closer, I'd invite you," she says with a smile and I know—and hope— she's lying through her teeth.

A few minutes pass, and I try not to let the silence turn awkward and bother me. I tap my fingers on the steering wheel in tempo with the music. Danielle makes small talk the rest of the way, and the fifteen-minute drive to the restaurant seems to take twice as long. If this girl wasn't marrying my brother, I'd never talk to her. We have nothing in common.

We get to the restaurant at 6:23 and hurry through the rain. Five well-dressed women are already seated. I guess they had more than ten minutes notice of this event. Supposedly I did too, and really, I probably did. I'm spacey like that.

"Sorry we're late," Danielle says and I can see her side-eye me, letting her friends know it's my fault.

I slide into a chair, glad there is already a glass of red wine in each spot. I don't consider getting somewhere seven minutes before a reservation "late."

"Hi," I say. "I'm Jake's sister."

The women murmur "hello" and go through introductions. I sip the wine and nod along, trying to remember everyone's names. I'm not really a shy person, but sitting here with a group of girls who've been friends for years makes me retreat inside myself a bit. My cheese ravioli is good, and I get out my phone and Google costume ideas when the conversation turns to sharing sex stories. I have no recent sex stories to share, unless my adventures with the neon-pink Silent Knight count.

"What about you?" a pretty blonde asks. Her name is Chloe. Or Zoey. Hell if I know. "Do you have a boyfriend?"

"Not at the moment," I respond.

"Oh, well, never mind then." She doesn't look surprised by my response.

"Do you have a boyfriend?" I ask.

"I just got rid of mine," she huffs. "Total pain in the ass and so clingy. I want to date casually for a while, ya know, just for fun. You're only young once!"

I smile and go back to looking up costumes on my phone. This is going to be a long night.

Since my parents have the worst internet connection in the whole wide world, I ended up going to bed early and waking at eight, which is early to me when I don't have to be at work. I eat breakfast with Dad then go for a walk on the sandy path from their house to the lake. The rain has gone and so have the clouds. The morning still holds a chill, but as I look at the dawn light reflecting off the choppy water, I know it's going to be a good day.

The sound of the small waves crashing against the rocky shore soothes me, and takes me back at the same time. I spent more hours than I can count out here as a child, sitting on the dock, playing in the woods and water, pretending, imagining, fantasizing that my life was grand and adventurous and I was someone else, someone important destined with a world-saving task.

Losing myself in fiction and fantasy was my escape then, and it is now. There were many, many times when Mom and Dad sent Jake down to the water's edge to check on me, making sure I hadn't fallen asleep and rolled off the dock into the water. That happens once and no one forgets about it. I'd be down here with a book, and often times Erin was with me doing the same. Jake teased us a great bunch, though he ended up joining in on our reenactments a few times.

That led me to the world of Cosplay and finding solace in fandoms, in knowing there were other people like me who longed for more, for adventure, for feeling like more than a tiny ant on this planet we call earth.

Not everyone gets it, especially hormonal teenagers who were still trying to figure their own shit out. Erin and I weren't the only geeks at our high school, but we were one of the few, battling between being ourselves and being what was expected. I had my moments of "fuck societal norms" that quickly passed, and it wasn't until I was in college that it really stuck.

I'm not and never will be that girl. I tried and hated it, then hated myself for wasting the time and energy for trying. Fitting in didn't make me happy. Pretending to be someone I'm not makes me feel dirty, like I'm cheating on myself with Fake Felicity. Embracing my weirdness makes me happy.

I walk to the end of the dock and sit down, taking off my Toms and letting my toes dangle along the surface of Lake Michigan. I lean back on my elbows and let out a breath as the sun hits my face.

If I'm so happy, then why am I feeling a ball of dread in the pit of my stomach? It's deep, and I don't want to acknowledge it. I lay back on the dock and rest my hands on my stomach. My mind goes to my happy place, filling the day with something grand, something that makes me special, and something that'll never happen.

I shake my head, knowing I can't cover up this feeling forever, and at some point I need to come to terms with the fact that me—the older sister—is still as single as an individually wrapped slice of American cheese with no prospects in sight. And yeah, it does bother me. I'm not in a rush to get married, but I want someone.

Someone who loves me and all my flaws. Someone who can't live a day of their life without me. Someone I can give myself to completely and love as much as I can.

Someday, I'll find that someone.

Chapter Three

I unroll the last curler from my hair and carefully pull it apart with my fingers before blasting it with hairspray. After adding another coat of mascara, I scrutinize my reflection for a minute before nodding at it with approval. I don't wear a full face of makeup very often because it takes too long and I'd rather sleep than get up an hour earlier for work.

But I like it, and it surprises a lot of people to know that I am good at doing makeup. I picked up a lot of tips from doing Cosplay makeup. Putting all my gear back in a travel bag, I pad into my bedroom to get dressed. I pull on the white and blue polka dot dress, so thankful the slightly padded top is supportive enough to go sans strapless bra. Petite, slender Erin never understood my woe when it came to strapless bras. Those suckers never stay up.

Dressed and ready with half an hour before we have to leave to set up for the shower, I grab the Best Buy bag from my dresser and go downstairs.

"What are you doing?" Jake asks me when I kneel down by the TV stand in the family room.

"Hooking up HD cables. I don't know how Mom and Dad live, watching everything in standard def."

He rolls his eyes. "You're such a nerd."

I make a face right back. "You had me help you pick out a new TV and rewire everything last year.

35

You know it makes a difference. This has nothing to do with being a nerd. I'm just helping Mom and Dad keep up with the times. They probably don't even know the difference between SD and HD." I turn off the TV, ignoring Jake's protests that he was watching some motorcycle show, and get to work, muttering to myself that getting Mom and Dad to upgrade their cable will be a whole other feat.

I'm just about done and getting everything put back into place when Danielle comes through the door. Her hair falls in soft curls around her face, and she's wearing a pale pink dress and tall white heels. I catch the smile and faraway look in Jake's eyes when he sees her and resist the urge to throw up in my mouth. It's weird seeing my kid brother so in love.

I stand and smooth out my dress. Danielle's eyes land on me, and her brow furrows.

"Oh, Felicity," she says, blinking. She holds onto the banister and pauses when she steps off the last stair. "I didn't recognize you."

"Hopefully that's good?" I inquire.

Jake laughs. "You clean up well, sis."

"Thanks."

He gets off the couch and goes to Danielle, linking his arm through hers. "I loaded everything in the car. I'll come with to help you carry it, but I don't need to be there, right?"

Danielle's eyes widen as she looks up at Jake. Even in heels, she's a good few inches shorter than him. "I'd really like you to be there, but you don't *have* to. Most guys don't go to the shower."

"Well," he says and leans down to kiss her. "I'm not most guys, am I?"

Her full lips pull into a smile. "That's why I said yes."

They kiss again and the vomit I was holding back threatens to come up again. I turn to get my purse. Mom, who's still frantically getting ready, calls to me, making sure I'm ready. The house is pure chaos for the next ten minutes with people bustling about, checking the cars for all the supplies, a temporary freak out when the caterer calls and says one of the cooks is sick and they might be running late, and Danielle chipping her "chip-proof" nail polish.

Maybe I don't want to get married anytime soon. All this seems like too much work for just one day, and fuck, it's not even the wedding.

Finally, we load into the cars and drive half an hour to the country club, pulling around to the back to unload everything. The shower is starting with a cocktail and appetizer hour in the garden, before moving inside for games, lunch, then finally opening presents and cake.

Are all showers this fancy? I'd only been to a few, and they were for my cousins who came from families as laid back as my own. They were Mom's sisters' kids, after all. The wedding planner is already here, and greets Danielle like they're longtime girlfriends.

The other bridesmaids arrive within minutes, and soon we're all gathered around the wedding planner so she can assign us "tasks."

Along with two other bridesmaids who I met at dinner last night,—Michelle and Chloe or Zoey or whatever— my job is to carry the vases of fresh-cut flowers from the car and put them on the high-top tables in the garden. We each take a cardboard box and go through the well-maintained courtyard.

"Don't blink," I say when we pass a statue of an angel, her head turned down and covered by her hands.

"What?" Zoey says, looking behind her to see me. There is something familiar about her blonde hair and heart-shaped face, but I can't recall ever meeting her. Still, I swear I've seen her around before. I probably have, actually. Mistwood isn't that big of a city.

I motion to the angel statue. "Weeping ... you know what, never mind."

"Uh, okay," she says and keeps walking. I shake my head. *Remember who you're with.* We set up in silence. Half an hour later, things are in place and I'm wondering if they will let us have a few early appetizers.

I sit in the shade and pull out my phone. Erin is on her way with the cake, and the party starts in an hour. It's going to be a long day.

"Thanks for helping," Jake says and takes a seat across from me.

"Of course," I say, smiling. "You're my baby bro. I'd do anything to help you, you know that."

"I do. And you have," he says quietly, referring to the times I bailed him out of trouble when he was in college and never told Mom or Dad. Or maybe it was the time I paid his accumulated parking tickets, or helped him beat a level in a video game. Whatever it was, he's grateful.

He looks across the courtyard at Danielle, who's throwing a mini-fit about the mimosa bar not being how she wanted it.

"She's a bit of a diva," he blurts, then looks embarrassed to have admitted that out loud.

"Just a bit," I say and nudge his foot under the table. "But so are you. You were always the high-maintenance sibling."

"That is so far from the truth."

I laugh. "No, that's how it is in my mind. Diva or not, Danielle seems great."

"She is. I wish you got to know her more. Maybe you guys could go out or something. Have some sister-in-law bonding time."

I have to work to keep my face neutral. "Yeah, maybe. That'd be fun." I push my hair over my shoulder. "Is she always like this or is the diva-ness an offshoot from being a bridezilla?"

Jake laughs. "Bridezilla. She likes things to go as planned." He shrugs. "It's her day. You know I don't care about weddings and whatnot. But I want to give her this, make her happy, ya know?"

"Don't make me cry," I say with a smile. Really, though, I'm so proud of Jake for growing up and changing from pain-in-the-ass younger brother to a man. Someone walks over to the mimosa bar and begins setting up. "Oh, booze!" I say, perking up. "Can the husband-to-be score me a mimosa, hold the OJ?"

"You just want a glass of champagne?"

"I do. You know I don't like orange juice."

He puts his hands on the table to stand. "I'll see what I can do. Then I'm going in to sit at the bar and watch some ESPN until it's time to open presents." He makes a face and rolls his eyes.

"Lucky," I say, even though sports aren't my thing. "I'll be here, uh, sitting and having fun."

He smiles and shakes his head. "Be a good sport."

"I think I am."

Jake goes over to the little bar, talks to the lady behind it, turns to me and shakes his head. Dammit. I lean back in the chair and look around the garden. Other than the creepy statue, everything is perfect. Flowers in full bloom outline the stone patio, and little crystal ornaments glisten in the sunlight on the surrounding trees. It looks like something out of a fairytale, and I kind of love it.

Weddings are all about coming together and celebrating love. They should make me happy, right? I let out a sigh. So why do they make me feel so lonely?

I get up and ask Danielle if there's anything else she needs me to do—there isn't—and then wander around until Erin gets here. I help her carry in the surprisingly heavy cake and set it on the table at the front of the banquet room. The event planner swoops in and puts decorations and candles on the table, giving it the "finishing touches" that it requires.

Erin and I sit in the back, chatting and watching everyone buzz about. Soon, family and friends filter in and the party gets started. I come back to my table with a plate full of appetizers and another mimosa, sitting next to Erin and across from my grandma and a few cousins.

"How's work?" my grandma asks.

"It's good," I say and hope she doesn't ask me what I do again. I tried explaining what an internet browser is to her before and that convo only ended in confusion and frustration. "Keeps me busy, but I like it."

"That's good, honey. And how's that guy you were dating, Mike? Or Matt?"

"Mike," I say and internally shutter. "We're not together anymore."

"Oh, what a shame," my grandma says. "He was such a nice guy. But you'll find someone else, someone better."

"I'm sure I will." I flick my eyes to Erin. She picks up her glass and smirks.

"Can I ask what happened?" my grandma asks.

41

"We just weren't compatible," I say, making Erin snicker into her mimosa. Grandma was right about one thing: Mike is a nice guy. But he has particular sexual interests that I just couldn't deal with. I need a drink just thinking about it, and feel the need to hide my feet under the chair cover.

Mike is nice all right, but he has a foot fetish. His dick spent more time rubbing against the soles of my feet than it did actually inside me, blow jobs included. I gave it my all, kept my toenails manicured and polished, and went months without any actual penetration before I called it quits.

"Good thing you found that out before you got in too deep," my grandma says.

"Yes," I say and take another drink. Though there was little *getting in deep* with Mike. "It's a good thing for sure."

The event planner calls everyone's attention, and we start playing the typical bridal shower games. Not knowing Danielle, I think it's safe to say I lost.

Once the shower ends, we help my brother and Danielle pack everything up to take back to their little house by the water. Danielle doesn't officially live with Jake yet, and she tries to pass off as a virgin to her parents and my own, but I know my brother and know he wouldn't stay in a relationship if he wasn't getting some. Because he's a pig like that. Then again, I wouldn't stay in a relationship like that either.

Erin stays for dinner at my parent's house, and we

spend the rest of the night sketching out our costume ideas and ordering materials online. I hug her and my family goodbye, take one last look at the remaining twilight glistening off the lake, and get in my car to start the drive home, reminding myself not to speed. I have Mr. Silent Knight and a DVR'd episode of Game of Thrones waiting for me, after all.

"You should dress up like this more often," Cameron says, scrolling through Facebook. "You're hot."

I look up from the computer and make a face. "Would you pay me more if I dressed up?"

He raises his eyebrows. "No, but I—"

"Then it's not worth it." I quickly type out a code, press enter, then save my progress. "What do you think?" I ask and push my feet against the floor, causing my rolling chair to scoot away from the desk. I yawn and grab my coffee at the last minute, before I'm too far to reach it. It's Monday morning. I need all the coffee I can get today. Cameron leans in, clicking through the website.

"It looks great! Way better than what the client paid for," he only half jokes. "Seriously. You're good, Lissy."

"Thanks. And really, it was easy."

"I don't know why you're here," he says quietly. "As much as I don't want to lose you, I feel like you're wasting your talents here."

I shrug off the compliment. "When the CIA seeks me out to be part of a top-secret hacker group, I'll quit."

Cameron rolls his eyes. "Why don't you apply? You don't have to be kidnapped in a black windowless van to get a job with the government, you know."

"I do," I say. "And I've looked into it. I'll think about it." I've opened the online application many times. Not just the CIA either. The FBI or Homeland Security would work too. And I'm sure there were other even more secret groups out there too. I wouldn't exactly be Black Widow, but fighting cybercrime would be badass enough for me.

"So," I say with a sigh. "Do I have to go to that appointment now?"

Cameron checks the time. "You got some time. What do you want for lunch? Thai food?"

I smile. "Aww, you know me so well."

"More than I wish I did," he shoots back. "Your usual?"

I nod and log onto my company email to message the art director about the garden website. Assuming he approves the graphics I added this morning, I'm done. I grab my phone and scroll through Pinterest, pinning fan-made memes of my favorite shows until

Cameron texts me to tell me lunch is here.

No one really cares that I'm friends with the boss, but Cam worries about his boss coming down hard on him for being so casual with me. There are no official policies against it, but it's "frowned upon" by the guys upstairs. Whatever. Buying me lunch as a thank you is harmless, if you ask me. I sit in the breakroom, half paying attention to the Steve Wilkos show as I eat my spicy noodles until I have to go.

I tell the people at On Star the address and get directions sent over, then drive halfway across town to a fancy art gallery, owned by a Mr. Hartford. I park and pull down the mirror, running my hands through my hair, which had gotten messy from the wind blowing through the open windows.

A little bit of dread goes through me when I get out of the car. I take a breath, finding my resolve, and think about Black Widow again. I push my shoulders back and walk into the lobby. Cold air hits me, making goosebumps break out over my arms.

I'm standing in a small foyer-ish lobby, with dark wooden floors and what I guess is the original tin-tiled ceiling. The lights are dimmed and weird; abstract art hangs on the walls. There are teeny-tiny handwritten price tags under each painting. My eyebrows hike up and I shake my head. Those things each cost my month's rent.

"Can I help you?" someone asks, and walks out from behind a satin curtain that's hanging by a desk.

"Yeah," I say and turn. "I'm here to—" I cut off when the familiar face of Mindy fucking Abraham comes into view.

Her brows push together. "Felicity?"

Dammit. I can't lie about who I am now, even though my first thought is to switch to a British accent and call myself Emma.

"I'm here to help you with the computer issues you're having. Customer service and all," I finish, bypassing her question again.

She blinks a few times. "Right, right." She smiles pleasantly and turns, waving me to follow her. Her blonde hair is pulled up into a perfect French twist, not a strand out of place, and her pencil skirt is the perfect combination of tight and work-appropriate, as well as the gray satin blouse she has on. There isn't a single run in her panty-hose, and her tall black heels click on the floor.

I shake myself, digging my nails into my palms. I'm not standing in the high school cafeteria, cheeks burning from the heat of embarrassment as she points and laughs at how my Spiderman lunch box matches the patches of red skin on my arms.

I internally grumble and take a step forward. *Fuck you, Cameron, for making me do this.* I close my eyes, inhale, and channel my inner Hermione. She never gave two shits what anyone thought of her and she ended up being even more badass than Harry, even if the books don't admit it.

Mindy scoots a big leather chair out from behind the dark oak desk. There's a picture of her holding a toddler, smiling up at the camera. Of course she's married and has the world's cutest kid.

"I thought someone named Marissa was coming out," she starts and enters her password into the computer.

"Yeah, she's having a baby or something," I say. "I'm just filling in."

She nods. "Do you remember me? I'm pretty sure we went to high school together."

Of course I remember her. She, along with her popular friends, made my life hell for a few years. I turn and look at her, as if I have to recall her face, as if she hadn't impacted me as she did.

"Mindy," I say like the name suddenly came to me. "Yeah, I remember you."

She smiles. "Thought so. And I did totally see you at that store the other day."

I keep my eyes on the computer screen, wincing at how outdated everything is. Seriously, Windows XP? I shrug. "Maybe. So, what's the problem you've been having?"

"I think it has a virus," she says. "We bought some sort of Kasper-something or other but I don't think it works. Everything is so slow and I can't get onto the internet without clicking on this a million times." She points with a manicured nail to the Wi-Fi icon on the screen. "The website you guys made won't load, and I can't update it. So you can get rid of the virus and put new protection on then make the site work?"

I laugh. "It's not that easy, but let me run a few checks and see what's going on." I scoot the big chair closer and after a few clicks know one of the problems is the lack of memory and the old systems the gallery is using. It's not compatible with the website. The server can't support pretty much anything done in the last five years.

"When did you move to Grand Rapids?" Mindy asks. She's hovering over my shoulder, watching me work. It's fucking annoying.

"About half a year ago," I say.

"I've been here for four years," she says, like I care. "My husband got a job at the hospital here."

I nod, trying not to notice the way she accentuated the word "husband."

"And I've been here for a while. I just needed something to do, and Ben is so talented."

"Ben?"

"The artist," she says. I catch her rolling her eyes. "He owns the gallery."

"Gotcha," I say.

"He has a computer in his office that has the same virus. Same issues. Slow, bad internet connection."

"That doesn't mean a virus," I say. "Where's the router?" When Mindy doesn't answer, I turn to look at her. Her eyes are wide open.

"I don't know. Shouldn't you be able to figure that out? You're the expert here. Maybe in 'my documents'?"

Thank you, Mindy fucking Abraham, for reinforcing the pretty and stupid stereotype.

"It's not in the computer," I say. "It's a little box-looking thing. What other computers do you have?"

"There's this one, and one in Ben's office."

"I'd guess the router is in there. Is he in there too, by any chance? I can go take a look at it now."

She looks at me like I just asked for free backstage passes for a sold-out concert. "No. He's busy, and he doesn't like to be bothered when he's busy."

Sounds like a nice guy. "Uh, okay. You don't have a virus, but your computer is horribly out of date. It can't support the site, which is why you can't get it to load."

She puts her hands on her hips. "You can tell that already?"

"I'll run a full diagnostic test," I say. "But I promise you that's the issue."

"Is it going to take long? Because I have stuff to do."

"I'm not sure how long it will take yet. Your computer needs a lot of updates, and the lack of memory is going to make that hard. I'll see what I can do."

Mindy leans in. "Can you put more memory on it?

I have a Google Drive thing."

"That's not really the same," I say and feel like I'm talking to my grandma. "It can help if you delete things from your hard drive, but it would have to be a substantial amount."

Mindy straightens and crosses her arms. "So you have no idea how long this will take?"

"No, I don't," I reply and remind myself to stay professional. I'm working a job, not catching up with an old high school nemesis. "You're way overdue for an upgrade. I'll do that and try the site again. Well, update if I can." I click through a few more things, growing annoyed and irritated with Mindy hovering. "I'll let you know when I'm done," I inform her with a smile.

"Okay," she says and turns, only to return a minute later with another chair. "I need to sit at the desk."

"Makes sense."

She's still too close, and I feel her eyes on me, not the computer. "I haven't seen you since college," she begins, pausing to see if I'd say anything.

"Yeah, it's been a while."

"I almost didn't recognize you without that skin issue. It seems to have cleared up."

I freeze. Seriously? I don't know if I should be embarrassed or pissed. It took a while to find a good combo of creams and meds, but I'd finally gotten the red flakey skin from psoriasis to go away. I'd have to stop taking the medication if I ever got pregnant, but I figure if a man loved me enough to intentionally knock me up, he'll be okay with the red spots for a while.

Mindy waits a beat for me to answer. When I don't, she goes one. "What have you been up to?"

I know this game. She's asking me so I'll have to ask her and she can show off her amazing life. I guess some people never change. You can take the bitch out of high school but you can't take the bitch out of, well, anyone.

"You know, normal stuff," I tell her.

"That's good. Do you like Grand Rapids? Was it hard to leave your friends?"

I don't take my eyes off the computer. "Yes, but I have lots of friends here and we hang out all the time," I lie right through my teeth. Ninety-nine percent of them are online. Okay, fine. Ninety-eight percent since I count Ser Pounce as a friend. Hanging out on forums and talking over games is pretty much the same thing as hanging out in real life though. Who is she to judge?

Calm your tits, Felicity.

"Do you still talk to anyone from high school or college?"

"Not really. Just my best friend Erin."

"Erin?" I can see her tip her head. "I don't remember her."

"Too bad. She's pretty awesome."

Mindy giggles. "High school was so long ago. And that's good you're liking it here. So funny to think we both ended up here!"

"Hilarious," I say dryly. Hilarious in a way that this is proof the universe hates me. I scoot closer to the computer.

"Are you married?" Mindy asks. She can clearly see the lack of a wedding ring on my finger.

"Nope."

"Oh. I got married young, a few days after I turned twenty-one. I just couldn't say no!" She laughs like it's actually funny. "So you have a boyfriend then?"

"Nope."

"Ah, must be nice to do whatever you want then."

"It is." I yawn and wish I'd stopped for more coffee. I'd downed my second cup on the way here. Why did Mindy still feel the need to put me down in a passive-aggressive way? Mom would tell me it was some deep psychological issue and she was actually insecure. While I did believe that, I also believed some people were just assholes, and Mindy fit that bill.

The front door opens, and an older couple comes in to buy a painting. Mindy gets up and greets then, then disappears into the gallery.

Adios, bitchachos.

I work in silence for a while, and figure out pretty

fast that the computer is loaded with cookies. The problem isn't a virus, but a computer so old it belongs in a museum. I can't even install the new protection they bought. I run a few updates and look around for the bathroom. That coffee goes through me fast. I tap my nails on the desk, hating that I have to ask Mindy where the bathroom is, though it's not like she doesn't use it herself.

The couple comes back to the front, and Mindy rings them up using an old-fashioned looking register. I hear her say the painting will be delivered tomorrow morning since it was too big to fit inside their car. They write her a check for over a grand and leave with smiles.

"Are you done yet? Did you get rid of the virus?" Mindy asks before the door closes behind the old couple.

"You don't have a virus," I tell her. "The issues you described can be fixed with updating your computers."

"Can you do that?"

"Not on this one. There isn't enough memory to support the update to the newest version of Windows."

"Can't you fix it?"

I put on a pleasant smile. "Yes, in theory. This whole computer is really old though. I think it'd be better in the long run to consider a new one."

Mindy purses her lips. "That's up to Ben. He's

very stuck in his ways."

Without seeing Ben, I assume he's older. And probably gay. This gallery is way too chic to come from someone straight.

"The register is slow for credit cards too," Mindy adds.

That's a whole other issue. "I don't think this building is wired for high-speed internet," I say. "Upgrading can help with that too. Really, you gotta stay current with everything to get the fastest speed."

"I'll let Ben know." She smirks. "And I'll let him know you weren't able to do what he hired you to do."

"Well, he hired the company to create a state-of-the-art site that is only compatible with a new operating system."

Her lips go into a thin line. "I'll let him know."

I don't move, assuming she's going to go talk to him now and then I can be on my way and find a damn bathroom. My bladder is not happy right now.

"I guess I'll have him call your company then. I said he's busy now, remember? He does *not* like to be disturbed. And he's not going to be happy to hear you can't fix this."

I press my lips together and smile. "All right then." I scoot the heavy chair away from the desk and stand, gathering my things. Someone else comes into the gallery, and I'm able to sneak out without saying any sort of awkward goodbye to Mindy. I call

Cameron as I hurry across the street to a coffee shop. I don't really need another coffee now, but they have a bathroom and my bladder is raging at me.

"Hey, boss man," I say, holding the phone between my head and shoulder as I sit on the toilet, and quickly explain the situation.

"Are you in the bathroom?" Cameron asks when the toilet flushes.

"Uh, no."

"Sure." I can see him rolling his eyes. "And don't worry about it. I'll call later and get it sorted out."

"Thanks," I say and wash my hands. "Need me to come back?"

He hesitates. "Not really. Just act like you're still busy over there."

I smile and feel some of the stress melt off. It might not be so bad of a day after all.

Chapter Four

I'll learn to go to bed at a reasonable hour someday, right? Maybe next year, when I'm older and wiser. But not now, when staying up playing games trumps sleep until the sun creeps up then I scramble to bed, trying to force myself to sleep before my alarm goes off in a few short hours.

I drag ass through work the next day, crashing when I come home. I wake up at nine-thirty, eat dinner, do a bit of cleaning, then take a book onto my small backyard patio and reading until mosquitos force me inside. The long nap makes it hard to fall asleep, so after using Mr. Silent Knight once or twice (or three or four times—hey, a girl has needs), I get out of bed to lay out the fabric for my costume and watch just one Harry Potter movie.

And then I'm dragging my ass into work Wednesday morning, just as tired as the day before. Having fallen asleep after I got out of the shower, I twisted my hair up into a bun as I walked from the parking lot into work. I did my makeup at stoplights, and had my favorite R2D2 tank top on under a white button up. I put off doing laundry and had been forced into the section of my closet I refer to as my "sexy librarian clothes," which isn't helping my issue with the top button of my shirt continually popping open.

"Look at you," Cameron says as I put my lunch in the fridge in the break room.

I let the fridge door swing shut and give him a look. "I know. I overslept and look terrible."

"I'm thinking the opposite," he says. "You are rocking that tight skirt."

"Really?" I turn my head to look at my ass. "I think it looks double its size."

"Maybe I'm biased," Cameron starts. "Or not biased, I guess, since I don't find you sexually attractive."

"Thanks," I say dryly.

"Oh shut up," he spits back. "I don't find any woman sexually attractive, not with your breasts and vaginas." He shutters. "Been there, tried that. So not my thing. But I do know you look good dressed up, by anyone's standards. I don't know why you don't dress up more often."

I hold my hand up and rub my fingers with my thumb, reminding him dressing up for work doesn't benefit me. It's not like I'll do a better job if my skirt hugs my ass than if my pants bag around my cheeks.

He rolls his eyes and puts cream cheese on a bagel. A few other people shuffle in, grabbing donuts and fresh coffee before starting the workday. I make small talk and eat a donut, yawning the whole time, then retreat to my desk, talking with Mariah as I work. I keep Facebook open, chatting with Erin as I answer emails and convert codes for clients, and then help

Mariah with a snag she hit in one of her projects.

At lunch time, Cameron comes and takes a seat at the table next to me. He doesn't have food, or his phone.

Crap.

"Unless you have Comic Con tickets, no," I say.

"A little presumptuous, aren't you?"

I stab a strawberry with my fork. "Am I wrong?"

He sighs and laughs. "No. I just got off the phone with that gallery."

"Not doing it," I say. He doesn't know about Mindy, and I really don't want to bring it up.

"Oh come on. The owner bought all new computers. Brand new and ready to be played with."

"I don't want to play with his. I like to play with my own, thank you very much."

Cameron's lips push together as he tries not to laugh.

"You know what I mean. Please don't make me."

"You are so stubborn, you know that, right?"

I shrug. "I prefer strong willed."

"Call it what you want. But I already said you'd be there to help set shit up."

"Fine," I huff. If I never see Mindy fucking Abraham again it would be too soon. "When do I have to be there?"

"Half an hour."

I nod and get back to my food. "I'm only doing this because I love you. And you told me my ass looks good today."

He stands with a smile. "Thank you, Felicity. Seriously, this saves me *so* much trouble."

I quickly finish my food, refill my Little Mermaid travel coffee mug, and stop at my desk to get my purse. I yank the band out of my hair and let the wind loosen the tight ringlets the bun created. I'm halfway to the gallery when I realize I left my coffee at my desk. I debate on turning around, but don't have time. I might, just might, be able to run across the street to the Starbucks by the gallery and hit up the drive through. I yawn. Yep. There isn't enough coffee in the world to get me through the rest of the afternoon with Mindy.

A text comes through from my brother, saying that Danielle is working on "tightening the guest list" and needs to know if I'm bringing a date. I pick up my phone, dangerously reading the text while driving. I won't actually text while driving, no sir, not worth the risk. Besides, what am I going to say? Chances are I won't have a date, and that makes me feel all sorts of low.

Fuck it.

I can have fun on my own. And Erin makes a pretty great date. I'll think of a response later. Right now, I need coffee. Of course, the drive through line is a mile long. I park, hoping I can quickly run in and get my order. Luckily, the inside line is nothing compared to the dozen cars lined up around the store. I put on lip gloss and rake my fingers through my hair then hurry into the cafe.

I order an iced mocha and a brownie with chocolate frosting that looks way too good to pass up. I pay, then stand to the side and wait for my drink, feeling the panic start to build as each minute passes. I check the time on my phone. Yep. I'm officially late.

I try to tell myself it doesn't matter, and that I probably won't need the whole appointment time anyway. Still, it bugs me to be unprofessional. If Cameron gets a complaint, he will get it from his boss and will be forced to handle it. Plus, after hearing how particular this Ben guy is, I can't imagine he'll be too pleasant when I walk in ten to fifteen minutes late. I need him there for part of the time to let me in his office and to put in passwords. And I'm sure he'll need step-by-step instructions on how to do pretty much everything.

Finally, my drink comes and it's a balancing act to hold my brownie, phone, wallet, and vente mocha. Somedays I really question my own judgment. This would have been exponentially easier if I had brought my purse in. I gather everything up, take a step, then stop, knowing I have to rearrange something or everything is going onto the floor.

The man who'd been behind me waiting on his drink grabs his coffee from the counter and abruptly turns around, probably thinking I was long gone. Yet there I am, just a foot from where I'd been.

He collides with me, smashing my brownie against my phone and sloshing my cold coffee down the front of my shirt. My mind whirls, going from *what the fuck*, to *holy shit this is cold*, to noticing that he's impossibly gorgeous. He's well over six feet tall, with a shock of thick, black hair that matches his dark eyes. Stubble covers a strong jaw and tattoos peek out from the sleeves of a black T-shirt that's filled out by strong muscles. His jeans are washed out and tight in all the right places, and I find my eyes trailing down his body on their own accord. That's one hell of a bulge he's got going on.

"Fuck, I'm so sorry," he blurts and takes a step back. Some of my coffee splashed on him, but the majority is running down my front and dripping onto the floor. "I didn't see you there. Well, I did, but then you moved," he goes on.

"It's okay," I say, feeling breathless as I watch his full lips move as he speaks. I blink. No, this isn't okay, actually. I'm covered in coffee.

"Let me help," he says and sets his own drink down to grab napkins. I'm standing frozen, not sure what to do. My items are barely in my grasp and any movement might send them falling. *Not the brownie!*

"Here," he says and takes the smashed coffee from my hand. I shake myself and take a step forward, setting my phone, wallet, and brownie onto the counter, and take the napkins from his outstretched hand. I wipe off the mess from my hands first, then move to my shirt.

"I'm so sorry," he says, eyes on my chest as he takes in the damage done. "I'm in a rush and I ... I ... fuck. Can I at least buy you another coffee?"

Rush. Right. I'm in a rush too, and my brain automatically goes to the universe cursing me for being selfish enough to show up late to an appointment just so I could get coffee.

"No," I say. "There's still some left."

He wipes off my phone. "I feel awful, really."

I toss the napkins and get another handful, sticking them inside my shirt and retrieving a chunk of ice from between my breasts.

"Hey, at least it wasn't hot coffee," I say and force a smile.

He smiles back and I just might have quivered. "Right. I don't want a lawsuit on my hands."

A barista comes over with a damp towel. I thank her and wipe at my shirt, knowing it's a futile attempt at most. This sucker needs to soak in some cold water and detergent. Fuck. I have to work like this now. I close my eyes, silently seething as I imagine Mindy's smirk as she asks what happened.

"You're pissed," Hot Guy says.

"Well, can you blame me?" I blurt and run the towel over my sticky hands before taking my phone from him. I wipe it off the best I can, knowing I have to take it out of the case ASAP.

"Is that the new iPhone?" he asks, eyebrows

going together. "It's not out yet."

"I have a beta," I say. One of the benefits of being a techie nerd, thank you very much.

He shakes his head. "That's besides the point. I think I ruined your shirt."

"It's too tight at the top anyway," I say then realize I basically said my boobs are too big. Or that I gained weight and it doesn't fit. Should I be embarrassed?

"It looks good on you," he says, eyes going past the coffee stain to my cleavage. "Even covered in coffee."

He's hitting on me. I haven't been hit on in … a long time. Suddenly, I need more ice running down my skin.

"Thanks," I say and blink up at him. His skin is a gorgeous light tan with hints of olive. He has an air to him that demands respect, a confidence that can be seen.

He dries off my wallet and wipes the mess from the outside of the plastic cup, eyeing my name hand written on the side.

"Felicity," he says and my name rolls off his tongue, his deep voice holding me captive from just speaking one word. "Are you sure I can't buy you another drink to make for this?"

"I'd like that," I say honestly. "But I'm running late to meet a client, and I hear the guy's a real asshole." I shake my head and sigh. "I'm already

63

dreading going in."

"Ouch, now I feel even worse. Asshole client and I ruined your shirt."

"The shirt is the least of my worries," I say with a smile.

"Then your client must really be an ass."

I raise my eyebrows. "Yeah, he seems that way. And his secretary isn't much better." I wrinkle my nose. "I'm only doing this as a favor to my boss since he's my friend." I inhale and slowly let it out. I hook my wallet around my wrist grab my phone and brownie.

"Can I walk you out?" Hot Guy asks and picks up my coffee. "And your hands look kind of full."

I'm smiling and nodding before I can get any logical words out. "Sure, thanks."

"I still want to make it up to you."

"Nah, it's okay. I really should go and get this over with."

He laughs. "Hopefully this guy takes it easy on you. Tell him some idiot ran into you and it's not your fault."

"I'll say just that." My heart flutters when he pushes the door open for me. "That's me," I say, motioning to my red Malibu parked right outside the door. I set the brownie and phone on the roof and open the door.

"Sorry again, Felicity," he says. "Maybe I'll see you here again. I pretty much live on coffee."

"Me too. Well, coffee and wine," I say and laugh at myself. *Did I really just say that? Why not tell him that the wine is drunk out of a plastic Butter Beer mug while Ser Pounce circles my feet?*

"Both are essential," he says and hands me my drink. "Good luck with the asshole client."

"Thanks, I'll probably need it." My eyes flick to the gallery across the street. "This day can't get much worse, can it?"

"Let's hope not." He lets his eyes run over me, slowly, deliberately. He wants me to know he's checking me out … and liking what he's seeing.

Holy shit.

I'm fairly confident only this guy can make a coffee shop parking lot an erotic experience. I'm blushing as I turn to get into the car. I close the door and pull my shirt up, untucking it from my skirt. I undo the buttons and yank it off. It's way too stained and wet to wear. I toss my head back against the seat. What the fuck should I do?

I sigh and hang the shirt on the passenger seat, hoping it might dry if I blast it with the A.C. I look at the clock.

I'm now fifteen minutes late. I put the car in reverse, realize that my phone and brownie are on the hood, and frantically grab them. Then I high-tail it across the street. I get out, get my purse, and gather my composure, catching my reflection in my window. If only I'd worn any other shirt under my blouse than

65

this … Whatever. R2D2 is awesome.

My heart skips a beat. I lean against the door of my car, taking a few minutes to text Erin and calm down. Plus I need to process Hot Guy.

What is wrong with me? I should have flirted back, right? Maybe asked for his name at least? Oh well. I'll never see him again. I shake my head when I realize that I've wasted another five minutes. Now I'm twenty minutes late.

I fluff my hair, take a deep breath—I smell like coffee, though I say that's not a bad thing—and push my shoulders back. It is what it is. I'm going to go in, set this shit up, then get the hell out of dodge.

I grab my work bag from the back, heft it up over my shoulder, and hold my head up as I walk into the gallery. Mindy looks up when the door opens. Her eyebrows go up as she takes in my Star Wars tank top. It's form fitting with a scoop neck, showing more of my tits than is appropriate.

"I'm ready to get started," I say, cutting right to the chase.

"Uh, okay," she says, blinking back her shock. "I'll let Ben know you're here."

"Thanks." I set the bag down on her desk, eyeballing the sleek computer that takes the place of the old dinosaur that sat in its place a few days ago. Mindy gets up, repulsion of my fashion choice clear on her face. She's looking good again today in a cream suit, hair in loose waves pinned back by shiny barrettes. Her makeup is flawless. Seriously, people have skin that even and clear?

Maybe she had some sort of procedure done. I doubt it. I'm sure my tainted high school memories glorified her a bit, my teenage mind thinking her better than she really is, but I'm pretty sure her skin had always been that way. Mine isn't particularly bad, but I don't look like a centerfold come to life.

Her heels click on the hardwood floor and she disappears into the gallery. Two of the paintings from Monday are gone, making the entrance look bare. I didn't doubt the talent of this Ben guy, but I doubted the price tags. Not being into art or anything classy like that, I had no idea what the going rate was for a custom piece like that, though.

I click my nails on the desk as I wait, disliking this Ben guy even more as each minute ticks by. Finally, Mindy trots back to her desk.

"He'll be right down. You can start with his computer. He's busy, you know. You should hurry so he can get to work."

I swallow the retort that's on the tip of my tongue. I'll hurry because I want out of here, not because Ben-Diva needs his precious time.

"Sure," I say and take another breath. A door opens and closes from inside the gallery, and I hear heavy footfalls come downstairs. Ben rounds the corner and it's all I can do not to let my jaw drop onto the floor. Color rushes to my cheeks.

Son of a bitch.

It's worse than any Shyamalan twist: Asshole, little-miss-diva Ben is the hot guy from the coffee shop.

Chapter Five

We stare at each other, neither speaking, for several beats. Mindy looks back and forth, not following our expressions of abhorrence.

"Felicity," Ben finally says and his eyes settle on my breasts. "Nice outfit choice."

"Some idiot ran into me and it's not my fault," I say back. "*Ben.*"

"You two know each other?" Mindy asks.

"Yes," Ben says the same time I say "No." Ben clears his throat. "Why don't you get started," he says to me. "I'd hate for that asshole client to get upset."

I purse my lips together and glare at him. Then I blink, grab my bag, and hurry past Mindy. We go to the center of the gallery and up a flight of wooden stairs that have been painted black.

My pulse is pounding, and I can't take my eyes off of Ben's ass as he ascends the stairs in front of me. It's so perfect and tight. A quarter would bounce right off that thing. There is a door at the top of the stairs that creaks open. The smell of paint and clay hits me hard.

"Close the door," Ben says and I just know he's going to yell at me and call my boss or something of the like. He turns around and crosses his arms. He's grinning. "You're not the fat, ugly nerd I was told was coming to install the new computers and fix the website."

"And you might not be the asshole client I thought you were."

"Just might not be?"

I lift my left shoulder in a shrug but can hardly move it under the weight of the bag. "I don't know you yet. You can at least tell what I look like in a second flat."

"That is true," he says and runs a hand through his hair. He leans against an L-shaped desk that's cluttered with books and messy stacks of paper. "Why do you think I'm an asshole?"

I swallow, trying to will the blood rush to leave my cheeks. "The way Mindy talked about you. You sounded like a high-maintenance diva, to be honest."

His face brightens as he smiles again. Then he raises an eyebrow. "You know Mindy?"

Crap. I could lie, right?

"I mean," he continues. "She saw you, and you're clearly not fat or ugly." His eyes do one more sweep of my body. "Not at all. So why would she lie?"

"She's sadistic?" I offer, voice going high pitched.

Ben tips his head like he's studying me. "She is, but not that much."

"We went to high school together," I admit and am surprised by the relief I feel in saying that. "And we weren't friends."

"What, were you the popular hot girl and she wasn't?"

I let out a snort—yes, and actual snort—of laughter and give Ben a "what the fuck are you smoking?" look.

"Other way around?" he asks like it can't be true.

I put my hand to my chest, meaning to draw attention to the giant R2D2 on my shirt as if that proves my point. "Very much so."

"Because you like Star Trek?"

I blink and look down at my shirt. Nope. I just … can't. I shake my head and stare at him with wide eyes. The adrenaline is wearing off and things are feeling more and more awkward. I wave my hand in the air.

"Look, sorry I called you an asshole, though I really didn't call *you* that. Just show me the computers and I'll get things set up, fix your site, and leave."

Ben still has that stupid grin on his face, and I hate how attractive he is with it. "You're making me want to prove to you I'm not an asshole."

"Really, you don't have to. You did seem like you were legit sorry you ruined my shirt back there—"

"You said you weren't upset," he interjects.

"I'm not that upset. That shirt really doesn't fit that well and I only wore it because I'm slacking on laundry. I don't think I've even worn it in years." Color rushes to my cheeks. Why am I saying this? *Stop talking, Felicity.* "Now … let's just get this over with and be on our separate ways. Then you'll never have to see me and think of this awkward moment again."

"I'll definitely be thinking about this again," he says and pushes off his desk. I just now notice the flecks of paint on his hands and arms. If I hadn't been so dumbstruck by his damn good looks, maybe I would have put two and two together and figured out he was Ben.

Though, I highly doubt that.

It was already in my mind that Ben was an older gay man, not a super attractive guy in his thirties with muscles and tattoos and a rather large bulge in his—

Stop.

"Feel free," I say and hold onto the strap of the heavy bag. Ben notices and steps forward to take it. Okay. Maybe he really isn't an asshole. "So, your computers," I start. "They were seriously old. How did you function?" I can be blunt right? We are past fake formalities by now.

Ben laughs. "I don't use it much." He must notice my shocked expression. "I bring my laptop with me everywhere I go and use that instead."

"Oh good," I say. "Because if you were one of those people that didn't like computers, I'd ... I'd really do nothing because I don't know you and it wouldn't matter at all." I laugh, nervous. Fuck, why am I so awkward?

"We can change that," he says, his dark eyes meeting mine and it's like he's looking into my soul, seeing how desperate I am for a good, hard fuck by something other than my neon-pink vibrator.

72

Seriously, my wrists hurt from doing myself every night. Thanks, Mom, for forcing me to take piano lessons that started the wrist pain. Wait, no. Mom should be nowhere in this thought process. I blink and shake my head.

"But first," he says when I just stare at him like he's an all-you-can-eat cupcake buffet and I'm on a carb-free diet. "The computer situation. I did update what we have here. It's easier to do bookkeeping in the office rather than brining my personal computer back and forth."

"I bet. So you want me to set that up too?"

"I can do it."

"I'm sure I can do it faster."

He gets a devilish glint in his eyes. "I'm sure you can."

Is he making a sexual joke or do I have a dirty mind? Fuck. Thinking about Ben and sex makes me warm and tingly all over. "Well, I'm here to help so … uh … I'll help if you want my help, because that's why I'm here. To help." I internally wince at my own choice of words.

"So you can help?" he teases and goes around to his messy desk. I take a minute to look around the space. The "office" part opens into a large studio, with floor-to-ceiling windows looking out onto the street. Sheer curtains have been hung over them, several feet of fabric gathered on the floor. The walls are a mix of cracked plaster and exposed brick, and

73

I'm not sure if it was done on purpose or if it happened over time. It is very fitting for an art studio, nonetheless.

Shelves are pushed against the wall, every inch covered in paint, brushes, and other various materials. Several easels have been set up in the middle of the room, and some sort of statue was shoved in a corner, looking forgotten. The entire place is a mess, but it's working. In fact, it wouldn't work any other way. Chaos and creativity go hand in hand.

"That's the new router you got?" I ask, wrinkling my nose.

"What's wrong with this one?"

"It's not very good."

"The guy at the store recommended it."

I put a hand on my hip. "You believe some teenager in a blue shirt over me?"

That grin is back on his handsome face. "How do I know you're any more—or less—qualified?" He runs a hand through his thick hair. "Where did you go to school?"

"MIT," I say right away then wish I could take it back. I got the majority of my schooling done there but actually graduated elsewhere.

"Fair enough," he says. "What router should I get?"

"Considering the old wiring in this building, I'd get something stronger with a better range. I can write down some recs for you."

His eyes fall onto my chest again. "Or we can go out to the store and get something together and then have dinner."

"No," I say right away, surprising myself. Hot Guy, aka, asshole-not-asshole Ben, just asked me out. Why is my gut telling me not to go? I'm not in high school anymore. This isn't some setup to mock me. We're adults. He wouldn't ask me out if he didn't actually want to go with me.

He looks taken aback, like he's surprised at my insta-rejection. "Do you have a boyfriend?"

"Nope. I don't have a husband either. I'm single." Might as well get it all out there. "You?"

"No boyfriend or husband. And no official girlfriend or wife."

"But you have something unofficial?"

"I date," he tells me. "But it's nothing serious." I'm not sure what to think of that. "Look," he says. "It's not every day I spill coffee on a hot chick that thinks I'm an asshole."

I smile. "That doesn't happen to me every day either. Or ever. Really, it's never happened." I don't remember the last time someone called me hot. Well, someone other than people at Comic Con admiring my accurate yet revealing costumes.

I put the router back in its package the best I can so Ben can return it. We start setting up the new computer.

"Do you have plans this weekend?" he asks me. I

don't, other than playing video games, working on my Comic Con costume, and binge watching *Firefly* on Netflix. "If not, I'd really like to take you out."

"I think I can rearrange a few things," I say. "Where are you going to take me?"

"What do you like?"

"When it comes to food? Uh, everything."

He laughs, flashing perfect white teeth. "That's easy. Friday night, eight o'clock?"

"Sure," I say, a little breathless, and try my best to hide my smile. No harm can come of this, right? I push aside my initial fears to give this a go. I fire up the new computer and sit down. Ben goes into the studio and turns on music, streaming from his phone. It's set to random, and goes through everything from Mozart to Pink Floyd. I keep stealing glances at him as I install the updates. Half his body is hidden behind an easel. His movements are frantic and jerky, unlike the smooth, graceful sweeps you see in a movie.

I catch a glimpse of his face and see he's totally relaxed and in his element, even though I'm here. It doesn't take long to get everything running. I use the old router to set up the internet, and even with the new computer, it's slow as fuck. Or it is by my standards. But the website loads without a hitch. I love being right.

"It's done," I say and scoot the rolling chair back. I move my gaze to Ben. He's enthralled in whatever he's painting. Mindy said he doesn't like to be bothered when he's working. Did that still apply? He likes something about me, and I don't want to mess it up before we have a chance to even go out. I pack up everything and wait.

"Ben?" I finally call, voice soft.

He doesn't look up.

"Ben?" I say a little louder. He flicks his eyes to me, seeming annoyed. There's something dark in the way he looks at me, but it quickly vanishes as my name rolls of his tongue.

"Felicity. Are you done already?"

"I am." I say. "Told you I was fast."

"You most certainly are." He blinks a few times, like he has to bring himself back into the here and now. He takes a handful of brushes to a sink, the white porcelain stained with paint, and washes them with care, not bothering to wipe the paint from his skin. He comes over to me, standing close to see the computer screen.

The smell of paint mixing with his cologne is intoxicating. It's been so long since I've dated, well, anyone really, let alone someone like Ben. Someone cool and confident and probably totally normal. I always hope new people are just as weird as I am. All I can go on with Ben is his outward appearance and the little bit of himself he's put into this office space.

He's muscular, so he works out. He likes art—duh—and works in a chaotic mess. There's one thing we have in common, at least. There is a Samurai sword hanging on the wall above his desk, and while it's still in amazing shape, it looks antique. Other than that, he's a mystery, and it scares and excites me at the same time. I suddenly feel so transparent: what you see is what you get when it comes to me. One look at the graphic T-shirt I'm wearing or hearing the Game of Thrones theme song play when my phone rings clues you into a lot about me.

"Is there anything else I can do to you—for you—before I go down ... downstairs?" I swallow the lump in my throat. I'm not sure how to act around someone like this, and it unnerves me. *Just be yourself.* I nod at my own thought, earning a curious look from Ben.

His dark eyes meet mine again. "I can handle it. Really. But Mindy needs help."

"Not the kind I can give," I mumble. A few awkward seconds pass, and Ben's brow furrows like he feels bad I have to do this. "It won't take long," I say and grab my bag. "So I'll see you Friday?"

"Friday."

I turn to head down the stairs, but Ben stops me. I whirl around.

"I need your number," he says, hand still gently holding onto my wrist. I can feel my pulse pounding under his fingertips.

"Right. And I should probably get yours." I take a few steps back and set the bag down on his desk, pulling out random items until I find my phone at the very bottom. We exchange numbers, and Ben says he'll call me Friday when he leaves the studio in the afternoon with details.

I walk down the stairs smiling. Not even Mindy fucking Abraham can ruin this day.

Chapter Six

I'm still smiling as I pull into the small garage and wedge myself between my crap and my car. I let my mind wander to an impossible future, most likely setting myself up for disappointment because that's just how I roll.

I'm not thinking about what our babies will look like, where we'll spend our retirement, or anything crazy like that. No, I have limits. They might be way fucking out there, but they exist. I let myself think about Friday's date turning into something more and that Ben can be my Plus One to Jake and Danielle's wedding. Everyone would be impressed with him of course, not just because he's drop-dead gorgeous, but because he's a rich and famous artist.

Okay, I might have made that part up. I did a bit of online investigating when I got into the parking lot. Ben does make a decent living—very decent, in fact—and while he's well known in the area, he's not really famous. Which is good, because I wouldn't fair well with paparazzi. He used to live in New York and has pieces in the Museum of Modern Art. He moved to Grand Rapids a few years ago, which seems odd. But oh well. It is what it is.

Ben is a real man. A living breathing man with rippling muscles and a tight ass. And he asked me out. I can't stop thinking about our date, and my excitement is turning to nerves. I have all tomorrow and most of Friday to obsess about it.

"Dammit," I mutter when I remember I left the sprinkler on. I'm tired, it's past my bedtime, and I just want to lay down. For a few seconds, I consider leaving it until morning, but I won't be able to sleep knowing I'm wasting so much water. I pad into my bedroom to grab my phone to use as a flashlight, see it plugged in, and take a Lightsaber out of my closet instead. I flick it on, green light glowing around me, and head to the front door. I open the door only to quickly slam it shut. Bugs swarm around the porch light. I sigh, shut off the light, and grab my boots to go out the back where it's a bit safer from killer mosquitos and moths.

Using the Lightsaber to illuminate the way, I go around the house and turn off the water. I start to coil up the hose when a dark figure catches my eye.

I freeze. Someone just walked up to my front porch. My heart skips a beat. It's after 11:30. No one good comes knocking on your door after 10 PM.

I hold the Lightsaber in front of me like it's a real weapon, the green glow reflecting off the cream siding of my house. I'll just take a peek at who is on my porch before I run inside. If things go south, I'll run and bang on my condo-neighbor's door and beg Pearl to protect me.

She's from the south and hasn't lost a bit of her spunk at seventy-three. Plus she owns a shotgun.

A black Audi is parked in my driveway. It's off, and I don't see anyone else inside. I swallow and creep forward, heart hammering when the outline of a man in dark jeans and a dark T-shirt comes into view.

My mind goes a million miles an hour again, but instead of imagining drunken wedding reception sex with Ben, I'm thinking of this guy kidnapping me and running experiments.

I trip over the garden hose that I'd been coiling up, catching myself at the last minute. The man turns, having heard something rustle in the grass. Light from the street lamps hits his face.

It's Ben.

What the fuck? Is he some sort of stalker?

"Felicity?" he calls.

Crap. I've been spotted.

I inhale and hold my arms down, trying to look casual. "Hi," I squeak out and walk through the wet grass to the porch. Green light illuminates his face. "What are you doing?"

He holds up my wallet. "You left this. I figured you'd need it before Friday. I tried calling you, twice," he adds quickly. "But you didn't pick up."

"Oh, shit," I say. "I had my phone charging in another room."

His eyes slide down my body and settle at the Lightsaber in my hand. "You're a Jedi?" He gives me that infamous grin.

"I wish." I hold up the Lightsaber. "It makes a great flashlight in a pinch."

An eyebrow goes up and amusement sparkles in his eyes. He just nods. "And you needed it because?"

"I was turning off the sprinkler, and then I had no idea who was creeping around my house in the middle of the night."

"It's only eleven thirty."

"Oh right," I laugh. "That's not late at all." Normal people are still out of the house and socializing with friends at that hour. "Lost track of time. Feels later than it is. I stay up, I go out with friends." Why can't I stop talking? My lips are moving and words are coming out even though my brain is yelling at me to stop. Another thing I can't stop is my gaze from sweeping down over his body. He's got more paint on his clothes, and his hair is rumpled like he just had sex, which is incredibly attractive and off putting at the same time.

And I should clarify—it's only off putting because that sex wasn't with me.

"So you drove all the way out here to give me my wallet?" I open the front door and step in, mentally yelling and thanking myself for not locking the front door. I turn off the Lightsaber and toss it aside, and then flick on the porch light. Ser Pounce winds

83

around my ankles, trying to make a sneaky escape. I push him back with my foot.

"It wasn't a far drive."

"Wait, how did you know where I lived?"

"Your license has your address," he says and gives me my wallet. Our fingers touch as I grab it from him.

"Right, right. I just changed it too, like a month ago. I haven't lived here that long and put off changing it because, well, who likes the DMV?"

He laughs and meets my eyes. "I don't think anyone does."

"Thanks," I say. "Really. I'd be screwed in the morning without it. My car is on E." I swallow. I should invite him in, right? Will that give the wrong implication? Do I care if it does, is probably the better question. I stare at him, suddenly terrified, as if he's a vampire and by inviting him in, I'm giving him some sort of power over me.

Maybe I should wait for our date Friday. I'll be prepared, dressed up, and maybe a little drunk.

Mosquitoes swarm around my door already, and when a moth swoops in, I know I have to close it or bust out the leftover tulle material from my fabric bin and make a net to sleep under.

"Want to come in?" I ask.

Ben is still looking at me. He hesitates, then smiles. "Sure." He steps in and I close the door behind him. "You look like you're ready for bed.

Sorry if I woke you."

"I was still up. Just playing games." I step out of my little foyer and toss my wallet onto the recliner chair in the living room. Silence comes between us and I regret asking him to come inside. I have no idea what *should* happen next. What would happen in a book or movie?

We could hook up, have passionate semi-one-night-standish sex then go out Friday? Yeah, don't think so. Sleeping with Ben tonight would make our first date not really a first, and then, shit. I don't know.

I need to get better at this thing called being social.

"What game were you playing?" he asks, eyeing the PlayStation.

"The Witcher 3: Wild Hunt," I say and try with every fiber of my being not to fear the Gamer Girl stereotypes. I fucking hate them. The whole Nerd Girl stereotype pisses me the fuck off, to be honest. I'd been quizzed more than once on my "knowledge" at a convention, and I only resisted punching the misogynistic asshat in the face to avoid being kicked out.

"I haven't played that one yet," Ben says. "But I want to. I haven't—is that a Nintendo 64?" His eyes go wide.

"Yeah, saved from my childhood."

"I haven't played one of those in years. It still

works?"

I nod. "It does. I have all the controllers and games from it too. Mario Kart on the 64 is still my favorite."

Ben looks back at me with a smile. "Can we play?" He blinks quickly, as if he's embarrassed for asking. "I mean, if you have to go to bed, I understand. Sometimes I forget most people get up early and have set hours since I don't."

My heart is about ready to jump out of my chest. "Yeah, we can play a few rounds." I know I'm tired and need sleep, but a *few* rounds won't hurt anything. "And I'm jealous of your lack of hours."

He takes off his shoes. "It's nice."

I get out the game and two controllers, handing one to Ben. I let him chose his character first, watching intently like it's an online personality test. It won't tell you anything worthwhile, but it's so important nonetheless.

He chooses Mario.

Safe move. You can't go wrong with Mario. I'm Toad, and we start the first Grand Prix race.

I win. Ben gets third. Not too shabby for not having played in years. A small part of me wonders if I should let him win the next race, since he's in second the entire third lap. I can't do it. I'm too competitive when it comes to games. Is that a flaw?

We end up placing first and second when races are over. The little celebration comes up on the screen. I watch it like I care, a little nervous to look at Ben. I want him to stay and play another round, but at the same time I'm so fucking tired from staying up so late.

"Well," he says and set the controller on the coffee table. "I should get some sleep. I'm a guest speaker at an art class early tomorrow." He stands and offers me a hand to help me off the couch. "And by early, I mean ten AM."

"That's almost my lunch break," I say with a smile. Our eyes meet and he parts his lips. My heart skips a beat like a school girl eyeballing her crush across the cafeteria. "What kind of class are you talking to?"

He shrugs. "I'm not too sure. I'll find out when I get there."

I shake my head. "Thanks again for bringing me my wallet."

"I'm glad I did," he says and turns. We walk to the door together. "Good night, Felicity. See you Friday."

"Yeah, Friday," I say. He doesn't lean in for a kiss or even give me a hug. He flashes that grin, and now I know he's completely aware how charming he looks when he does it. I close the door and practically skip into my room for bed.

❧

"You have got to knock it out of the park Friday night," Cameron says to me, holding a spoonful of yogurt in the air. It's Thursday morning, and I'm sitting in his office. "I'm talking tits out, dark eyeliner, and red lipstick. Stuff straight guys like."

"Red lipstick doesn't look good on me," I say, stomach churning.

"It's supposed to make you look more sexual, like remind men of how they want to put it in you or some nasty shit like that."

My eyebrows push together. "What the hell are you talking about?"

Cameron shrugs. "I saw an article on Facebook about it, and that's the real reason behind lipstick. To remind men that women have holes to stick it in." He holds his hand up. "Their words, not mine. But isn't the point of makeup to make you look more sexually attractive?"

"Maybe. Or maybe it's just to make you feel pretty?"

"You are too innocent sometimes with your viewpoints," he sighs. "But seriously. You gotta take it up a notch."

"You really think the gaming friend-zoned him?" The knot in my stomach tightens.

Cameron shrugs. "I can't say. Adam thinks so."

"Why can't I be friends with a guy *and* go out with him and have sexual feelings or whatever? Why does it have to be one or the other?"

"You do become friends with people, but that's later."

I nod. My dream guy is the hot and sexy knight in shining armor, but he's also my friend. He's someone I can have steamy sex with, and can lounge around the couch in my PJs playing video games with. I want the best of both worlds.

Am I wrong to think that's possible?

The strong, brooding, alpha-male is fine in fiction, but in real life, all that pushing up against a wall and fucking does not a real relationship make. I'll have days when I'm not in the mood. I'll have days when I'm sick and not attractive. I want the orgasm-so-hard-I-can't-walk sex *and* love and friendship.

"And you think I can fix this?"

"Oh of course." He takes another bite of yogurt. "You just have to show him you're more than one of the guys."

I nod, thinking I should probably listen to Cameron. He's always given me great advice before, yet there is a knot in my stomach—a separate knot from the friend-zone knot—that says I should just be me. I want a relationship, not a one-night stand. Yeah, sex with a hot guy would be great too, but I can't deny the deep-down longing for something long term.

Someday, right?

Someday I'll figure this crap we call life out and

learn how to fully ignore society's definition of what a woman should be, from the way we look and dress to the way we're supposed to clean the house, raise the kids, and have dinner ready and waiting on the table.

Someday.

Chapter Seven

I stand on the closed toilet, precariously balancing on tall heels, and snap a picture of myself in the mirror. I carefully jump down, wishing I had another way to get a full body shot of my reflection in the mirror in my bathroom, and send the picture to Erin.

I rush into my closet and change my top, slipping a silky black tank top on, and quickly shimmy into a pair of dark jeans. I ditch the heels, opting to holding them in my other hand instead of risking falling and breaking my neck before the date with Ben. I send her another picture, then move to the sink to take the hot rollers out of my hair.

A few seconds later she replies, saying both her and her hubby like outfit number two better. Good. I won't have to change again. With much care, I loosen the curls and create a new hole in the Ozone with hairspray, touch up my makeup, and accessorize with a red-jeweled necklace, matching earrings, and a black bracelet. I sit on the closed toilet to put on a pair of tall black heels, tastefully spotted with gold and scarlet gems. Yes, they are Gryffindor shoes, and yes, I fucking love them.

I put them on, spray myself with perfume, and look in the mirror.

"You are awesome," I tell myself. "The shit, actually. If Ben doesn't like you, then fuck him. His loss." I nod at myself, trying to believe the pep talk. Can I have a glass of wine? Just half a glass?

I'm so nervous.

I tighten my bra straps and reach inside my shirt to give my breasts a boost. I have on a push-up bra and might have done a super-light version of Cosplay cleavage, which entails using contouring to make my breasts look fuller and rounder ... not that they need much help though.

I leave the bathroom and straighten my bedspread. Ya know, just in case we come back here and things get physical. When was the last time I washed my sheets? Last week? Two weeks ago? Maybe longer since I can't even fucking remember.

I cringe and go crazy with the Febreze. I shove my dirty laundry into the closet, force the doors closed, and go into the living room. I have about ten minutes before Ben gets here to pick me up. We're going to Osteria Rossa, a fancy Italian restaurant in Grand Rapids. I'd yet to go there, and am really looking forward to yummy food.

I sit on the couch, getting the evil eye from Ser Pounce because I pushed him off my lap, not wanting to get covered in cat fur, and flip through channels. I end up watching the tail end of an episode of *Naked and Afraid* until the doorbell rings. I shoot up, count to ten, run my hands over my top, and go to the door.

"Wow," Ben blurts when I open the door. His dark eyes widen and he slowly looks me up and down, clearly not caring that he's obviously checking me out. "You look amazing."

"Thanks," I say, trying to brush off the compliment and not smile like a goon. "You don't look so bad yourself." He's wearing dark pants and a black button-up shirt. He's effortlessly put together. I take a step to the side. "Come in."

We move into the living room and he turns, eyes fucking me all over again. He closes his eyes in a long blink and bites his bottom lip. The he shakes himself and smiles.

"Hungry?"

"I am," I say. "You?"

"I'm always hungry." He sees Ser Pounce and reaches out to pet him. The fat cat hisses and turns his nose.

"He's an asshole, don't take it personally," I say. "I wanted a dog, but my old apartment didn't allow dogs. I think Ser Pounce knows that he was my second choice and resents life because of it."

Ben laughs, and I'm relieved. Not everyone understands my weird sense of serious-sounding sarcasm. "We should probably take off. Ready?"

"I am," I repeat and grab my purse. Ben waits for me as I lock the front door, then opens the passenger side door of his Audi for me. I get in, breathing in the scent of new leather and paint. I turn and see a sheet draped over the backseat, protecting the leather from all the art supplies he has thrown in the back. Yes, definitely a chaotic mess creative type. We make small talk, mostly Ben telling me how Mindy still can't figure out how to use the website.

He opens the door and offers me his hand when we get to the restaurant. I carefully step onto the curb, clutching my purse in the other hand. Ben locks the car and pockets his keys.

And he doesn't let go of my hand.

We have reservations, and only wait a couple of minutes before the hostess leads us to a table in the back of the restaurant. The lighting is low and it's supa fancy. I feel nervous again.

You're the shit.

Yes. I am. We sit opposite each other. Ben orders a bottle of red wine—thank God—and the waiter brings us bread to nibble on as we look over the menu.

"You said you haven't lived here long," Ben starts as he takes a drink of wine.

"No, I got a new job and moved from Mistwood about seven months ago."

"Mistwood?"

"It's a small-ish town near Lake Michigan."

He nods. "Do you like it here?"

I shrug. "It's been okay so far. It's kind of fun being somewhere new, and the job is pretty easy."

"I'd think so," he comments. "What's someone who graduated from MIT doing working in customer service?"

"Oh," I say and put another piece of bread on my plate. "I don't actually do customer service. I was filling in for someone else at the company I work for."

"What do you actually do, then?"

"Code websites. Easy-peasy stuff." I wave my hand in the air. "I used to be a software programmer before this. Loved the job, but the place I worked didn't offer much room for growth. Or raises," I add with a wry smile. "Who knows where I'll be in a year or two."

Ben is smiling. "You've got the wanderlust bug."

"I do," I agree. "I like traveling and going new places."

"So do I." He dips his bread in oil and takes a bite.

I take another drink of wine. "Have you always been here?"

"I grew up in Detroit," he says. "My father was in the military so we moved around a lot until I was a teen, and he was done with the army for good."

"That must have been hard," I reply, knowing how hard middle and high school was for me and I had the same friends throughout both.

"It wasn't so bad." He shrugs. "When you're constantly going somewhere new it forces you to not be shy. I think it pushed me to be an artist too."

"Really? How so?"

"I liked sports, but you can't join teams mid

season," he starts to explain. "Which makes it harder to make friends. But you can always join art clubs no matter what point it is in the school year."

"I wouldn't have taken you for an art club type," I admit. "You don't look the type."

"You said it: looks can be deceiving." He lets out a breath. "I always liked art, liked being able to get lost in something."

That's how I feel about Cosplay and fantasy. I feel another connection to Ben. "And you're good at it, right?"

He smiles. "That too. I really don't think anyone can be *bad* at art. It's expressing something. If you can't paint landscapes, sculpt. There's always another way to get what you feel on the inside onto something on the outside." He shakes his head. "It wasn't always easy moving around, and art gave me that outlet."

I like seeing this deeper side to him. "That makes sense."

"I did eventually get used to moving, and used to making new friends. And that's how my parents met," he goes on. "My dad was stationed in Japan for a while. Brought my mom back with him." He laughs softly. "I think my grandparents are still pissed about it."

"Have you ever gone there to visit them?"

He moves his head up and down as he finishes chewing. "A few times. I haven't been there in years though, and I'm wanting to go back."

"I've never been there," I say. "I'd love to go. So much."

"It's beautiful. My grandparents are a bit old school too, so it's almost like going back in time. And Tokyo is just … so much. There are so many people and there's always something going on. It's nonstop, but it's awesome." His eyes grow big as he talks, and the passion and excitement takes over his face. "It's easy to get that lost in the crowd feeling when thousands of people pass you buy unnoticed, but it has an energy about it that's just contagious."

"Why haven't you gone in a few years?" I ask and hope it's not prying.

"I opened the gallery here a few years ago," he says. "And it's kept me a lot busier than I expected. But I love it too."

I don't really know what being an artist entails, though I imagine it's pretty fucking awesome, like getting paid to get up and do your hobby. Making websites isn't art, but it's creating something, and seeing something come from nothing.

"I like to sew," I declare. "Not really the same thing."

"I've never attempted sewing," he says. "What do you like to sew?"

"Costumes," I answer. "I like to Cosplay."

"So you're one of those people who go to Comic Con all dressed up?" There is amusement in his voice, but it's not judgmental.

"I am. It's so much fun."

"I've never been to Comic Con."

"Wizard World in Chicago is coming up at the end of summer," I tell him. "My friend Erin and I are going. We go every year."

"Are you dressing up?"

"Of course."

The smile is back on his face. Before he can ask me anything else, the waiter comes over to take our order. I hadn't looked over the menu at all, so I order the same thing Ben does.

"So," I start once the waiter leaves. "What do you do other than paint?"

"Hang out with friends, work out." He shrugs. "Usual stuff. I've been going to a lot of galas and art shows lately," he says almost like it's a surprise. I nod like I have no idea either, although his pictures came up when I searched him on the internet, smiling next to one of his paintings, with the buyer on the other side. And the buyers ranged from politicians to CEOs of huge companies. He hasn't said it out loud to me—yet—but I know he has a piece in the Museum of Modern Art in New York. Once that went up, his popularity increased tenfold … and then he moved here. Weird. Or at least that's what the research says. "And I like to read."

"Me too. I read a lot. What do you like to read?"

"Anything, really. I've been into the classics lately. You?"

"I love paranormal romance."

"I've never read that," he muses. "Is it like that Fifty Shades stuff with vampires?"

I laugh. "There are some like that."

Ben wiggles his eyebrows. "Then maybe I will read it. I do like to be bitten."

My cheeks flush at his blunt confession, and I'm not sure if he's joking or telling the truth. I think he's telling the truth. If things get hot and heavy tonight, should I go in for the kill and nip him with my teeth? The extent of my BDSM knowledge goes so far as tips from *Cosmo*, and after that last article about poking a man's tender regions with a fork—don't break the skin, they said, like that was even a question—I'm doubting all their advice.

No surprise, my brain gets ahead of me again and I get a flash of flesh and see Ben on top of me, thrusting those glorious hips into me, and I gently clamp my teeth down on his neck. Blood warms my cheeks, going through me and making me feel hot between my legs.

The waiter brings us more bread and refills our wine glasses. I pick mine up, fingers trembling slightly, and take a big sip. I set the glass down and look at Ben, unable to get the image of him naked and on top of me out of my head.

We keep talking about normal first date things, like our families and work. The food comes and we get words in between bites. The silence isn't awkward,

99

but I'm so worried it will be I keep saying stupid things, things no one cares about, like how long it takes me to clean my house. I like talking to Ben, and the more time that passes, the more comfortable I feel. There is still a formality in the way he talks to me, like he's not really being himself. He's "on" and his game is good.

Suave, smooth, confident. Yep. He's got it all.

I get sauce on the side of my mouth when I take a bite of cheese ravioli. Some splatters on my shirt. Thank God the fabric is dark and you can't see the stain. I don't have it all. And I never will.

I mentally sigh.

When we're done with the main course, Ben orders two pieces of cheesecake without asking me what I want. Should that bug me? Or should his dominance turn me on? (Because it does.) And I like cheesecake. Pick your battles, right?

I'm nowhere near drunk after the wine plus all the food, but my mind is a little buzzed and it helps me relax. I slowly eat the cheesecake, legit full from filling up on so much bread—but it was so good! Whoever doesn't fill up on bread, or chips and salsa, or whatever you get before a meal at a restaurant has no soul, I swear—and feel Ben's eyes on me.

I look up and smile. "Do I want to know what you're thinking?" I ask and pick up my water.

He gives me a wicked grin. "You might be interested in it."

"Then you better tell me." I slowly run my finger down the stem of my wine glass.

His eyes drop to my chest then go back to my face. "I don't see how you weren't the popular girl in high school, like you said. You look like you would be."

I drop my gaze. "Looks can be deceiving." He's meant it as a compliment, but his words make me feel self-conscious. Damn it.

"They can."

"I didn't always look like this," I offer and know I should just shut my stupid mouth and stop talking.

"That doesn't matter," he says. "I didn't know you then. And I like the way you look now. A lot."

I can't help the smile that pulls up on my lips. "Yeah, it's not so bad," I say back. The waiter brings us the check; Ben grabs it before I can even look at it and pays, leaving a rather large tip.

I waited tables in college. Ben just earned major bonus points from me.

He takes my hand when we leave the restaurant. The night is still warm, and a light breeze rustles my hair. Stars do their best to shine above us, despite the light pollution. It's perfect.

"I don't know about you," Ben says, "but I'm not ready to call this a night yet."

"I'm not ready either."

Hand in hand, we slowly walk to his car. He opens the door for me again, then gets in the driver's seat. "What do you want to do?" he asks as he pushes the start button. "We could get drinks at Stacks."

That's another place I'd never been but had heard of. Stacks is an upscale bar that caters to white-collar businessmen. So not my thing.

My nose wrinkles and Ben laughs. "You have another idea?"

"It's so nice outside. We could ... uh ... go mini golfing and ride go-karts," I blurt, saying the first thing that comes to mind. Plus I rock mini-golf.

Ben's face goes slack and I'm sure he's thinking that's the stupidest thing in the entire fucking world to suggest we do on a first date. We're adults, after all. He puts his hands on the steering wheel. "That sounds awesome," he says and the smile returns to his face.

I sit back in the seat, grinning ear to ear.

"You're cheating!" Ben laughs after I get my third hole-in-one. "I don't know how, but you're cheating!" He sets his beer down on the bricks that outline the eighth hole and drops his ball, using his foot to line it up with the hole.

I grab my ball and hop off the AstroTurf, piña colada sloshing down my hand. "Yes, cheating with my telekinetic powers," I laugh back.

Ben hits the ball. It bounces off the side of the little brick path, rolls halfway up the sloped course, and comes back down. We both laugh. It takes him five more attempts before we can move on.

"I didn't know these places served booze," Ben says, grabbing his beer. "Well, the last time I was at one, I wasn't old enough to drink."

"I assume they started doing it for the parents who come with small children," I say. "You know, the ones that take even longer than you. They have to drink to keep their sanity."

He takes my arm as we walk across a wooden planked bridge. It's not the easiest thing to do in heels.

"You're probably right."

We stop at the next hole, and I step aside. "Go ahead. Let's see if you can get it in the hole on your first try."

Ben turns to me, a devilish glint in his eyes. "I always get it in the first try."

Oh boy.

I open my mouth, wanting to say something sexy and witty back to him. But only a garbled, "I bet" comes out. He flashes me his bedroom eyes and sets the ball down.

I stare at his tight ass, thinking of it sans clothing with my nails digging into his flesh as he goes to town, pumping and thrusting into me. I get hit with a hot flash, and I know it's not from my oncoming period.

I take a big gulp of my drink and shake my head. A group of teenagers shriek and laugh across the course. It's a group of three couples, and they are all over each other in a typical juvenile public display of affection.

"Young love," Ben muses, looking up. "They don't know how easy they have it."

"No bills, no jobs, just homework and parents to deal with," I say. "But still, I'd never go back to high school if you paid me." Unless I was undercover, like in a movie. Then maybe I'll consider it. Maybe.

Ben's ball rolls into the little white hole next to a fake pond filled with water so scummy the fountain is clogged and just spitting up bubbles instead of spraying the water into the air.

"You really hated it that much?" He steps off the course.

I drop my ball, hit, and miss. It goes into the water. I grimace and walk up to get it, using my purple golf club to pull it from the water. "I'd never go back, if that tells you anything," I say. "But it was years ago. I'm over it."

"I loved high school," he admits and it doesn't surprise me. He's always been good looking, I can tell, and I'm sure he's always been athletic and talented too. "But I wouldn't go back either. College, yes."

"Oh me too," I say. I'd go back for a do-over. I fucked up big time in college. "That was fun."

I get a hole-in-two and Ben and I exchange party stories as we finish the course. I win, by a lot, but I stopped keeping score after the fourth hole and it became apparent I'd dominate.

"Are you up for go-karts?" I ask Ben when we turn in our golf clubs and balls. I finish my piña colada and toss the plastic cup in the recycling bin next to the trash.

"If it involves you, I'm up for anything," he says and I can't help but wonder if the "up" reference has to do with his penis.

I'm so fucking mature, I know.

"Let's see if your Mario Kart skills carry over into the real world," he teases and buys us tickets. There's not many people left this late, and the park closes in twenty minutes. It's more than enough time. We get into our little cars and the attendant comes over to check our seat belts. Ben revs his engine, wiggling his eyebrows at me.

"You're going down," he says. Another sexual reference? Gah, I need to stop.

"So are you," I threaten and rev my own engine, getting a stern look from the man in charge. Mine was a sexual reference, by the way. I love a man who goes down on a woman.

The green light flashes and we take off, passing the three other people on the course—who are all twelve years old or younger. Ben jerks his wheel, slamming into me. My car shutters and hits the wall, bouncing off the rubber tires lining it.

I laugh and hit him back but he swerves out of the way just in time. We fly down a hill and my kart gains enough speed to pass him. He catches up quickly and rams into me again, causing me to spin out and get stuck.

"Hah!" he calls out, smiling as he goes on. I have to wait for the stupid attendant to come over and turn the car around. Seriously, why isn't there reverse on these things? I'm off again, laughing when one of the kids hits Ben's kart, slowing him down enough for me to pass.

"That's karma for you!" I shout as I fly by. Ben's on the go again, his kart picking up speed, and he T-bones me. We both spin out, laughing. The attendant comes over, muttering about how this "isn't bumper cars" and turns us both back around. We have one lap left, and Ben gets ahead by just a few feet. He wins, and waits for me at the finish line.

He hops out of his kart and comes over to me, offering me a hand. I climb out, a bit unsteady on my Harry Potter heels, and I stumble. He catches me, hands closing on my waist, and he holds me a moment longer than necessary, not letting go even after I get my balance back.

I feel his muscles through his clothes, smell his cologne, sense the warmth of his skin. I shiver. He turns, letting one hand drop to his side. The other stays on my waist. Once we're back on the sidewalk, heading to the parking lot, he slides his hand down to the curve in my hip. Cameron's words about wearing Spanx come back to haunt me, and I hope and pray Ben either doesn't notice or doesn't mind the extra fat I have sitting on my hips, stored there and waiting for me to go into hibernation or something.

His fingers press into my flesh and I'm suddenly so hot between my legs. I hook my arm around him and rest my head on his shoulder.

"Thanks," he says when we get in the car. "I haven't had fun like that in, fuck, too long."

"You're welcome," I reply and more of Cameron's words come back, worse than haunting. It's full-on demonic possession and I'm internally panicking that this "fun date" has put me even more into the friend-zone. What was I thinking? I should have played off the smart, sexy girl Ben thinks I am instead of letting my inner dork come out and beat him badly in mini golf.

I bite my lip and pick my purse up from the floor of the car. On auto pilot, I grab my phone and see I have a missed call from my brother followed by two texts. I never replied to his question about having a plus (or minus) one for the wedding. I have another "good luck!" text from Erin that makes me smile. I love that girl. I put my phone down and fret over being labeled as one of the guys the rest of the way back to my house.

Ben glances at me from time to time, the

happiness in his eyes turning to confusion by the time we pull into the driveway. I'm about to get out and walk myself up to the door, because at this point I've convinced myself nothing more is happening. I'm such a good self-cheerleader, I know.

Ben beats me to it. He cuts the engine and gets out, rushing around to get the door for me. He takes my hand and slowly laces our fingers.

"Do you want to come inside?" I ask. "I have wine."

He pulls me to him and my body crushes against his. The heat is back between my legs and my body longs to feel more. "Yeah, I want to come inside."

"Good," I blurt.

He chuckles. "You sound surprised."

"No, I'm not, I'm just, uh, uh, glad because I want you to come in too in case, uh, in case you want to, and we, uh, can play games or something," I stammer and my cheeks are suddenly as hot as my lady bits.

But not in a good way.

Thank the fucking lord it's too dark out here to see the blushing. I need to learn to stop talking. Seriously. I say the dumbest things when I'm nervous. Ben's fingers inch along my back, until the tips are just under the waist of my jeans.

"I'd like to play games with you," he tells me, voice deep and commanding. My head goes up on its own accord, and his lips are just inches from mine.

He moves a hand up, cupping my cheek, then brings me to him as he parts his lips.

I'm suddenly nervous and forget how to kiss. Do I close my eyes? Open my mouth now or later? And my hands? What the fuck do I do with my hands?

His soft, full lips crash against mine and everything falls into place.

I hold onto his waist, sliding my hands up his back. His tongue opens my mouth and slips inside, causing my knees to weaken as I hold tighter to him. The kiss intensifies and he pushes me against the car before finally breaking away, tipping his head so his lips brush against my ear.

"You have no idea how much I've wanted to fuck you all night," he whispers.

For once, I don't speak, don't say something to kill the mood. I put my hands on his face, turn his head back to mine, and kiss him again. I take his hand and lead him to the house, desperately feeling around in my oversized bag for my house keys.

Bugs swarm around the porch light. I swat them away and finally get the damn key. My hands are trembling as I push it into the lock. I turn the key, madly opening the door. We step inside and I throw my purse onto the ground. Ser Pounce hisses at Ben from the couch.

That's right. Be jealous. Someone else is sleeping in my bed tonight. Maybe. Probably? We'll end up in bed, I'm sure. But I don't think much sleeping is going to happen.

The heat of the moment has cooled down a bit. I swallow, take my shoes off, and look at Ben with wide eyes, not sure what to do now. He steps out of his shoes and reaches for me, hands sliding around my waist and under my shirt.

My heart lurches in my chest. He draws me in until my breasts smash into his firm chest. He's looking right into my eyes, confident, calm, so damn sure of himself and what he's going to do next.

He brushes my hair back and kisses me softly, pulling back and moving his lips to my neck. A shiver runs through me, and I'm so fucking wet. I want him now. Like *now* now.

My breath leaves me and he takes a step forward, and now I'm pressed between Ben's body and the wall. In the heels, I'm close to his height. Without them, I can feel his cock harden against my stomach.

He breaks away and rests his forehead against mine. "Want that glass of wine?" he asks.

I want a tall glass of you.

I nod, but don't move. Ben is still holding me against the wall, after all. "If you do," I pant. He grinds his hips into mine and sucks at the skin on my neck. I run my hands through his hair and gasp when his teeth clip me.

Fuck the wine. Actually, fuck Ben. That's what I want to do. I want to fuck him. My hands drop to his waist and I'm untucking his shirt from his pants without really knowing what I'm doing. His mouth is on mine again and his hands go from my waist to my breasts.

I unbuckle his belt next and pull it through the loops, letting it fall to the floor. My hand finds its way to his thigh and runs up it, feeling his erection through his pants. His tongue pushes into mine and he can't kiss me hard enough. I move my hands up to his chest and give him a gentle shove. He takes a step back, not letting me go, and stumbles over our discarded shoes. We take another step back then pause to grope each other.

"Wine?" I say between kisses.

"Later," he growls. "I fucking want you."

Holy shit. "Okay," I say and am too swept up in the moment to get embarrassed. I take his hand and turn, leading him into my room. As soon as I'm through the door, Ben's arms wrap around my waist. He lifts me up, and my legs go around him. He takes a few steps to the bed then tosses me down and advances, pinning me to the mattress with his body.

I'm so hot for him I can hardly stand it. He kisses me, slowly trailing his mouth down my neck, kissing my collarbone. He sits up just enough to grab the hem of my top. I push up and hold my arms above my head. He pulls it off and lets it drop on the floor next to us.

He looks at me, and all I can think is how I ate too much at dinner. Booze makes me bloat. These pants are too tight along my waist and my pushin' for the cushin' spills out too much. I should have worn the mother-effing Spanx.

He lets out a moan. "Fuck, you're beautiful."

I'm so glad I don't have the stupid Spanx on. It's awkward to take them off, anyway.

"You really think so?" I blurt and he nods. "Tell me again."

His eyes glimmer and I realize he thinks I'm attempting to dirty talk and dominate, not seeking reassurance.

Desire burns in his eyes, and he looks at me like I'm the most beautiful woman in the world. "You're a fucking knock-out." He buries his head between my breasts, sucking and kissing. He reaches behind me and unhooks my bra with one hand, faster than I can unhook it myself and I wear the damn thing every day. Well, nearly every day.

I roll the straps down my arms. Ben moves it out of the way, grinding his cock into me as he gazes at my breasts. He groans and dives down, taking one in his mouth, tongue circling my erect nipple. I toss my head back and rake my fingers through his hair. I've never gotten off on nipple stimulation. Really, it did nothing for me.

Until now.

My whole body is alive, humming with pleasure of what's to come. It's going to be fucking epic, I know it.

I don't even realize he's unbuttoned my jeans until he starts to pull them down. I lift my hips to allow them to come free, bending my knees and pulling my legs out. The jeans join my shirt and bra on the floor.

I'm laying here in just dark-purple panties, and Ben is fully clothed. This isn't right. I put my hands on the side of his face and gently push him off of me.

"Something's wrong," I say.

Is that disappointment that flashes through his eyes? "What's wrong?"

"You still have your clothes on."

The disappointment quickly transforms into lust, and he gives me that grin, the famous grin I'm now forever going to associate as the "I'm going to fuck your brains out and make it impossible for you to walk in the morning" grin. He sits up and unbuttons his shirt. I watch like he's my own personal Magic Mike warming up before a show. Slowly, he peels his shirt back.

Holy sex on a stick.

Black tattoos cross his chest, going over his shoulders and down his biceps. It's too dark to discern exactly what they are, but I'm able to make out a skull and a few Japanese characters. He's muscular, with abs I'd lick chocolate—fuck, I'd even lick ranch dressing off those babies—and biceps too big for me to come close to wrapping my hands around.

My heart is pounding, blood rushing through me. I've never wanted anyone so badly before in my life. I lick my lips and unbutton his pants. The force of his erection pushes the zipper down, and the tip of his dick is sticking out the top of his black boxers. It's glistening and wet and abso-fucking-lutely perfect. The only thing that could make it better is it being inside me.

He's back on me, putting himself between my spread legs, kissing me like I'm the last woman on earth and his life depends on it. I'm so hot, so wound up that I feel like I might come just from him brushing against my clit through my panties.

He moves slightly to the side and hooks my leg over his, holding onto my thigh. We kiss for another moment and then he breaks away, moving down. His lips trail from my neck to my stomach. Holy fucking lord. He's going to—

I cry out when his fingers sweep against me. The muscles in my thighs tighten when he pulls the panties off. I twist the comforter in my hands, opening my eyes to watch him go to town.

He moves slowly, knowing he's a fucking tease. His hands slide under my thighs, spreading me and pulling me against him. His tongue lashes out against my clit, hard, then soft, then hard again.

Oh. My. God.

He turns his head and kisses my inner thigh, the same time he runs his fingernails along my stomach.

It's almost too much and we just fucking got started. I twist the blanket in my hands, not trusting myself not to grab his head and force him against me until I came. Twice. Three times, maybe.

He turns back, mouth against my core, and licks and sucks. My chest rises and falls and my mouth is open. I curl my legs around his shoulders, breath quickening even more. I'm so close.

Ben knows it, too, that fucker. He slows down, pulling back and only giving me soft, gentle kisses, making me arch my back so that my center stays in contact with his sweet, wonderful mouth and that oh-so talented tongue.

After a minute of torture, he goes back in full force, sliding a finger inside me. I moan out load, pleasure erupting. My abs tighten and I don't breath as the orgasm rolls through me, ending with a shudder that leaves me quivering and pulsing against his mouth.

I'm panting, vision blacked out. He keeps his mouth on me, drawing it out, waiting until I stop floating in bliss to let me go. He wipes his mouth and moves back up. It takes all I have in me to reach down and grab his cock and guide him inside me. My fingertips feel all tingly from that strong orgasm.

Fuck, yes.

I wrap my fingers around his thick shaft, pulling his wetness down and using it as I pump my hand. He moans and kisses my neck. I keep working my hand until I can bend my legs again. Then I flip him over, yanks his pants off, and start returning the favor.

Ben tangles his fingers in my hair, breathing heavily as I flick my tongue over the tip of his dick. He reaches for me, fingers stroking my clit, bringing me close to coming. Again.

When he's close, he pulls me onto him, cock rubbing against me, then begrudgingly sits up to get a condom from the wallet in the pocket of his pants. I clench my jaw, impatiently watching him put it on. I wipe my face and quickly run my hands through my hair, hoping I still look as hot as I feel.

Ben drops the condom wrapper on the bed and is on top of me in an instant. I open my legs and bend my knees, urging him to me. He cradles my head in his hands, lowers his lips to mine, and kisses me as he slides inside.

His dick is large; I know that since I was just all up in its business, but I underestimated how big now that it's inside me, thrusting, pulsing, pushing in and out. Ben's holding himself up above me, muscles tight and bulging. I feel his biceps, imagining the tattoos beneath my fingers. I slit my eyes open just enough to get a look at his handsome face.

Arching my back allows his thick, wonderful, magic fuck-stick to hit my g-spot. I let out another moan as I come, holding him tighter. He moves his head down, nuzzling my breasts. I pick my head up and flick my tongue along his ear. Ben softly groans,

116

and his movements quicken.

I nip at his earlobe with my teeth and he pushes into me as deep as he can, moaning as he finishes. He lowers himself, cock still pulsating inside me, and rests his head against mine. A few beats pass before he slowly slides out and rolls onto his side. His arms slip around my waist and he kisses the side of my neck.

I let out a satisfied breath and relax against Ben. I want to enjoy this moment, relish in the fact that I'm all tingly and warm and can still feel Ben's big dick between my legs. I'm sure I'll feel it in the morning too.

But of course, with me being me, I start thinking that something has to be said before this gets awkward. We'll have to face the music sometime soon, and I have to pee so it's not like I can pretend to be asleep.

Ben trails his fingers up my stomach and gently fondles my sensitive breasts. I shiver and tip my head toward him. He leans over and kisses me.

Could this be any more perfect? I'm convinced he's the perfect lover.

"That was really nice," I blurt. "I enjoyed it." I'm not rating a video game. I squeeze my eyes closed. *Fuck, what is wrong with me?*

"I'm glad you did," he says. "I did too."

I just nod and try to relax. I'm tensing at my own lack of social skills. Is after-sex talk even considered a social skill? I clamp my jaw shut, resisting the urge to ask him "now what?"

He runs his finger over the curve in my hip and presses his lips to my neck. He's not acting like he wants to jump up and run home. That's good, right? Another few minutes pass before he gets up and goes into the bathroom, grabbing just his boxers.

I'm overanalyzing everything and it hits me that I really want things to work with Ben. I want a second date. Then a third. And a fourth. I want to see where this can go. I like him, and I think soon I can really like him, given a few more dates and another (okay, more than one please) fucking awesome cooter clash like he'd just given me.

It also hits me that I'm not really sure what to do now. I'm far from being a virgin, but I haven't had that many relationships. I lost my virginity the beginning of senior year in high school, dated that loser for a while then hit a dry spell until college, where I met, dated, and bedded an even bigger loser—but that's another story. I swore off men for a while after that, not getting back into the game until after I turned twenty-one. Things were casual, and I had one good fuck buddy until he decided to grow a vagina and develop feelings for me.

Then I dated Mr. Foot Fucker. Yeah ... no need to bring that up. But we had actually dated for a while before we hooked up, which, thinking back on it, was probably done on purpose. He made me have feelings

118

for him, made me care *before* he asked to suck my toes while he beat himself off.

Because I would have grabbed the polka-dot stilettos he always wanted me to wear and booked it the fuck out of there if I didn't care deeply for him.

And that brings me back to Ben.

Ben.

The cool, confident, sophisticated, sexy artist. I'm not romanticizing him, not at all. I didn't know him very well yet, we'd only been on—hold the phone.

One date.

We'd gone on only one date. Not two. One. And we slept together. Did that make me a slut? Do I care if it does? (No, I don't.) But what I do care about is what Ben thinks of me. I'm not easy. I don't give it up to anyone who wines and dines me. There's something about him, something that makes me unable to hold back any and all passion, something that makes me so comfortable to be around him even when I'm nervous.

And none of that makes sense.

What is he doing to me?

The toilet flushes and I hear water running. Ben's coming out any second now. I run my hands through my hair, pushing it out of my face, and throw back the comforter, pulling down the sheets. I slip underneath, moving it up to cover my breasts. Not because I don't want Ben to see, but because that's what they do in movies.

It's sexy, right?

Or maybe it's just a sexy way to censor nipples?

(Fuck censorship, by the way.)

The bathroom door opens, and I know I have to be realistic. Ben can very well tell me he has to go, has work in the morning, blah, blah, blah, and I can't blame him. I can't get mad at him.

His eyes meet mine and his lips pull up in a small smile. He picks up the rest of his clothes and my heart sinks a bit. Yep, he's leaving.

"Well," I start. Should I thank him? No, that doesn't feel like the right thing to say. Hope to do this again another time? Yeah, that might work. It's the honest truth, anyway. He lazily folds his clothes together and tosses them on the chair next to my dresser. Then he's climbing back into bed.

I'm in that bed.

I blink, heart skipping a beat as it rises back into place. He doesn't get under the covers, but he lays down and drapes his arm around me, resting his head against my stomach, which in turn presses on my bladder and reminds me I have to pee. Stupid bodily functions ruining the moment. I run my fingers through his hair.

"My turn," I say softly and try to be as graceful as possible when I get out of bed and walk into the bathroom. I'm still naked, completely naked, and I know he's watching.

I pee, wash my hands, and debate on taking my

makeup off now or later. I decide on later mostly because I'm lazy. I'll actually end up falling asleep with it on, like usual. There is a short nightgown hanging on the back of the bathroom door. It barely covers my ass, and is outlined in lace.

But it's dark green with the Green Lantern symbol on the chest. Oh well. I pull it on, noticing that my nipples are still hard and very visible through the thin fabric. That's definitely not a bad thing, not right now.

I go back in the room and get in bed next to Ben.

"So," he starts and reaches for me. "How about a glass of wine?"

Chapter Eight

I wake up around ten AM that next morning. I have a slight headache, thanks to the two bottles of wine Ben and I polished off last night. We stayed up way too late drinking and drunk racing each other in Mario Kart. I think it was nearing four in the morning when we had sex again on my living room floor then wobbled into my room and passed out in bed together, naked and sweaty, and cuddling until we drifted off into a booze and sex-induced blissful sleep.

My mouth is dry, I need to use the bathroom, and probably brush my teeth. I run my hands over my face, feeling little crusts of mascara on my cheeks. Thank God I woke up before Ben.

He's still sleeping, breathing deep and steady, and he's lying on his stomach, arm wrapped around a pillow. He's sprawled out, hogging over half the bed, and has the blankets tangled around his legs like he tried to kick them off in his sleep. I admire his bare ass for a minute then quietly get out of bed and slink into the bathroom.

Turning on the shower, I brush most of the knots from my hair while waiting for the water to warm, then jump in, brushing my teeth while the shampoo rinses from my hair. I re-shave my armpits because those fuckers grow a full head of hair overnight, but skip my legs for the sake of saving time.

I towel dry my hair the best I can, rake my fingers through it, and decide that's good enough. Ben is still sleeping when I get dressed and pad into the kitchen to stick a K-cup in the Keurig. While the water is heating up, I preheat the oven and grab a can of cinnamon rolls from the fridge. I peel back the label and put it on the counter, pressing a spoon to the seam. Before I can actually push down, I close my eyes and turn away, like I'm clipping the red wire of a homemade bomb with three seconds left until detonation.

I fucking hate opening cans of biscuits.

I stick them in the oven before it's at the optimal temp, but that'll help them cook faster, right? Breakfast now cooking, I get a cup of coffee and pick up my phone. I need to talk to Erin. Stat.

I sit at my little island counter and send her a text.

Ben and I hooked up after one date! HOLY SHIT! But seriously, WTF do I do now? He's still sleeping in my bed.

I add creamer to my coffee, waiting for Erin's reply. I'm not sure if she's working today or not, but if she is she's probably busy decorating a wedding cake. My phone buzzes a minute later with a response from her.

Make him breakfast in bed, suck his dick, and tell him he's the best you've ever had. Then offer anal. Definitely anal.

I raise an eyebrow. *Hi, David,* I type back. *Is Erin around?*

She's at work, he replies. *Left her phone at home. You really hooked up on the first date? Boo, you whore.*

I smile and shake my head. He won't admit *Mean Girls* is one of his favorite movies, yet he quotes it all the time.

Haha, thanks. Have Erin call me when she gets home, please, I type. He responds with a thumbs up emoji and I exit out of my texts. I scroll through Facebook, not really paying attention to what I'm looking at, as I wait for the rolls to finish baking, or for Ben to wake up. Whichever happens first.

They end up happening at pretty much the same time. I open the oven when Ben walks into the kitchen.

"Smells good," he says.

"Thanks," I say and set the hot pan on the stove. "There's coffee too, if you want some."

Ben rubs his temples. "I think I need some." He gets himself a cup and sits at the island. I frost the rolls before they've cooled and the cream cheese frosting melts down the sides just the way I like it. I dish two up and take a seat next to Ben.

"What are your plans the rest of today?" he asks

and slices his cinnamon roll apart with his fork.

"Nothing really," I say. I have nothing planned for the whole weekend other than gaming and working on my costume. "You?"

"Nothing really either," he replies. "I have a work thing tonight." He makes a face. "I told you I go to events a lot."

"You say that like you don't like them."

"I do and I don't," he explains then takes a bite. Once he's finished chewing, he continues. "It's work. I like selling paintings, of course, and getting recognized for it, but it's all fake smiles and bullshit small talk. I didn't start painting so I could go to things like that."

It's an honest confession, and I feel like I can see the real Ben right there in front of me.

"Makes sense," I say. "I don't go to many black-tie events though, so wearing a pretty dress and sparkly jewelry seems fun."

"For maybe an hour," he says dryly. "Then you'll get bored, trust me."

"How's the food at those things?"

He chuckles. "Not too bad, actually. But I don't get to sit down and eat. I'm busy walking around and talking."

"Aww, poor baby," I tease.

He nudges me. "Shut up. Yeah, yeah, I should be thankful and all that." He raises an eyebrow. "But it's still boring as fuck."

I hold up my coffee cup. "Here's to a non-boring-as-fuck night."

"Thanks," he says and picks up his own coffee mug. "If you were with me, it wouldn't be boring."

He's referencing sex again. I think. Or maybe I'm good company to keep? Hell if I know.

He finishes his cinnamon roll and set his fork down on his plate. "Are you up for one more round of Mario Kart?"

Ben said he'd call me when he left an hour later. I didn't ask when he'd call, even though I wanted to. It's a legit question, after all. Sunday came and passed with no word from him. So did Monday. Tuesday morning I get up and think what we had was a fling. I'm feeling a little down as I drive to work, and stop at the McDonald's drive thru to get something greasy that will kill my stomach later as comfort food.

Around eleven, I'm nodding off as I code a custom template for another client. My stomach grumbles and I can taste the two hash browns I ate earlier. I lean back in my rolly chair and rub my eyes, thankful I didn't bother with mascara this morning. I'm thinking about what I should get for lunch when Ben texts me.

When do you get off work?

Five-ish, I type back. *Why?*

I want to see you.

I smile and read his two texts again, making sure I read his message right. Before I can reply he asks me when I go to lunch and asks if I want to meet with him somewhere. My smile broadens and we agree to meet at noon at a locally run cafe not far from my office.

The next hour drags on forever.

Ben is already in the cafe when I get there, absent-mindedly stirring his coffee with his straw, eyes down on a book. He looks up when I'm a few feet away and smiles.

"Hey," he says and checks me out. A flash of regret over my outfit choice goes through me, but I quickly squish it down. I like my World of Warcraft Alliance Polo shirt. And Polo shirts are sexy ... or at least they were in the early 2000s. Whatever.

Ben is wearing jeans and a light blue T-shirt that is covered in something dark, but looks too thin to be paint. The closer I get, the more I can smell the varnish. He doesn't give a fuck how he looks, though to be fair, the messy artist look is working for him.

"Hi," I say and take my purse off my shoulder. He puts his book down and stands, extending an arm, putting it around my waist and pulling me in for a quick kiss.

"How long do you have?" he asks me.

"Like forty-five minutes. You? Oh wait, it doesn't

127

matter, does it?"

He smiles and shakes his head. "Not really, though I try to set hours for myself or I'm at the gallery all night." He shrugs. "Not that I mind."

"Lucky."

"I know. We should order food now so you don't run out of time. What do you want?" He pulls his wallet out of his pocket. Is that a subtle way of saying this is a date? Fuck. Why is everything so awkward when it comes to dating?

"I usually get the veggie pot pie here," I say.

"Sit down, relax," he says. "I'll get it."

"Thanks." I take a seat across from where he'd been sitting, and see that he's reading a contemporary thriller. It's a popular book, one that's been on the lists for a while now, but hadn't caught my interest. My phone is dinging like crazy from inside my purse. I had texted Erin on the way over to tell her that I'd heard from Ben, and she was already asking for deets.

I turn my phone on silent. I'll text her later, like when I'm sitting at my desk and am supposed to be doing work. Ben returns to the table.

"How's work?"

"Meh, it's work."

"Are you going on any more customer service calls?"

I shake my head. "The temp is there to take over, thank God. I really don't like dealing with people," I admit and Ben laughs. "Though I'm glad I took that one call with that asshole client."

"I'm glad you did too." He reaches across the table and takes my hand, gently pressing his thumb into my palm. "Want to go out again this weekend?"

"I do," I say without even having to think about it. "Have anything in mind?"

"Dinner … movie … sex," he says casually and it takes all I have not to look around and see who heard. Not that I'd mind, since that sex is happening with me.

"I can live with that," I tell him. "Friday?"

He makes a face. "I have a gala Friday. Is Saturday okay?"

"Yeah," I say then wonder if I should act like I have a life. Why lie? My ideal Friday night is one spent at home anyway, with fictional characters and wine to keep me company. We talk and laugh throughout lunch, and soon it's time for me to head back to the office. Ben walks me to my car.

His hands settle on my waist and he pushes his hips into mine. I can't help but get turned on. I hook my arms around his neck.

"If I called your work and personally requested you, would you get sent out to help me plug in my router?" he asks, voice heavy with innuendo.

"Possibly," I say. "It's worth a try. Because that's definitely a problem I can help you with. And my boss is out sick, so whoever you talk to won't really know what's going on."

I want him, and my lady parts that were oh so lonely until recently agree. I'm getting wet just thinking about doing the sex again. Screw work. There's an alley behind this cafe…

"I'll call," he says. "Say you messed up something else and act like I'm pissed."

"Good thing my boss is out sick or this wouldn't work," I say. "Because I'm *very* good at plugging in routers." Then I shake my head. "He wouldn't buy it if you said I messed it up. Not that I've done it personally for him. He swings the other way, actually." I need to stop talking. Like yesterday. I shake my head and look down, letting my vision focus on his crotch.

"Well, that works in my favor then." He tips my chin up and kisses me, leaving me breathless. We part our ways and I smile like a goon for a few minutes. Then I shake myself and call Erin. I give her a brief recap of our lunch date.

"I told you he likes you!" she says.

"It's still too early to really know," I argue and ignore that nagging feeling of dread bubbling inside me. The one that questions *why* he likes me. I'm just me, nothing special, nothing overly memorable.

Just plain, 'ol Felicity.

"Though," she goes on. "I do wonder why he didn't ask you to go to that gala with him. I assume he'd take a date. You usually do to fancy events."

"I half wondered the same thing."

"Half wondered?"

"Yeah," I say. "The thought entered my head but I didn't want to think about it because I knew you could take dates to those events, and why am I not his date. I can be sophisticated. Well, I can *act* sophisticated."

"Sorry, I shouldn't have brought it up."

"No, it's fine," I insist and push down on the gas to get through a yellow light. "He did tell me he dates. Like we didn't specify that we're exclusive or anything, and he said early on that he used to—still does—shit if I know. Whatever. He's free to date other women until some rules are laid down, right?"

"Right. And you can date other men."

"Good, since I got a line of 'em outside my door."

"Hey, you never know."

I let out a snort. "True. But it's whatever. I like Ben, even if it's all casual for now. There's always a later."

"I love your outlook," she says. "I wish I was like that."

"You can be," I say. Erin is a worrier. Stage four, incurable worrier. "Just loosen up. Or drink more wine. That's what I do."

"I had a glass last night."

"I had a bottle last night," I say, and I'm only exaggerating a bit. "I'm back at work," I sigh. "How's the bakery today?"

"Slow," she replies. "Which is kind of nice. This weekend is going to be crazy with orders. Someone ordered a five-hundred dollar Ninja Turtle cake for their kid's first birthday."

"I'm kind of jealous."

"It's an awesome cake," she says. "But that much for a one-year-old?"

"Yeah, that's pretty crazy. Don't babies smash and drool all over their first cakes too?"

"Oh, they ordered a separate 'smash cake' for the kid."

"Entitled little asshole."

"You're telling me." I take a spot in the back of the parking lot, knowing it's not even worth driving up to the doors to look for my spot I had earlier. I swear there are parking vultures around here, watching for anyone a row up to move their car. Maybe they can't do simple math, because walking out to move the car, then back in, then back out, comes to more walking than just in and out like a normal person. "All right, later, bitch."

"Bye, hun," she says and we hang up. I gather my stuff, grab my pink lemonade, and go into work. I sit at my desk for all of two minutes before Cameron's assistant calls me into his office. I get a few stares from my fellow employees, and Mariah tries to meet my eyes. They think I'm in trouble. I can't look at her. I'm not ashamed, but I can't contain this either. If Ben's plan goes as, well, planned, I'm basically being

132

summoned for a booty call.

That's kind of fucking epic.

"What's up, Jason?"

"Some girl named Mindy called from that gallery you went to last week."

I can't help the abhorrence that shows on my face and the nausea that twists in my stomach. Mindy fucking Abraham is even worse than the aftertaste of grape-flavored cough syrup.

"Oh, and?"

His thick eyebrows push together. "She couldn't even explain what the problem was, just that there was a problem. And she'd like you to come back and help fix it, since you installed new software or something."

Jason is an older man, rocking the dad-bod. He rubs his head. "Good luck with this one. I couldn't get a decent answer out of her. Can you head over and see if you can handle it?"

I sigh. "I guess. Want me to leave now?"

"Yeah, just get it taken care of. Hell of a day for Cameron to get sick."

"You've been busy?"

"Just one of those days, ya know?"

"I do," I say and feel a little guilty. I didn't want to stress anyone out. "I'll go now. Don't worry. I can handle it."

"Thanks."

I was hoping he'd say to leave once I was done,

but it is early in the second half of the work day. I keep my eyes down as I walk to my desk, which probably furthers everyone's thinking I got yelled at.

"Follow-up customer service," I quickly explain to Mariah. "Still covering those."

Her mouth forms a little "o" and she nods. "Have fun," she says.

"It shouldn't be too bad." Hell, it's going to be good.

I step into the gallery, having almost forgotten about Mindy. Seeing her sitting behind the desk with her perfect blonde hair in perfect curls, and her perfect silk blouse perfectly showing off the right amount of perfect fake cleavage is like a sucker punch.

"Felicity," she says, lipsticked lips pulling back into what she would call a smile. "The computers aren't working. Ben's isn't working at all." She says each word slowly, and blinks several times. Are her eyelashes real? No one has eyelashes that long. Though, if anyone did, it'd be her.

"Then I better go up there and get to work."

"Yeah, you better. I thought you were supposed to be like super smart and you can't even do something simple like this," she says with a sigh. "No wonder you failed out of MIT and had to go to that little community college."

I push my shoulders back. "I didn't fail out of MIT," I say, not even addressing the fact that she insulted herself by insulting the college we both graduated from. "And it's none of your damn business."

She opens her mouth and puts her hand to her chest. "Stay professional," she says. "We are paying your salary, after all. Wait, you probably get paid hourly, not salary."

I'm fuming, and I don't want her to ruin things for me. She will *not* be on my mind when I'm screwing Ben in a few minutes.

"And it is my business," she goes on. "Ben will want to know if someone incompetent is coming in. Maybe we should have requested someone else."

Shit. No, don't tell Ben I didn't graduate from MIT. He thinks I did. I really don't want to have to tell him that story. I don't even want to think about that story. "I should get to work," I mumble, and silently pray that Mindy steps on a Lego tonight.

I keep my eyes on the stairs and walk past Mindy, trying to get satisfaction in knowing that I was summoned here for fun, not work, and that I'm sleeping with her boss. I'm halfway up the stairs before I realize I'm stomping, though the black Toms I've paired with my dress pants—that Cameron says don't go together—don't have the same clacking echo

135

heels would have.

I open the office door and find Ben near the windows welding something. I stop, taken off guard. I thought he just painted. Sparks fly around him, and the anger and frustration melt away. The door catches in the breeze from the open windows and slams shut.

Ben jerks up and turns off the, uh, welder? What the heck is that thing called? I suppose it doesn't matter. He looks hot holding it, and right now, that's all I care about.

"Sorry," I say.

"It's okay. There's a wind tunnel in here when the windows are open," he says and takes off the protective eyewear. He wipes his hands on his pants, takes a step back, and looks at his work in progress. It's abstract, and to be honest, I have no idea what the fuck it is.

I don't really get modern art, and it makes me feel stupid, like I'm missing something that should be obvious to the rest of the world.

He strides over, taking me in his arms. He dips me backward and kisses me. He smells like metal and fire. I wrap my arms around his torso and drink him in. Once the kiss has ended, he reaches behind me and locks the office door. My heart is in my throat, and the heat is back between my legs, rivaling the heat of the blue flames that were just in his hand.

"You're tense," he says and I don't know how he can tell so soon. "Nervous?"

"No," I say then wish I played it off that way. "Just a little stressed. But I'll be fine."

"Sit," he orders and waves to his chair. I let my purse fall from my shoulder to the floor and sit in the desk chair. It's surprisingly comfortable. I need one of these bad boys for my desk at work. "Relax."

I nod and let my eyes fall closed. Ben puts his hands on my shoulders and starts rubbing. Holy shit that feels good. I can't even remember the last time I got a massage. I think it was from Erin, actually. And only because I had a knot in my shoulder so bad it kept me up at night and at the time I was way too broke to actually go get a massage.

"That feels so good," I moan as he works my stiff muscles. My head droops forward. I didn't stay up super late last night, but I still didn't go to bed as early as I should have. I could fall asleep like this. It's so fucking relaxing.

He's very thorough, rubbing my neck, then my shoulders, and working his way down. He takes his time on my lower back, and then untucks my shirt. His warm fingers slide into my pants and he continues to massage the top of my ass. He bends over and kisses the nape of my neck. I shiver and let out a breath. He moves his hands around to my front and I lean back in the chair, giving him access to his favorite parts.

He unsnaps my dress pants and reaches inside, softly stroking my clit. In no time at all, I'm wet for

137

him. Suddenly, he turns the chair around, grabs my waist, and picks me up, moving me to his desk. He's so strong, lifting me as if I weighed nothing at all. He's right there in front of me, one hand around my waist and the other cupping my cheek.

I wrap my legs around him and reach out, pulling him into an embrace as we kiss. His semi-hard cock stiffens, pressing into my center. I slide my hands down and unbutton his pants. He pulls my shirt over my head then takes his own off. In full sunlight, I can see how intricate his tattoos are. The scars came after a few had inked his skin, and I want to ask what happened. Maybe after we have sex. I don't want to ruin the mood and know we don't have much time.

I trace my finger over a long scar on his left pec muscle and he shivers, temporarily stopping kissing me. Then he dives in like he's starving and I'm the first meal he's had in days.

His lips move from my neck to my collarbone, teeth lightly clamping into my skin. He unhooks my bra and pulls it off and lowers himself, leaving a trail of kisses until he reaches my breasts. He takes one in a hand and the other in his mouth. I toss my head back and realize the windows are wide open. We're on the second story and deep inside the office, but can still be seen.

Fuck it, who cares?

The risk of being seen—and heard by anyone in the gallery—turns me on. I've never done anything like this before. Never had someone who makes me feel so passionate, who turns me on so quickly, and makes me so hot.

Desperation comes on and I'm taking Ben's pants off, stroking his beautiful cock, and urging him to me. My pants come off next and Ben drops to his knees, tossing my legs over his shoulders. I go back on my elbows, knocking a stack of papers and something heavy off his desk. The papers scatter and the three-hole punch lands with a thud.

Oh well.

His mouth is pressed to me, five o'clock shadow rough on my delicate skin. The combination of rough hair and soft, smooth tongue almost pushes me over the edge. He stops when I'm on the cusp of coming and I want to slap him, push his head back between my legs, and tell him not to stop until I'm finished.

I'm still panting, head still back when I hear a little crinkle. Oh right, condom. Duh. Once it's on, he puts his mouth back to me and finishes the job, keeping his mouth tight on me, licking, sucking, flicking, as I come, contracting against him. Without giving me time to recover, he pulls me forward and pushes in.

I can't help but cry out. My body is alive with pleasure, unlike anything I've felt before. I never knew I could feel this good, be so turned on. My ears are ringing and my toes tingle. Ben thrusts in and out, with short, fast movements. I hold onto him and he takes a handful of my breasts, circling my nipples with his thumb.

"You're so fucking hot," he pants and bends down to nuzzle my neck. I'm still riding the pleasure train, not caring where the fuck I'll get off. Because I'm getting off again right now.

I clamp my hand over my mouth to muffle a moan as I come the second time, the orgasm rolling through me with so much force my body shudders. I open my eyes for half a second and see that Ben is watching me, and seeing me orgasm turns him on. He pushes me back onto the desk, grabs my thighs, and pushes in deeper than before. So deep it almost hurts.

Almost.

He pulls back until his dick is almost out, then rams in again. And again. And again. Then we both moan and climax together. My legs quiver and he pitches forward, panting. I hold onto him, unable to catch my breath or slow my heart rate.

Holy fucking shit.

He lets out a final deep breath then brushes the hair back from my face. My breasts rapidly rise and fall as I gasp for air. His eyes meet mine and he gives me that devilish grin, then straightens and pulls me upright as he slides out.

"Hopefully that solved your computer issue," I say, still breathless.

"Hopefully," he says back. "Because if there is another problem next week..." he trails off, raising his eyebrows. I laugh, wishing I could get called out for this kind of customer service call every day, but I know Cameron would catch on.

"Mmmm," I say as he grabs my waist. He gently kneads the extra loving I have on my sides and I feel self-conscious … but I actually think he finds it—dare I say—sexy? Because he's looking like he wants to bend me over the desk and fuck me again.

"You're something else," he says and right away I know that one is a compliment. "What are you doing to me? I can't get you out of my head." He pulls me to him and kisses me passionately. Wind blows the curtains wide open and rattles the locked door. Ben tears himself away, turning to take the condom off. He tosses it in the trash and I vaguely wonder if he's going to cover it up later, which gives me a flashback to my pretending-to-be-a-virgin days when I'd double wrap used condoms in toilet paper or paper towels so my parents wouldn't see. I did the same thing with tampons for a while so my mom wouldn't know I started my period and give me "the talk."

"Same to you," I say back. Ben hands me my bra. I put it on, watching him get dressed. Someone knocks on the door, and I freeze.

"It's okay," he says when he sees my panic. "The door is locked."

I nod and get my pants up. Ben pulls his shirt on, straightening the hem as he walks to the door. I madly reach over the desk for my shirt and put it on, then take a seat at the desk, putting my hands on the computer keyboard.

"Someone is downstairs, looking at the bronze statue," Mindy says when Ben opens the door. He only opens it halfway, and I can see Mindy craning her neck to look at me. "They want to talk to you. They are thinking about buying it."

"I'll be right down," Ben says and turns to look at me. "You're logged in, right?"

"Yes," I say and press down on random keys. Then I realize the computer isn't even on. Oops.

"Good," he says, eyes meeting mine. "I'll be back as soon as I can to assist you."

I nod again, cheeks flushing, though they're still red from fucking. Ben opens the door all the way and steps out. I keep my eyes focused on the black computer screen. I know Mindy is looking at me, waiting for me to look up and meet her gaze so she can give me a snarky smile or make some bullshit comment.

Finally, she turns and goes down the stairs, heels clicking on the wood. I lean back and let out a breath, realizing how close we were to being caught. Maybe Mindy had come up the stairs earlier and heard? Then that means she stood there and waited, listening for us to finish. What a sick freak.

Or maybe not.

Probably not, or she would have knocked sooner. I pull out my phone from my purse and log onto a gamer site instead, checking for updates and reading through forums for entertainment. People lose their shit over the littlest things. Five minutes turn to ten, then fifteen. Twenty minutes later, Ben texts me, saying the people interested in the piece are talkers, and want to discuss getting a few custom paintings. It's going to be a while, like an hour or more since they have to draw things up and go over some sort of contract. He says I can leave if I need to get back to work and he'll call me later.

I gather up my things, knowing I can't stay that long even though I want to. I have some work left to do on the site I'm coding, and I don't want to stay at work late. I text Ben back: *I do need to get back to the office, as much as I don't want to. I can plug in your router anytime.* I add a winking emoji and smile after I send.

I take another minute to gather my composure. My panties are damp since I pulled them on without cleaning myself up, and Ben makes me pretty fucking wet. I'm feeling pretty damn empowered as I go down the office steps. A middle-of-the-workday fucking is always something I wanted to do, but never thought I'd be with someone who could give that to me.

Ben glances at me and smiles when I step off the last stair. He's standing next to a tall statue that kind of resembles a tree. I haven't stopped to get a good look at anything yet, but I remember the price tag on that thing could pay for four months' worth of rent for me. Holy shit.

"Felicity," Mindy says when I walk past her desk, voice sickly high pitched. Why does she purposely talk like that? I turn around to see her staring at me, lips pressed together, and eyes narrowed. I rack my brain for a witty comeback to whatever the hell kind of insult she's planning to throw at me.

Then her eyes widen. "Your shirt," she starts and for a brief moment I think she's going to make fun of my WOW polo, then I realize she wouldn't recognize the emblem.

"What about it?" I ask and realize it's not tucked in. But I never tuck in my shirts for work. It's wrinkled? No, I did my "mist with water and throw in the dryer" trick this morning. Maybe it wrinkled in the few minutes it spent on the floor? Nah, I doubt that.

Then she says it the exact moment I realize what's wrong.

"It's inside out."

Fuck. It is. There is no mistaking that seam. I blink a few times, trying to come up with a lie. It was always this way. Yes. I put it on inside out this morning. Silly me.

"It wasn't like that when you came in." Her wide eyes narrow as she puts two and two together.

Damn it, Mindy fucking Abraham, calling me out. Oh well. I'm fucking your boss, so ... so I have no idea what that makes me. Probably a whore in her eyes.

"Oh," I stammer. "Maybe? I don't know. I didn't really pay attention." I scurry toward the door, catching one last glimpse of Mindy's face. For a moment, it's pulled down with sadness. Then jealousy takes over and her jaw sets in that I'm-gonna-cut-a-bitch way that sends a shiver down my spine.

She's fucking pissed, and then I realize something else. Married or not, she's crushing on Ben. Big time.

Chapter Nine

"You're such a better sewer than me," Erin sighs.

"Not really," I say back, leaning in to get a better look at the computer screen, and in turn, her costume. We're talking via Skype, going over the progress of our Comic Con costumes. "That looks awesome."

"Meh, it's not so good in person."

"If you need me to help with the fine details, I can," I say. "I'll be home for my parent's annual Fourth of July party," I remind her. "We can work on costumes then."

"I might take you up on that offer." She sits down and pulls her hair into a clip. "Are you inviting Ben?"

I make a face. "I don't know."

"Why not? I think it's safe to say he likes you after the office booty call yesterday."

I smile. "True. He likes having sex with me, I know that. But I still can't decide if he likes *me*."

Erin waves her hand in the air. "You're too hard on yourself. Why wouldn't he like you? My best friend is awesome."

"Thanks. And I don't know … It's just a feeling? He said he dates other women, remember? I assume he goes out with plenty of other chicks who are…" I trail off, not wanting to voice my concerns out loud, not even to my BFF of over ten years. Compared to anyone else Ben is dating, seeing, fucking—whatever, I'm just not going to measure up. I want to believe I can, but the realistic part of me wins this one.

"We'll just see," I conclude. "He's busy a lot anyway. That weekend might be big for art shows."

"Sure," Erin says with a roll of her eyes. Something clatters inside her house and David shouts. Erin lets out a slow breath, trying to stay calm. "I should never have let him get a puppy," she says through gritted teeth. "Yeah, the little pooch is adorable, but my house, and my sanity, cannot handle this."

I laugh. "Aren't huskies like super high-energy dogs?"

"Yes," she says. "But that's what he wanted. Something that reminded him of Balto." She shakes her head and I laugh again. "I better go see what kind of trouble they got into now. And clean up the mess. I swear, David is such a child himself he cannot take care of a dog. It's a good thing neither of us want kids any time in the near future. Or ever." Erin isn't a "kid person." It surprised me when she let her hubs get the dog, honestly. She's laid back and so fun, but she likes things neat and orderly in her house.

"Just call him Grey Wind and pretend he's a dire wolf in training? That doesn't get his head cut off," I suggest.

"Maybe." She shakes her head. "Bye, Liss."

We end the Skype call and I go about working on

the top of my femme Batman costume until I can hardly keep my eyes open anymore. Instead of putting away my sewing gear, I close the door to the spare room, aka my work room, to keep Ser Pounce from stepping on pins or fucking with my material. That asshole likes to fuck with my material.

I shower, realize I haven't eaten since lunch, and bring a bowl of Fruit Loops to bed, too tired to make anything else. I flip through channels and grab my phone, wanting to meaninglessly scroll through Facebook as I eat. I have a text from Ben, sent over two hours ago. Whoops. I didn't hear my phone dinging from the other room.

He wants to know if we can meet for lunch or dinner tomorrow. Or both. He says he misses me. I'm smiling as I respond, telling him that both would be nice. He responds quickly, telling me to let him know when I'm taking my lunch break. We plan to meet at the cafe again.

I drift to sleep with Ben on my mind, eager to see him in the morning.

"Hey," I greet Ben as I step into the cafe. It's lunch time and crowded, and if Ben hadn't gotten here early, we wouldn't have gotten a table. He gives me a hug and a kiss, then we sit. I put my purse and umbrella on the chair across from Ben and slide in next to him on the booth seat.

"I ordered already," he says, arm going around me. "Same thing as before. Hope that's okay. It was getting busy and I know you're on limited time."

"Thank you," I say, eyeballing the long line and the frazzled girl behind the counter.

"It should be here soon. Hopefully. I'm starving."

"I usually am," I say. "But there was a birthday at the office so we all got cake."

"Nice."

A college-aged boy brings us two iced coffees and says the food should be out soon. I peel the wrapper off the straw and stick it inside the cold mocha.

"I heard something interesting today," Ben says, taking a drink of his own coffee.

"And what is that?"

His eyes narrow just a bit. "Mindy said you two had a class together in college. I know she's not smart enough to get into MIT."

Crap. Shit. Busted.

Fuck.

"Yeah … we did." I grab my straw wrapper and start twisting it between my fingers, heart hammering.

"So you didn't go to MIT?"

"I did," I say and let out a breath. "But I didn't graduate from there."

"Why do I get the feeling there is a story behind this?"

149

"Because there is, but it's not a good one. Trust me." I tie a knot in the wrapper and pull it until it breaks. I still feel sick about it, the fact that I was so close to getting a degree from one of the best tech schools in the country. I still feel humiliated that I was dumb enough to let someone control me, manipulate me, trick me into doing something that could have ruined my whole life.

He was the first guy to tell me he loved me, that he didn't want to live without me, that we were meant to be.

And I fucking believed him. I trusted him. I *loved* him. He was my first long-term boyfriend, and finding out I'd been used caused all the confidence I'd gained since high school to crash and burn into a pile of oblivion, not to resurface until adulthood. Hell, I'm still trying to get some of it back, still trying to have faith in the people of the world not to bend me over and screw me in the ass with no lube.

I take a breath, drop the straw wrapper, and look up at Ben. "This guy, Micah, I was dating convinced me to hack into the grade book and save him from failing pretty much all his classes." Ben doesn't say anything. His face is neutral and he patiently waits for me to keep going. "It was untraceable, but one professor noticed his grade went from a 48% to an 84%. And then something was said and the other professors noticed and called Micah out on it. He didn't even hesitate to tell them I did it."

I run my finger down the outside of the plastic coffee cup, collecting condensation on my finger. "The dean and the head of the tech department were actually impressed at my hacking skills—they didn't word it that way though—and were disappointed I did something so stupid my last year. They let me transfer my credits instead of kicking me out. Hence the degree from the local college. I was young, and I made the mistake of believing Micah when he said he loved me. Live and learn, right?"

A few seconds of silence tick by. Then Ben reaches out and puts his hand on mine. "You're a hacker?"

I tip my head up. "Only by night."

Ben chuckles. "That is impressive, actually."

"You're one of the few to think so," I say. "But thanks. It fucking sucked, but I was, and maybe still am, a little proud of being able to get into the system."

"Have you hacked other sites before?" he asks.

"Maybe," I say. "But I never really did anything bad like that again. I swore to use my superpowers only for good after that. A few were just to see if I could do it. And once was to change my best friend's ex-boyfriend's Facebook page. But I don't consider that really a *hack*. It's so easy."

"I don't know how to do it," he tells me and leans back in his chair.

"Not many people do," I say. "Which is good." I

shrug. "Cybercrime is still a crime, ya know? I don't want to get caught—again—and screw myself again. I got lucky with MIT. I probably won't get lucky again." I wipe the condensation from my cup. "So … that's the story."

"It's not that bad of a story," he says and puts his hand on mine. "And I think it's fair to say you went to MIT. You said you were one semester away from graduating?"

"Ugh, yes. I can't bring this up to my parents yet either. They're still pissed at me."

"I'd still consider you an MIT graduate, even though you lack the degree."

"All I had left was one core class and electives. It would have been the easiest semester ever. But oh well, right? I made a bad choice, let someone convince me to do something I shouldn't have, and learned the hard way. Dwelling isn't going to change that."

"Right. You have to move on or live in agony."

"Exactly. Yeah, I regret it, but whatever. Every mistake made me who I am, and all that shit."

Ben chuckles and laces his fingers through mine. His eyes sparkle and he opens his mouth to stay something when our food comes. We dig in, eating a few bites in silence before speaking.

"Did you and Mindy have a falling out?" he asks. "She seems to be holding a grudge against you, and I don't know why."

I shake my head and push my fork through the crispy crust of the veggie pot pie. "We were never friends." I flick my eyes to Ben, and I'm shocked at how *not* self-conscious I feel. Thinking about my glory days as a teen usually zap me back to feeling like crap faster than the TARDIS can leave an exploding planet.

But not right now.

Because right now I'm having lunch with this gorgeous guy who's looking at me like I'm his favorite person in the whole world. And maybe Mindy fucking Abraham can still make me feel like dog poo on the bottom of her expensive shoe with one belittling glare, but I don't have to cower and let myself stink like shit this time around.

"I really don't know why she didn't like me then, or why she still cares now. She moved to our town our sophomore year and just needed someone to pick on, I guess." I take a bite of food and sigh, feeling my give-a-damns go out the window. "She became the Regina George of our school in just weeks, and everyone flocked all over her. You know those types." I shrug. "But that was years ago, and she's never grown up, never moved on." The realization crashed down on me as I speak. "Being the queen bee of high school was her peak. It's kinda sad when you think about it."

"Peaking in high school is sad," Ben agrees, looking into my eyes.

153

I smile and nod. I don't want to tell him that I'm still insecure about it, that Mindy brought me to tears and bullied me to the point of faking sick so I wouldn't have to go to school and face her. I shouldn't be ashamed of that.

Shouldn't.

But I'm still scared he'll think less of me, that hearing it out loud will somehow slap sense into him and he'll see me as the nerdy looser Mindy and everyone else saw in high school. I'm so logical it kills me, I know.

"Well," Ben says. "She's still jealous of you if she's talking shit."

Still jealous implies that she was once jealous of me, and that's not the case. I just nod again. I came into this conversation with a dozen fucks. I wanted to leave with all twelve of them. I want to get to the point where I don't give a single fuck about Mindy. She's not worth it.

"Have you been to the Gardens and Sculpture Park yet?" Ben asks.

I shake my head since my mouth is full. Once I swallow I say, "No, but I keep hearing about it. I want to go."

"How about this weekend?"

"Yeah, I'd love to."

"And tonight," he says carefully, and for half a second I think he's apprehensive about asking me out again, like I might for some crazy reason turn him down. "Dinner and a movie?"

"Oh yes, that's perfect. A movie I want to see just came out."

"Great," he says with a smile.

"It's so big!" I exclaim.

"That's what she said," Ben says with a grin.

I laugh and roll my eyes. He swings my hand as we walk down a path that leads through a peaceful section of tall grass, wild flowers, and statues and sculptures in the park. "Really," I say. "I can't believe I've held out on coming here. It's beautiful."

"I'm glad you think so," he tells me and slows when we cross a wooden bridge. People mill about, enjoying the nature and the artwork spread throughout, soaking up the warm June day. We stop walking and Ben wraps his arms around me. I'm not wearing heels this time, just my Hufflepuff Toms, and Ben is several inches taller than me. I go up on my toes and kiss him. "Want to finish the tour or do you want to go back to my place for dinner now?" He raises his eyebrows and I know he's thinking about dessert.

And by dessert, I mean sticking his P in my V.

That's a pretty good dessert.

"It's up to you," I say. "I like it here. It's very

calming. And pretty. I like calm and pretty."

He slides his hands along my side and takes both my hands. "We can keep going. I come here from time to time when I want to think. And this place is really inspirational. Then again, so are you."

We cross the bridge and walk in silence, taking in the sights for a few moments. I'm completely comfortable with Ben, which is kind of weird when I think about it too much. Not counting meeting for lunch during the week, this is our third date. We spoke on the phone Thursday night for several hours, and he called me Friday before the art event thing-a-ma-bob that he had to go to just to say hi and see how my day was going.

I'm starting to like him a lot.

We both slept in this morning. The event Ben went to was a few hours away, and by the way he spoke, he didn't get in until late. I stayed up doing important things like arguing on an online forum about the sexism in Cosplay. And playing League of Legends. That's important too, of course.

I called Ben when I got up, like he wanted me to, and we made plans to visit the gardens then go back to his house. He's cooking me dinner. I assume I'll be spending the night, like he had with me, but, again, I'm not sure the protocol on this kind of thing. Since he picked me up from my house, the ball is in his court. To an extent. Maybe? Hell if I know.

Instead of looking presumptuous and backing a

separate bag, I used my biggest purse and loaded it with a few overnight things, like face wash, my toothbrush, and my travel makeup bag. I folded a new dress and a fresh pair of undies for tomorrow and put it inside, and for tonight, I'm wearing a matching bra and panty set. I like to be prepared.

Speaking of preparedness, I debated on bringing condoms. I didn't, assuming since Ben puts them on his dick, he probably has more. I'm currently not on any sort of birth control. I stopped taking it six months into my dry spell because I was too lazy to take it every morning, and really, what's the point when I'm not getting any? I have no problem getting back on it, but I don't want to jump the gun and assume what Ben and I have will turn into anything … uh, lasting?

I'm afraid of jinxing this.

Because this—whatever the hell it is—is pretty fucking awesome.

"What do you think about that one?" Ben asks me a while later. I follow his gaze to a glass sculpture rising from the ground. It's twisted yet graceful and is every color you'd see if you looked up at a starry sky.

"I like it," I say as I inspect it. "It's pretty, and reminds me of … I really don't know. I'm bad at interpreting art, don't be mad."

Ben chuckles. "I wouldn't be mad, and I think the interpretation is so open. What one person feels and sees is so different from another, and even more different from what the artist was thinking and feeling at the time."

I nod. "Like maybe this artist only had midnight colors to work with, but everyone else says blue means depression or some psychological stuff like that. I happen to think blue is calming, by the way. And open at the same time. That makes no sense, I know."

"I think I'm following," he says.

"It's probably because the TARDIS is blue," I try to joke, then remember Ben isn't a Whovian. *That'll have to change if this thing develops further.* "And it reminds me of magic and the sky. And the sky is magic, really. The sky is the literal sky, but it's so much more than that too. It's like a symbol of not putting limits on things, and a dark sky reminds me that there is so much out there left to be discovered."

He nods, eyeing the glass shapes. "You did a good job interpreting that one. Don't say you're not good."

I shrug. "But who knows if that's what I'm supposed to feel."

"You're not *supposed* to feel one thing or another. Just feel." His arm goes around me and my heart does a skip-a-beat thing. I rest my head on his shoulder and close my eyes for a long blink. "And the artist would agree with you about blues and limits, well lack thereof."

"How do you know?" I ask, then realize Ben is the artist who made this. Duh, Felicity. "Oh, right.

Do you have anything else here?"

"Yes, but we don't have to search it out," he says and I get the feeling he's too humble to take me on a tour to show off his work. "And we've already been by one other one."

My eyes widen. "I didn't insult your work, did I?"

He laughs again, and fuck, I love when he does. "No, you didn't insult anything. And I take criticism really well. I know not everyone is going to like something I make. You can't please everyone anyway, so why try?"

"Very true," I reply and his statement resonates deep inside. I take the words personally, thinking of how it's taken me years to figure that out.

You can't please everyone.

Not in art, not in life. Why waste the time and emotion fretting about it?

"Haters gonna hate," I say and lace my fingers through Ben's. We continue walking the path. "Life is too short to worry like that, ya know? It took me a while to realize that, to be honest, but I like doing my own thing. It makes me happy, so who cares what others think, right?"

He pulls me in for a kiss. "Exactly."

159

Chapter Ten

Ben lives in the historic district of Grand Rapids. It's yet another place I'd heard of but hadn't invested the time into seeing. There are historic home tours I meant to go on, but forgot. And it's not like I can just go knocking on doors. Though I have driven down his road a time or two.

His house is one of the larger old homes, and he tells me it was built in the early 1900s. He parks around back, inside a detached garage. The sun is setting, but when we get out, I slow.

"Wow," I say and look up at the large, dark-gray Victorian house. "It's beautiful."

"Thanks," he says and gives the house the same starry-eye look I'm giving it. "It's been a lot of work restoring her, but I love it."

Hearing him refer to his house as a female is oddly charming. "Was it in bad shape when you bought it?"

He shakes his head. "Not horrible shape, but the previous owners attempted to do a lot of upgrades themselves when they weren't skilled enough to do so. I had to take a lot out and redo what could have been left original."

He holds my hand as we go up the wooden steps of the back porch. They creak under my feet. The old wood has a new shine to it, and a cast-iron table and chairs are positioned against the house on the covered porch. I imagine waking up and having coffee out here, looking across the way at the other historic homes. Oh, I wonder if his house is haunted! That would be terrifying and neat at the same time.

A dog barks when Ben sticks the key in the door. Huh, that's interesting. He's never said anything about having to go home and let a dog out.

"Settle down, Harumi," he says when he opens the door. A yellow lab shakes her tail so hard her whole body is wiggling. She wildly greets Ben like she hasn't seen him for days, then comes over to me. "She's very friendly," he says with a smile. "She'll lick you to death."

I bend over, heavy purse falling forward. I drop it on the floor and pet the dog—Harumi, I think Ben called her. "You smell my kitty, don't you?" I ask as she presses her nose all over me and inhales. "He's going to smell you and be mad at me. But that's okay. He's an asshole anyway. It'll serve him right."

Ben holds the back door open and calls the dog out to go potty. I pick up my purse and look around. We entered in through a mud room. A washer, dryer, and ironing board are on one side, with a stack of neatly folded towels on top of the dryer. The other side houses a shoe rack. Most of the shoes are Ben's, but I spot a few that belong to a woman. A woman with small feet, to be exact.

I take my shoes off and go through the mudroom,

which emerges into a large kitchen. The cabinets and granite countertops are white, contrasting with the dark wooden floor. The backsplash above the sink looks like stained glass, no doubt handmade by Ben. Everything is neat and orderly, looking like something from a magazine. There is an oval breakfast table by a large window that looks out to the back porch. I can see Ben toss a ball for Harumi in the small yard.

I set my purse on a chair and stand by the breakfast table, watching Ben for a few seconds before turning to look at more of the house. I'm assuming the woodwork is all original, including the ornate crown molding. I can see a large dining room with a big table off of the kitchen, and a living room to the other side.

The house has that old feel to it, but it's clean and smells like paint, which automatically reminds me of Ben and makes my heart go pitter-patter (and my insides tingle). I want to look around the rest of the house, channeling my inner Winchester and check it out for spirits, but don't want to be rude.

Just then, the door opens and Harumi runs in, followed by Ben.

"I didn't know you had a dog," I say, petting the overly excited lab.

"Yeah," he says. "She's an easy keeper. She's ten, don't let her spastic behavior fool you, and sleeps a lot."

"Awww, she looks good for ten!"

"Thanks," he says and runs his hands over the dog's head.

"This is one of the coolest houses I've ever been in," I say and look around. "I love old houses."

"They have character," he tells me. "Want a tour?"

I eagerly nod. We go through the kitchen in the dining room. I recognize the artwork as Ben's right away. I can't really say he has a style, because everything is so different. But there is something so irrevocably *him* about it.

The dining room opens to the foyer, with a grand staircase front and center. It's U-shaped, with a balcony looking down from the second floor. On the other side is a fancy living room, set up with period appropriate furniture and lots of bookshelves. The other living room that I saw through the kitchen is completely modern, and feels almost out of place. There's a small bathroom tucked away near the basement stairs, and a sunroom in the back of the house. It has easels and other art supplies set up, with paint splattered cloths draped over the floor. The smell of paint is strong in here.

"I try to do most of my work at the studio," he says. "But I bring work home with me." He gives me a smile and turns to take me upstairs.

There are three bedrooms and two bathrooms up here. There must have been more bedroom at one point, because the master bathroom is so big I'm sure

163

it used to be an entirely separate room.

"This is my room," Ben says and waves his hand to his side. I peek in. This room is modern and normal too. Well, normal but still impressive. The bed is lazily made and there is a pile of laundry on the window seat, and a few dog toys on the floor. A stack of papers clutters his desk, burying his laptop, and the top drawer of his dresser isn't closed all the way.

This looks more like the Ben I know.

"We'll see more of that later," he adds. "That's a guest room that Harumi has taken over, a bathroom, and another bedroom. And that's it."

"It's huge and really pretty," I say, noticing that the last bedroom's door is closed. If it's just a guest room, he doesn't need to show me it, really. But the other doors are open, so it seems odd … as well as his "art room" and his bedroom being messy like his office yet the rest of the house is spic-and-span. And I really want to know who took care of his dog when he spent the night at my house last weekend.

"Thanks," he says. "I might be odd to say I see a house like a giant canvas. It can give off feelings just like a work of art."

I can't help but think what kind of feeling does my little condo give off? Shabby-geek? Is that even a thing? If not, it needs to be.

"Hungry?" he asks, turning back to the stairs.

"I pretty much will always answer yes to that," I say with a smile. "Maybe I shouldn't, but I'm not gonna lie."

"I do always answer yes to that," he says and jogs down the stairs. We go back into the kitchen and Ben opens the fridge. "I'm not really a good cook," he says apologetically. "But I'll try my best for you."

"You're sweet," I tease. "And really, I appreciate it. But if you want to order pizza or something I won't hold it against you."

Ben considers. "Pizza does sound good. Extra cheese and pepperoni?"

"And breadsticks?"

"Always breadsticks."

He orders the food and then we go into the modern living room to watch TV. He pulls me into his lap as soon as we sit on the couch. I snuggle close to him, breathing in his cologne and feeling his firm muscles press against me. I'm tempted to kiss him and slip my hand inside his pants, but know the pizza guy will be here soon and we'd have to break up the hanky-panky in a few.

"What do you want to watch?" I ask him.

"I don't really care," he says and leans over to kiss me. "Whatever you want to is fine with me."

I take the remote and flip through the movie channels, finding the second Hobbit movie starting in a few minutes. "Have you seen the first one?" I ask.

"I've seen them all, and all the Lord of the Rings movies," he replies and it takes all I have not to jump his bones right there. "And read the books. *The Hobbit* was my favorite book as a kid."

I'm smiling and I can't stop. "I loved—still love it too! I got in trouble in the seventh grade for reading it during class."

"You really were a rebel in your day," he jokes.

"Oh, the worse. Reading in class, sneaking comics into church, and then it all went to hell once I got a cell phone and computer. I was a girl on a mission and my mission was trouble."

Ben's laughing, eyes sparkling as he looks at me. "And now?"

"I only use my superpowers for good, remember?"

"Oh, right. How could I forget?"

"What games do you play?" I ask, eyeing the Xbox. He has a PlayStation too, thank God.

"I haven't played much lately," he confesses. "I've been busier than I thought. I like Halo."

I slowly turn to him. "We can play for a bit."

"You know how to play?" he asks.

"Uh, yeah. And I'm good. I'll probably kick your ass."

"I doubt that," Ben says, playfully elbowing me. "Loser gets naked?"

"Get ready to take your clothes off," I challenge and straighten up.

He looks me up and down. "Yours will be hitting the floor first."

"Sure, they will."

He gets two controllers and pops in the game and sits close next to me. I haven't played in a while but don't doubt my skills. The virtual arena is my stomping ground. We get started and I again consider letting Ben think he's the better player and beat me, but damn it, I just can't. I've killed his character four times by the time the pizza gets here.

We set up the food on the coffee table, and Ben brings out beer from the fridge. We keep playing as we eat, getting louder and louder the more we get into the game, and the more beers we down.

Two hours later, we're still playing, still drinking, and still having a blast. Ben's phone rings and he takes his eyes off the TV.

"It's my mom," he says, letting me know why he's ignoring the call.

"I don't always answer my mother either," I say. "Especially now because she keeps bugging me about my brother's wedding that's coming up."

"When is he getting married?" Ben asks and shoots at me. I dodge out of the way just in time, but get hit by another player.

"Dammit!" I mutter. "The weekend after the fourth of July, but I don't remember the exact date. I should know this. I'm in the wedding."

Take that, cocksucker! I kill the online player who shot me, hoping I can heal before I get hit again.

"Nice," Ben says. "Are you close with your future sister-in-law?"

167

"Not at all," I chortle. "She's not a horrible person, but she's not someone I'd be friends with if she wasn't being legally bound to my family either." I shake my head. "Even my brother says his fiancé is a bridezilla. There's like over a month or so left until the wedding and she's freaking out over RSVPs. Hence my mom calling. I don't see why they even sent me an invitation. They know I'm going."

Ben chuckles. "You didn't RSVP for your own brother's wedding?"

"I kinda lost the invite," I admit. "But obviously I'll be there. I wouldn't have spent money on a bridesmaid dress just to blow it off."

"It's been a while since I've been to a wedding," Ben says. "My cousin got married two years ago, but that's it. Most of my friends are already married or living up the single life with no intentions on settling down."

"Same here," I say. "My best friend got married like right out of college." I risk my character standing still so I can grab the glass bottle from the coffee table and drink the last of my beer.

"Being in a wedding is fun," he goes on. "If you like the person."

"Hah, yes. Erin's wedding was a blast. It was small yet very elegant with a subtle Star Wars theme."

He looks at me, raising an eyebrow. "How the hell do you have an elegant Star Wars wedding?"

I smile. "It was like a regular wedding but with

168

small Star Wars stuff added throughout. Half of it probably went unnoticed by half the people. But things stick out when you're a fan, ya know?"

"Yeah," he says and I remember that he mixed up Star Trek and Star Wars when we first met. Ugh. Such a shame. "I've never been to a themed wedding."

"I go back and forth with wanting one and wanting something classic," I say, still focused on the game. "Something fairytale-ish would be perfect. Like Disney Princess approved. But honestly, I'm not too concerned about the decorations. That's not what it's about, right?"

"In the end, not at all. I have a buddy who took years paying off his wedding. The credit card debt almost ended their marriage."

"Yikes. It's just not worth it. I want to get married because I'm in love and don't want to spend the rest of my life without that person, not because I want a fancy party."

"Me too," Ben says. "I don't have many requests for my wedding, whenever it happens. Just an open bar and *All the Single Ladies* is not to be played."

I laugh. "Agreed. And no *Sexy Back*. Why are those two older songs go-tos for DJs?"

"I am okay with the chicken-dance song."

"Oh, you have to have the chicken dance." I laugh then realize we just discussed something mega important in a way that felt completely natural. We turn our attention back to the game, playing for another few minutes before Ben's mom calls again. With a sign he sets his controller down and answers it.

"Hey, Mom," he says then falls silent as he listens. I hear a female on the other end, talking fast—too fast for me to understand. Then Ben stands, saying something in Japanese, grabs the empty pizza box, and goes into the kitchen. I finish the round and stop the game. I can hear Ben talking to his mom, and although he's speaking a different language, it sounds like he's trying to calm her down. A minute later, he hangs up and comes back into the room, eyebrows pushed together.

"Everything okay?" I ask, taking his hands in mine as he plops onto the couch.

"Yeah," he says, but sounds distracted. "My mom can be a little high strung sometimes. She's a worrier over small things."

"I can relate," I say with a smile. I let go of Ben's hands and gather the empty beer bottles, taking them into the kitchen. "Do you recycle?" I ask, feeling the floor vibrate behind me as he comes into the room.

"Yeah," he repeats and pulls out a drawer that holds both the garbage and the recycling. "Thanks. You didn't have to do that."

"It was easy," I say. "Can I have some water?"

"Of course." He grabs a glass and fills it from the fridge. I down half in seconds. He lets Harumi out, stepping onto the porch. He seems upset, like

170

whatever his mother called about really is weighing on him more than he's letting on. I finish the water, go into the bathroom to pee, then go out on the back porch with him. He's sitting on the steps, throwing a worn-out tennis ball for the old dog.

I take a seat next to him. Ben wraps an arm around me, holding me tight against him for a few seconds before he speaks.

"It's a nice night."

"Very nice," I say. "I love summer nights like this. It makes me want to move somewhere warm where it's always like this."

"Hah, yes. Winter is coming sooner than we think."

"Winter is coming," I repeat, mentally smiling at his unknown reference. Harumi brings the ball back, her gait a slow trot. I reach forward and grab it, throwing it a few yards. I don't want to make her run too far. "I'm so not looking forward to shoveling my driveway or clearing snow off the car when I leave work."

"When it's really bad sometimes I don't leave the house," Ben says.

"A man after my own heart," I joke. "I don't mind winter, I mean, I grew up here so I'm used to it. But when it drops below twenty-five, I want to throw in the towel and hibernate."

He nods then flashes that grin. "I don't go to the gallery when it's bad. And by bad I mean snowing or

171

really cold."

"Lucky."

"I can work from home, so it's not a total day off."

"Still lucky."

"If you could work from home, what would you do?"

"Does it have to be a legit job, or can I get paid for just not destroying the world?"

His fingers slide down my shirt, inching the hem up. "Other than being paid to do nothing, what would you do?"

I shake my head. "I don't really know. Come up with video games?"

He laughs. "That's like doing nothing."

"Hey now. A lot more work goes into that than you'd think. I'm sure I'd love almost every second of it, but it's not like sitting down and playing."

He nods. "I'm sure. I consider myself computer savvy, but I know there is more to it than I can even think of."

"There is. Which is why I like it, and the field of technology is always expanding. It's limitless and always challenging. What's new and impressive now won't be in five years. Hell, it won't be in one year. And I love that."

"I am jealous of your phone," he says.

"Good, you should be. There are a few kinks to be worked out, but I like it much better over the current version."

"It doesn't come out until next fall, right?"

"Right. I might be able to score you a beta. Might is the keyword there though. I can try to pull some strings."

"You don't have to if it's a hassle."

"Nah," I say and nudge him. "You're worth it."

The smile returns to his face. "Glad you think so." His other arm goes around me, and before I know it, we're kissing under the stars. Though, it's not as romantic as it sounds, since mosquitoes and moths are buzzing and flapping around the porch light a few feet behind us.

Ben swats them away and takes his tongue out of my mouth. "Want to go inside and upstairs?" he asks. "I'm getting eaten alive."

"Me too." He stands and pulls me to my feet. "Maybe you can eat me alive once we're inside," I say it casually like a joke, but really, I'd love for him to go to down town on me again. He's quite good.

He gets that I'm-gonna-fuck-you glint in his eyes and wets his lips. "I think that can be arranged."

He calls in Harumi, who lazily runs over and jumps up the steps. Ben gives her a pet and opens the door, swatting at the bugs to keep them from coming inside with us. I fill my glass with water as he puts a scoop of food in Harumi's bowl and locks up for the night.

I get a few gulps down before Ben's arms clasp

around my waist. I set the glass down and spin around to face him.

"Did I tell you, you look beautiful tonight?" he asks softly.

"You did, but I don't mind hearing it again."

His lips brush against mine, and a shiver runs down my spine. My eyes close and my breasts crush into him. "You're beautiful."

I run my hand through his hair, growing wet as he grows hard. He turns his head and kisses my neck as his hands drop to my waist, sliding forward and unbuttoning my jeans.

We never make it upstairs.

Chapter Eleven

"Somebody looks happy," Mariah says to me at work Monday morning. A week has passed since Ben and I strolled the Statue Garden, and I stayed the night at his place. "Did you meet a boy?" Her eyes practically light up at the thought. She might live vicariously through other people's love lives.

"I am happy and yes," I say. "A very nice, handsome boy." I lean across the small aisle. "One who knows how to please a woman. Multiple times."

Her hand flies to her chest. "I remember those days. Enjoy them while they last," she only half jokes and gives me a wink. "I'm happy for you. Is he going to be your date for the wedding?"

My heart skips an actual beat. I'd voiced my "always being seated at the single table" woes to her during the week, but hadn't brought up Ben. I didn't want to talk about this amazing man only to have him ghost away from me. But after the last two weeks, I'm pretty sure he's not ghosting anywhere anytime soon. Or at least I hope not.

Ben made me breakfast in bed yesterday morning. We spent the whole day just lounging around, watching TV, talking, and making lame jokes we both found to be hilarious. Oh, and we had sex a few more times that day. Our goodbyes got longer and longer, words mixed with kisses and cuddles.

175

He doesn't want to leave. I don't want him to leave. It is like a high school romance where you can't get enough of the other. But that's how I feel. I can't get enough of him. I'm comfortable around him. I'm myself. I don't want to be anyone else when we're together.

Being me—and probably being a realist—that dark cloud looms in the distance. We're not exclusive. Nothing has been said, nothing has been promised or put off limits. He let me know from the start he goes out with other women.

Who am I to be the one to make him settle down?

I'm not. I'm just me, just little miss weird Felicity, a blunt nerd with occasionally poor social skills. After a long talk with Erin last night, she convinced me to enjoy what's going on and let it go from there. I can't control everything. I can't key in commands like a computer and use hacks and cheats at life.

"I haven't asked him yet," I confess. "I've got time," I say mostly to convince myself. I don't see why he wouldn't go with me. It's just one night and it's not that far, plus there is an open bar with top-shelf liquor. And cake. Awesome cake, made by my best friend, I should add.

"Yeah," Mariah agrees. "You do." Her eyes flick to the office door. Someone from corporate is doing an office visit today, and Cameron is going nuts over it, texting me how freaked he is when he gets the chance. He asked me to go out for drinks with him after work, like the minute we clock out.

I was hoping to see Ben again, but agree to drinks anyway. Maybe he can join us. He said he'd text or call me when he got done at the gallery today, whenever that is. I can't get him out of my mind, and for the first time since I started at this place, I don't finish my assigned work early.

The big wigs leave an hour before the office starts to shut down for the day, and the air is immediately less tense. I go back and forth between my work and Facebook, messaging some of my online friends to chat about random things.

I do twenty minutes of actual work, then switch back to Facebook to creep on Ben's profile. He accepted my friend request not long after we met, and rarely updates anything. Lame. I need to creep, mister. He gets tagged in events and by other galleries, but nothing that sheds light on his social life. He does post a lot of his art to Instagram, and has an impressive amount of followers.

I'm about to switch to Pinterest when the little friend icon notifies me I have a request. I click on it and almost shit my pants.

Mindy fucking Abraham.

My mouse hovers over "delete request" but I stop myself. I'd rather just ignore it, or not let her know friending me on Facebook is a big deal. Because it shouldn't be. It's fucking Facebook and I'm a fucking adult.

Like an evil force has taken over my body, I accept her request. But it's not because I want to creep through yet another profile. Everything was set to private before, though it isn't hard to get around that. I click on her profile then close my eyes.

Nope. Not doing it. I already know how she will come across. Picture perfect. So picture perfect that it will make me wallow inside, wishing my teeth were that white, or my skin that clear. I'll be jealous of her fake breasts, even though my real ones are better than hers. Just heavier, sweatier I'm sure, and slightly saggier.

But they felt better?

Yeah, sure. I can go with that. Instead of looking at her perfectly posed pictures of her perfect family, I unfollow her and exit out of the Internet. I should work. I'm at work, after all, and the day is almost over.

"So, give me deets," Cameron says as we munch on chips and drink margaritas.

"We did dinner Friday night, saw a movie Saturday afternoon, then spend that night and Sunday just hanging out, playing video games and watching TV. Super laid back, but super enjoyable. And we fucked several times, of course."

One of Cameron's eyebrows goes up. He looks at his drink and grabs another chip, dipping it in salsa.

"What?" I ask.

"Oh nothing," he says and flicks his wrist.

"Bullshit. What?"

He lets out a breath and looks at me, expression soft like he's going to break bad news. "Nothing is exclusive yet, right?"

"Nothing's been said."

"And he still dates other women?"

"Not that I know of, but I mean, if we haven't voiced the whole only see each other thing, then he can, right?"

Cameron nods. "Honey, I love you. You know that. I don't want to see you to get hurt. I'm saying this out of love."

My heart sinks into my stomach. Good thing there is a decent amount of tequila in there for it to float in. "Saying what?"

"You stay in. Play video games. Drink beer and eat pizza. You're one of the guys."

My eyebrows go together. "But we have sex. Frequently."

"All men would fuck their best friend if they had a vagina."

"You think I'm just friend material?"

"I'm not saying that's all you can be. I'm just saying it sounds like that's what Ben is doing. He still

179

hasn't taken you to his fancy art shows?"

"No, but—" I clamp my mouth shut. I'm not making excuses for Ben. If that really is the case and he's using me for fuck-able guy time, then I feel more violated than a cucumber at an all-women's prison. I gulp my margarita. "So, what do I do?"

"I'm not sure. Straight men confuse the hell out of me. Maybe just ask him?"

"No. If I don't like the answer, I'd rather not know. Ignorance is bliss, after all."

He pats my hand. "I shouldn't have brought it up. Look, it's early. You've been seeing each other for what, three weeks? Give it time."

"Right." Three weeks isn't that long. Not at all. But shouldn't it be enough time to decide if someone wants to be with you or not? I knew after our first date that Ben is someone I want a relationship with. I'm not talking marriage here, but something a bit more serious than just casual dating. Though, if Ben were seeing other women … when? We spent a lot of time together over the last three weeks, especially the last two weekends.

"Anyway," Cameron says and I know he feels bad. But not as bad as I'm feeling. Fuck. Fuck life. Fuck love. Fuck it all.

I take a deep breath and pick up my drink. No need to jump to conclusions. Nothing has changed between Ben and me, and I was super-freaking-happy just hours ago. I always knew being friends with your boss was bad news.

"Got plans for the Fourth?" he asks.

"Probably going home. My parents do this huge party on the lake. It's one of those invite your friend and their friends and anyone they've ever met—as long as they bring food or drinks—kind of parties They have boats and jet skis for their cabin rental business so it's actually fun."

"Did you invite your boy toy?"

I shake my head. "Not yet, at least. I'll mention it to him. Maybe if I promise hunting and fishing, and, uh, other manly things, he'll want to come."

"Liss," Cameron says sharply. "I'm sorry, okay? Don't make me feel bad."

"I'm not trying to make you feel bad. Just trying to give myself a reality check."

He looks at me sympathetically. "No need for that. Just keep realistic expectations. That's what I did, what I still do. It keeps this from breaking." He puts his hand over his heart. "It's a harsh world out there."

"Fuck, yes it is." I finish my drink and feel my head spin. I'm about to order another and drown my pretty much entirely imagined woes when Ben calls. My heart flutters like it did before. "Hello?" I say, not sure what I should feel.

Why do I let people get in my head so much?

"Hey," he says. "What are you doing?"

"Getting drunk with my boss," I answer, eyeing

Cameron. "You?"

He lets out a breath. "Just got done talking with a pain-in-the-ass client. I don't do completely custom work, ya know? Don't tell me what to paint then have me paint it. I don't work like that."

"Yeah," I say then fall silent.

"I was going to ask you out to dinner, but I guess if you're already out I won't. I miss you."

And just like that my heart melts.

"Want to join us?" I ask without giving Cam the chance to object.

"Your boss won't mind? And you don't mind? I don't want to bother you."

"Not at all. I'd love for you to join us. I'm kinda drunk, and could use a DD."

"Are you drunk and frisky?"

I laugh. "Always." I tell him where we are and hang up. "You don't mind, do you?" I ask Cameron.

"Actually, I'm really curious to meet this guy. So no, not at all."

"Good."

"You should call in sick tomorrow," Ben says, hands going under my shirt. He pushes me back on my bed. We got back from the restaurant a while ago, and I successfully convinced Ben to watch the first episode of *Game of Thrones* with me. Now he's hooked.

Mission complete.

"Cam would know I'm faking for sure."

"Nah, say you got food poisoning."

"We had the same thing." Ben puts himself between my legs. "But no one questions explosive diarrhea."

"Hah, so true. Is being hungover a good enough excuse?" He lowers his head and kisses my neck. "Or losing control over the lower half of your body after I fuck you so hard you can't walk?"

Hot damn. My lips press together and curve into a smile. My eyes widen and my vagina quivers. "I've never thought there would be any words I'm unable to say to my boss, but those might be it."

Ben laughs and kisses me, trailing his lips down my neck and across my collar bone. "And now you have to follow through on that promise."

"I won't disappoint." He sticks his fingers inside my leggings, which are navy blue and covered in glow-in-the-dark stars and moons. The TV is the only source of light in the room, but the pattern still gives off a soft glow. Ben peels them off and tosses them on the floor. He moves back, accidentally knocking the TV remote onto the ground. It bounces closer to me, and I lean over to get it but end up tumbling off the bed. I land hard, laughing.

"Are you okay?" Ben asks, holding back a chuckle.

183

"I think so," I say and push myself up, feeling super sexy on all fours. I whacked my shin on the nightstand on the way down. I stand and wince. "That's gonna bruise."

I toss Ben the remote and click on the bedside light to look at the angry red spot on my leg.

"Ouch," he says and takes my leg in his hands. I'm so glad I shaved this morning. His lips brush against my skin.

"They're going to have to amputate it, I just know."

"Most likely. That's a very serious injury. Looks infected for sure. We better cut it off now before the infection spreads."

"Just call me Peg-leg Pete, the pirate."

Ben laughs. "I won't be calling you Pete anytime soon, but I'd be okay with the pirate part."

"You have a thing for pirates?"

"I might. And it might have to do with the fact that the first-ever porno I watched was called Pussy Pirates."

I can't control the giggle that comes from my mouth. "You're not supposed to admit stuff like that, right?"

He shrugs. "Why not? It's not like it's a secret men like porn. And jerking off. Though I haven't watched porn since we've been together, if that makes you feel better."

"It does," I say and repeat his words in my head.

184

Not the ones about porn, because I don't really care. Some of the things I look at on Tumblr are pornographic, after all. It's the part where he said "since we've been together." We're together? We're an item? Officially? Is that how it works in the adult world? You just date and fuck and grow close then just assume you're together until one day someone drops down on a knee and offers a ring?

Shit.

I need to know this.

Cosmo, you've failed me. Again. Except for that tip about curling my eyelashes *before* I put on mascara. That's actually a good tip. Thanks for that one.

"I have a pirate costume," I blurt, needing to say something to keep myself from freaking out. Is Ben my boyfriend? Should I change my Facebook status? Why hadn't he changed his? Seriously, grow the fuck up, Felicity. That shouldn't be a first thought.

"You do?" he asks, voice dropping. His hands travel up my thighs. "Want to put it on?"

I smile. "I suppose I can. But only because you're asking so nice," I whisper and lean forward, brushing my lips against his neck as I talk. I get up and go into the spare room, which houses my sewing stuff. The closet is full of costumes. I remove my clothes and hang them on the chair by my sewing table. The pirate costume is in the back of the closet, and it takes for-freaking-ever to get the corset laced up by myself. I laced it backward, then pretty much scraped my

185

nipples off turning the tight leather corset around. I decided to forgo the white chemise that goes underneath.

I hike up the skirts, pull on fishnets and tall leather boots, then put on my hat and grab a LARP sword. It's shiny and made of real metal, but the edges are dull enough that I won't have to worry about skewering Ben as he plunders me.

I slow as I walk back to my bedroom. I've worn costumes a million times. I prefer them to "normal" clothes, anyway. Yet this is the first time I've donned something for this reason.

A *sex* reason.

Excitement rushes through me. Excitement, and desire. I step into the room, trying to think of something sexy to say that has to do with pirates. "Swab me poop deck" comes to mind, but there's something so non-sexy about poop, I can't use that line. Even if I was into anal—I haven't tried it … yet—reminding Ben that where he's about to stick it is next to my personal sewage system is a mood killer for sure.

"Ahoy, matey," I say instead.

Ben sits up, mouth opening just a bit as he looks at me. I come over to the bed and he grabs me around the waist. "I'm going to shiver your timbers, baby," he says and we both laugh. "I have no idea what that means, by the way. Just know I'm not going to stop fucking you until you're screaming my name."

"Yo ho—ohhh!" He puts himself between my legs, hard already.

"I kind of want to make up a story," he admits as his tongue runs along my ear.

"You mean like role-play pirates?"

"Why not?"

I haven't role played anything in bed before. My heart speeds up with fear of sounding stupid or messing this up somehow. "We're forbidden lovers? I'm a pirate captain's daughter and you're the general of the British army?"

He nods. "Stop trying to temp me to do the wrong thing," he says and lifts up my skirts. Is this really happening? Ben is actually into role-playing pirates of all things? Fuck being friend-zoned. If this is what the friend zone gets me, then I should have taken a seat here long ago.

Channeling my inner pirate wench makes me a bit of a dominatrix. I flip Ben over and climb on top, looking down over my tits at him. "You have to be quiet," I say. "Or my father will hear us. He will kill you if he sees us together."

He reaches up, hands resting on my sides, which are more pronounced in this tight-ass corset. "It's worth the risk," he says.

And then we're kissing, his hard cock pressing against me, begging to be let in and allowed to plunder me into oblivion. I hold out, even though I'm craving him just as much, slowly removing his clothes until he's lying there completely naked while I'm still fully dressed in my costume.

The light is still on next to the bed. It's the first time I get to take my time and look at Ben, to admire his naked body. He's like a work of art himself. Muscles and tattoos, tan skin, dark hair and eyes. Each is gorgeous on its own. Put them all together and he's a fucking masterpiece.

And then there is his cock.

Holy shit. That dick though.

I'm not one to inherently think a penis is beautiful. They're kinda misshaped most of the time, a little too veiny with an odd-looking mushroom tip. They serve one hell of a purpose, but to look at … not so much.

But not this glorious dick that's at full mast in front of me. Looking at it turns me on, makes me want it inside me—my mouth, my vagina, hell maybe I'll try it up the back door. His cock is long and thick, with enough girth to fill me completely and then some. The veins run along the shaft, and the whole thing is nicely attached to neatly trimmed balls.

His whole package is finely wrapped with a pretty bow. I inhale then bend over, hardly able to breathe in this fucking corset, and take it in my mouth, tasting salty precum, swirling it around with my tongue.

Ben lets out a gasp. I suck hard and pull up, just focusing on the tip before diving down again. His hands grasp my hair and he lets out a moan. I'm so wet and hot I wonder if I can come right here, not even being touched. Hearing Ben get off is getting me off.

I feel his cock pulsing in my mouth and his thighs tighten. I slow, wondering if I should keep going or not. I'm sure he's close to finishing, and I really want that beautiful dick to thrust inside me. I don't want him to be done.

I let him decide, which might be a mistake because I'm doubting he has much self-control right now. His closes his fists in my hair, letting out another moan as he comes, legs twitching. He's breathing heavy and I'm a bit proud of how intense that seemed for him.

I slowly sit up, letting his dick slide out of my mouth. I want to run to the bathroom and spit the semen out, rinse my mouth, then come back. Is it too soon? I have to act like I enjoy this, all of this, right? That's what women are supposed to do.

Fuck that shit.

I give him a closed lip smile and go into the bathroom. I turn on the water and spit, then quickly use my hand as a cup and rinse my mouth out. I'm back in bed in under sixty seconds.

Ben is still laying there, still panting. I don't think he noticed I was even gone. A few seconds tick by then he's over top of me, unzipping my boots and taking off my panties and tights. He's on his side next to me kissing me, and I'm sure he's glad I got that

189

water.

He puts his hand under my petticoat, stroking my clit. I shudder from pleasure. I'm so wound up, so ready for this. He works his fingers, taking his time rubbing, circling, stroking me. I hold onto him, feeling his muscles bulge and flex as he finger-fucks me.

He pushes two fingers inside me, finding my g-spot, then moves back to my clit. After a few minutes of going back and forth like that, I'm coming so hard my ears ring and my toes tingle.

And he doesn't fucking stop.

He moves his head between my legs, kissing the inside of my thighs before taking me in his mouth. Then his tongue lashes out and in just seconds, I'm welcoming my second orgasm.

He moves back up on the bed, holding me close. I get a moment to recover—and I need it—as he rubs my arms and shoulders. I'm starting to majorly relax when he trails his hand down between my legs again.

I moan and roll onto my back, giving him access. He's hard again, and wastes no time getting on top of me. The tip of his dick rubs against my clit, sending me over the edge again. I lift my hips and he slides into me.

He lets out a moan and I realize he doesn't have a condom on. Part of me doesn't care and doesn't want him to stop. His dick has been in my mouth multiple times; I'm just as likely to get an STD from him by sucking his cock as I am from him raw dogging it.

I just don't want to get pregnant. I have messed-up cycles and can go way over a month without bleeding, and never know when I'm going to start until I get crumple-into-bed-with-pain cramps. Then a few hours later Aunt Flo shows up. I haven't had a period since I've met Ben. I should be due for one soon.

But that's a big risk.

He pushes in as deep as he can and all logic goes out the window. I wrap my legs around him and move my hips along with his, needing this now. I come for the third time, clinging to him as my body goes haywire. He bites down at my neck, lets out a breath, and pulls out as he climaxes, coming onto my thigh. He pushes himself against me, trying to get some sensation out of it.

He relaxes against me, his weight crushing, and buries his head in the cleavage that's popping out of the tight leather corset.

"That was nice," I say and run my hands down his arms. "And by nice I mean fucking amazing."

Ben's still panting. He rises his head and kisses me. "You're fucking amazing."

My heart swells and I feel myself inching closer and closer to the edge. No. I'm not falling for him. Not now. Not yet. I can't when there is so much up in the air, so much unknown.

"Want me to get you a towel or something?" he

asks.

"Nah, it's already dripping down my leg onto the skirt. That'll work well enough." I use the material to wipe up my thigh.

Ben makes a face. "Sorry?"

"You should be. So sorry you do me again."

He rolls off me, chest rapidly rising and falling. "That can be arranged."

"Actually, you can unlace the corset and call it even."

"If undressing you is the price I have to pay for fucking you…" He grabs me and pulls me onto him. Our eyes meet and his lips part, like he wants to say something. He kisses me instead and sits us both up. Deft fingers unlace the corset and I go into the bathroom to undress and run a damp washcloth over my sticky skin.

I want to bring up the "since we've been together" thing but I'm not sure how to do it. I don't want to insult him if we have been together in his eyes. It's not like I'm seeing anyone else, or have any intentions to.

Why can't we go back to the days when we passed a note where you just had to circle yes or no? So simple. Black and white. Unless that fucker adds a "maybe" option to that note.

Ben has his boxers on, and he's lying on the bed flipping through channels. He's everything I want and everything I thought I'd never have.

"Hungry?" he asks.

"Not really, but I do have cookies."

"You like to bake, don't you?" he asks.

"I do," I tell him and open the top drawer on my dresser. I pull out panties and a Captain America tank top to wear to bed. I undress in front of him, knowing he's watching but not feeling self-conscious. "My best friend owns a bakery. She pretty much forced my love of baking from an early age. She's way better than me, which is good since she owns a bakery and all. Want milk with your cookies?"

"Is there any other way to eat them?"

I smile and leave the room, coming back with chocolate chip cookies and two glasses of milk. I'm surprised to see Ser Pounce sitting on the foot of the bed. He's not cuddled up with Ben by any means, but he's blissfully ignoring him. And hey, that's progress. I snuggle with Ben as we eat and watch another episode of *Game of Thrones*. Ben says he should leave since we both have work in the morning, but makes no attempt to get up.

I put the dishes aside and we cuddle under the blankets, comfortably tangled together.

"What are you doing for the Fourth of July?" I ask lazily, close to the point of being so tired my logic filter is off. I'm not worried about asking him anymore.

"A friend is having a party," he says and my heart sinks. "Why? Do you have plans?"

"Kind of. My parents own cabins and boats and stuff along the lake and have a huge hillbilly boat party thing."

"Did you say boats?"

I nod. "And a few jet skis. They rent them out to people who rent the cabins. But they always save a few for the party."

"That sounds fun."

"It is, actually. There's more food than you can eat and everyone is drunk. Even my mom, and she's a trip once you get enough wine in her. I haven't been home much lately. I'm kind of looking forward to it," I confess as it hits me. "Erin always goes. And makes a tasty cake."

"The one who owns the bakery?"

"Yeah. I should have mentioned it sooner so you could have gone with me." My eyes are closed and the steady beating of Ben's heart is relaxing. I don't want him to leave.

"My friend's party isn't something I'd be sad to miss," he says slowly.

"Really?" I sound too hopeful.

"Really. When are you leaving?"

"Sometime that Friday evening. I intended on spending the weekend there, since the Fourth is on Saturday and all. You don't have to go if you don't want to. I know it's a long time to be with me and all…"

"I do want to," he says. "I like being with you,

194

Felicity. You act like it's a surprise."

"Just making sure," I add quickly. I smile, and wrap my arm tighter around him.

"I have to go to an art exhibit opening Wednesday night, and I should spend tomorrow getting ready," he says. "I'll be at the gallery late, and Thursday I have to drive three hours to another gallery and be gone the whole day. So I won't get to see you the rest of the week. I'll be looking forward to the whole weekend together."

"Good. Because I am too."

Chapter Twelve

Tissue paper crunches under my ass, which is hardly covered in a disposable thong. I shift on the foam bed, nervously looking at the door. My heart is racing. Fuck. I shouldn't have done this. I can still get up, put my pants back on, and dash out of the salon before someone comes in, covers my cooter with hot wax, and rips my hair from my body.

There's a knock on the door. I smooth out the white robe I've been given over my lap. Crap. No time.

A pretty esthetician with her hair in a tight bun comes into the room. She looks like she could be my mother, which is both reassuring and awkward at the same time. Please be gentle with me. I'm a wax virgin.

"Felicity?" she asks, looking down at the paper I filled out at the front desk.

"Yeah," I say and swallow hard. The smell of the wax fills the air and my thighs clench shut on their own accord. I'm nervous as fuck and feel like I'm about to get a PAP smear or something invasive like that. Though, in the end, that'll probably hurt less.

"You forget check box," she says in a thick Russian accent. I can hardly understand her. "You want backside wax too?"

"Uh, sure," I say. After an hour-long debate Monday night, I decided to call and make an appointment today for a wax after getting my hair dyed back to its original color of brunette. That way I won't have to worry about shaving or having an unsightly bikini line while on the lake. And I thought it might be a nice surprise for Ben when he sees me tomorrow night, since his head is frequently between my legs.

And I hate shaving with a passion.

"First wax?" she says and sets the paper down.

I nod.

"Relax. Pain over quick."

"Okay. If you say so."

I lay back and squeeze my eyes closed. I'm about to freak the fuck out. Over a wax. Get it together, Felicity. I need to channel my inner Black Widow. Pretend I'm being tortured for info. Yes, that works. I'll think about how utterly messed up that is later.

The esthetician puts on gloves and gets to work. My fingers dig into the foam bed as she cleanses my skin, dries it, and preps for the wax. My heart is pounding when the hot wax is spread onto my skin.

The strip goes on next.

Holy crap, pain is coming. I start the countdown in my head. *Three, two*—she pulls that sucker right off. Oh, that wasn't so bad. I let out a breath. She spreads more wax on my skin and rips up another section of hair. I'm tempted to look but, having the feeling it will resemble something torn off Chewbacca, I don't to save myself the embarrassment. I had to forgo shaving all week to get this wax.

It takes longer than I anticipated, and when I'm told to roll over and spread my thighs, the realization that "backside" means "butt crack" hits me like a sucker punch to the stomach and I'm so stunned I can't do anything but lay there in terror and hope I don't fart.

I leave feeling smooth, sore, and just a little violated. My skin begins to burn as the fabric from my panties and jeans rubs against it, and by the time I get home it's on fire and super itchy.

Then I realize the lotion put on after the waxing was scented. I'm okay with scented stuff most of the time.

Most. Of. The. Time.

Freshly waxed, fragile skin plus a history of eczema and psoriasis going back years isn't most of the time. Damn it. I rip my clothes off as soon as I get through the door and run to the shower to wash off what I can.

I pause in front of the mirror while the water is warming up and stare in horror at my bikini line. It's red as hell. Yes, definitely a reaction to the scented lotion. This is the exact opposite of what was supposed to happen. I was supposed to make my fun zone more *fun*. Not angry and red, like it wants to kill anything that enters it.

I open my medicine cabinet and pop a Benadryl in my mouth, then get into the shower, taking a drink from the water streaming down to swallow the pill. I stand in the warm water, scared to touch my irritated skin, but curious as to how smooth it feels, and feel considerably better when I get out. I slather on cortisone cream, pull on a thigh-length nightgown, foregoing undies all together, and go into the kitchen to make dinner. I call Erin while my mac n' cheese is cooking and tell her about my poor lady bits and how I was too terrified to even think of being allergic to scented shit.

She can't stop laughing. A best friend, yes she is.

I eat, then crash into bed, feeling sleepy from the Benadryl. I watch a few episodes of *The Big Bang Theory*, get up to brush my teeth, check on my skin— yep, still red—and take one more Benadryl in hopes that I'll wake up better.

It almost works.

I sleep through my alarm. I'm a lightweight when it comes to anything, and two Benadryls knocks me out. I half ass my hair and makeup, wear a flowy dress and my granniest panties to avoid any chaffing during the day, and take one more Benadryl since I'm looking better. I'll counter act it with coffee and be fine once it wears off by midday.

I pack a lunch, feed Ser Pounce, and try my best not to fall asleep while driving. I trudge into the office and plop into my desk.

"Oh, like the new hair color!" Mariah says.

"Thanks," I mumble.

"Are you okay?"

"In a sense, yes. I had an allergic reaction to something and the Benadryl is making me so tired."

I stash my purse under my desk and fire up my computer. "I just need a few hours for it to get out of my system then I'll be fine."

"You're making me worried, honey," she says, sounding motherly. Do I look that bad? "Maybe you should go home and get some rest."

That is a great idea, but I can't ask to go home because of this. I blink several times, trying to get my head out of this fog. I didn't bring coffee with me since I didn't have time to make any. I push my shoulders back and walk to the break room.

There are fresh donuts on the table. I could kiss whoever brought them. I take two, and fill a cup with coffee, mixing in creamer. I run into Cameron on my way back to my desk.

"Sexy color," he says and touches my hair, then he flicks his eyes to my face. "Rough night?" he asks.

"You could say that."

"The boy toy?"

"Hah, I wish." I take a sip of coffee; I think I need an IV of it today. "Uh, actually I got a wax and then had a reaction to the lotion. It's pretty painful and rashy. I overdosed on Benadryl."

Cameron looks at me with a blank face. Then he busts out laughing. "That would only happen to you."

"Shut up," I say dryly. "It's not funny."

"It's hilarious." His face gets serious. "How bad of a reaction? Do you need to see a doctor or anything?"

"Nah," I say and take another drink of coffee. "The redness is almost gone, thank God. I'm just so fucking tired."

He gives me a watch-your-mouth-at-the-office glare. "Why didn't you call in sick? You look terrible."

"Thanks, and I'm not sick. I didn't even think of it, really." I sigh, feeling the drugs pull me back. "I should have."

He crosses his arms. "You know, you've never taken a sick day since you've been here. You won't be behind if you take the rest of the day off."

"Seriously?"

"Seriously. You can do some work from home anyway, right?"

"I can, and I don't have much to do with this current site anyway. The client is out of town for the holiday so we can't go over anything I've done for approval."

"Then go home. Get some rest and ice your cooter."

"Don't say it so loud."

He's laughing again. "Sorry. Really, I am. Now go, get some sleep and have a good weekend."

"You too."

"Oh, I will. Adam's sister's husband's family has a house in the Hamptons. We're flying out right after work."

"Classy. Sounds really fun though. I'm kinda jealous," I lie. From what I know about that area— granted, it's all from TV shows and movies—is that it's too fancy for my liking. Feeling grateful for befriending my boss the week I started here, I go back to my desk, shut down my computer, and gather my things. I say bye to Mariah on my way out and consider calling Ben, but decide not to.

I don't want to tell him why I'm leaving early, and I'd really like to go home and crash for a few hours before packing and getting dressed. Deciding to forego the rest of my coffee, I get into bed right away.

Four-and-a-half hours later, I wake from my drug-induced slumber. After a long, hot shower, I feel completely better. I look better too, which is awesome.

I get my packing done in under an hour, set things up for Ser Pounce to be alone all weekend (I need to remember to shut the windows and turn the AC on before I leave so the kitty doesn't cook in case it gets hot), and call Ben. His phone rings but goes to voicemail. I leave him a message, sure he's busy painting or sculpting or talking to people who come in to buy his expensive work, and go into the kitchen.

I need to make something to bring to the cookout, and I've been too lazy to go grocery shopping this past week. Lazy, and distracted with Ben. I have a lot of apples. I could make apple pie. That's easy and tasty.

I preheat the oven and start making the crust. It has to chill for a while, and I rationalize that I should probably finish the open bottle of moscato in the fridge so it doesn't go bad by the time I get back from the weekend getaway. I pour myself a big glass and sit at the island, scrolling through Facebook and Pinterest for half an hour before getting up to slice the apples.

The oven has been on for way too long now, and the kitchen is hot. I twist my hair up and use a pen to secure it in a bun. I'm sweating by the time I get the pie in the oven. My phone rings as I go around closing windows to turn on the air.

"Hey," I say to Ben. "How are you?"

"Better now." He sounds like he's smiling. "How's work?"

"I got out early," I tell him. "On good behavior. What about you?"

"I'm finishing up at the gallery. I need to shower. I'm covered in paint."

"I think you look rather good covered in paint."

He laughs. "That's good, because I am most of the time."

"You can come over earlier if you want," I say.

"I'm packed. I just need to shower again because I'm hot and sweaty."

"And why are you hot and sweaty?" he asks, voice seductive.

"I made apple pie."

A moment of silence goes by. Then Ben asks. "Is that a sex reference?"

I almost choke on my wine. "I can totally see how it could be interpreted that way, but I actually made apple pie. My kitchen gets hot when I use the oven. Curse of a small house, I guess." I look at the timer. "It'll be done soon-ish. Do you want to come over and enjoy a slice of my pie? And *that* is a sex reference. But you can eat real pie too. I made it to take with us to my parent's, but it smells too good not to eat now."

"Yes," he says right away. "Give me like an hour. I still have to pack a bag. Then I'm going to have a slice of your pie. Maybe two."

"Or three." I drink the rest of my wine. "See you soon."

"Bye, Felicity."

I hang up with a smile. My mission this weekend is to find out what exactly Ben considers me, because I really want to be his girlfriend. There's still a stupid part of me that's nagging about how he's not "my type" and is totally out of my league. Not wanting to think about it, I quickly rinse off in the shower and put on a bit of makeup. I pull on a blue cotton dress—comfy for traveling—and put a pair of Toms by the door next to my bag and my purse.

There. I'm ready. Mom will be proud of how light I packed. Though realistically, I'll be in my bathing suit most of the weekend on the boat. I don't need much. I sit in the living room, sprawled out on the couch, enjoying the cool air rushing down on me from the ceiling fan, and watch reruns of *Supernatural* until Ben gets here.

"You look pretty," he says when he steps inside. "I like the darker hair." My arms go around him, and I pull us together. Being away for a few days reminded me how much I love being together.

"Thanks," I say and we kiss. The timer goes off for the pie, and we both go into the kitchen to get it.

"It smells amazing," he says, arms locking around my waist. I close my eyes and lean back into him, dropping the pot holders on the counter. My mind goes to what Cameron says, that Ben sees me as a friend material only, and I get hit with sadness.

That was unexpected.

I force a smile, trying to push aside how strongly I feel for him. I don't want to be friend-zoned as a fuck buddy only. I want something more with Ben because even though he might be totally out of my league, he's my total dream guy.

"It has to cool for a while," I tell him. "It's too hot to eat."

His lips meet my neck and his teeth graze my

205

skin. "I know something we can do to pass the time."

I shiver, whirling around in Ben's arms and linking mine around his neck. He looks into my eyes, expression full of lust and ... something else.

I'm not sure what it is, but I am entirely sure you don't look at a friend that way.

"What do you have in mind?" I ask. I run my hands down his back and under his shirt. Just the feel of his warm skin against my palms makes me hot. Ben is spending the weekend with me.

With my family.

Meeting my parents.

My brother and his stupid fiancée.

Driving two hours and blowing off a friend's party.

Fuck buddies don't do that, right? It's too much effort. He's a good-looking guy with an impressive career. He could easily get some wherever he goes. And by now I know there is more to Ben than pussy seeking.

He shrugs. "We could watch TV, go for a walk ... you know, exciting stuff like that." His hands travel along my front and his fingers pull on the hem of my dress. "Or we could go into the bedroom and nap."

"Yes. Nap. How responsible of us. Since we're going to drive and all. Don't want to nod off in the car."

Ben takes a step back, bringing me with him "Not, not at all." With no warning, he picks me up and tosses me over his shoulder, then runs to the bedroom. He tosses me down on the bed and pins me down with his body.

His heart is beating fast against mine and he gives me that look again, a look that says he thinks the world of me. My first thought is what the fuck is wrong with him, to look at me that way. I'm laying beneath this incredible man, this incredible man with an incredible boner that's pressing into me, by the way, and I'm feeling self-conscious and shy like I did when I ran into Mindy fucking Abraham outside the Adult Toybox.

I close my eyes and push those thoughts from my head. Thoughts that I'm told I shouldn't have as an adult. I shouldn't care what other people think. I shouldn't worry about others' opinions.

But I do, even though I try so hard not to.

I open my eyes and see Ben still looking down at me like he wants to devour me. A moment of clarity hits me.

I do care about others' opinions. But that list of "others" just got a whole lot shorter.

I run my hands through Ben's hair. He matters. I feel so strongly toward him at the moment, I don't trust myself to speak. So I kiss him, locking my lips with his, sealing in any bumbling emotional words that might spill from my mouth.

He pushes his tongue inside and pulls my dress up. Things get heated quickly, and before I know it, my panties are on the floor and Ben is lowering his head between my legs. He runs his hands over the smooth skin on my bikini line. No pain, no bumps, and no redness. Thank the fucking lord.

I watch him work, tongue lashing in and out, harsh then soft on me, until I can't take it anymore. My eyes close and I ball the blankets in my hands as I scream, coming so hard my legs shake. Holy fuck. The more we mess around, the better he knows me and my body. And the stronger the orgasms are.

A girl could get used to this.

I'm panting like crazy, chest rising and falling as he move up next to me. I smile at him. "That was great, thanks. We can leave now. Totally rested."

He bites his lip and smiles back before grabbing my waist. He moves between my legs. "There's no way I'm letting you out of my sight, out of my reach, my grasp, my touch, right now."

All I can do is nod and fumble with the button on his pants. Somehow I manage to get them and his boxers down. His hard cock springs free, hitting me in the stomach when he lowers himself onto me again. He rubs against me, letting out a soft moan. I reach for him, taking his hardness in my hand, and pump my arm up and down a few times. I contort my body to be able to keep stroking him while gently biting his earlobe. He's like puddy in my hand. Well, not really, since puddy is soft and not long and thick and hard.

But he melts into me, practically squirming. Precum wets his cock and I swirl my thumb over the tip, spreading it down. He repositions himself so his dick rubs my clit. The wet warmth drives me wild and I need him inside me. He holds himself up on his elbows and brushes the hair out of my eyes, then kisses me.

I'm getting so wound up again. I widen my legs to urge him inside. We're kissing again, and the passion is like something from a romance novel. This is really happening, right? He reaches down and strokes me for a few seconds before sliding his hand beneath my head, bringing my mouth even closer to his.

"I need you," I whisper. "Now."

The tip of his dick is almost inside me. "Left condoms…" he stops to kiss me. "…In wallet in car."

"Well, fuck," I pant. "Just pull out again."

"Are you—" he cuts off when I lift my hips. "Sure?"

No, I'm not, but right now I'm not thinking logically. Again. Twice in a row…come on Felicity. You know better than that.

"I have some," I say. They're probably expired, but it's better than nothing, right? Ben moves off me and I madly dig through the top drawer of my nightstand to find the crushed box shoved in the back. He puts it on with haste and we pick right back up where we left off.

I come three times before we're through.

209

Once we've cleaned up, we settle back into bed together. I rest my head on Ben's chest and he lazily runs his fingers through my hair. I don't care what anyone says. Life seems pretty fucking perfect right now.

My phone vibrates on the nightstand next to us.

"Want me to get that for you?" he asks.

"Mhh," I mumble, feeling sleepy. "It's a text message. It's probably my mom, asking if I've left yet. She still worries about me driving and needs to know when I leave so she can time shit out. Does it say 'mom' on the message?"

He grabs the phone. "Uh, no. It's your friend Erin … and she wants to know if you're still experiencing severe anal itching and if your rash is gone."

I pull away from him, completely horrified and embarrassed. It's a joke. I can say it's a joke. Right? Oh god. Fuck.

"Do you have something?" he asks slowly, face paling. "I think I should know if you do. I mean, I've spent quite a bit of time down there." He grimaces. "Just tell me if you do. I know we never brought it up, and maybe that was my bad, but—"

"I don't have anything," I interrupt, burying my

face in my hands. "I promise, I'm clean."

"Then what is your friend talking about?"

I can't look at Ben. Not now. Not ever. Oh my God I want to die.

"Felicity?"

"I got a wax to surprise you and had a reaction to the lotion they put on me after. I have stupid sensitive skin and scented lotion makes me break out in a rash." My voice is muffled by my hands. I turn away dramatically and put a pillow over my head. "I didn't want to tell you because it's embarrassing!"

A few seconds tick by. Then Ben laughs. "I did notice how smooth you are. And you could have told me. I didn't hurt you, did I?"

"No," I say, still hidden under the pillow.

Ben is laughing again. He takes my arm and gently pulls me. "Don't be embarrassed."

"Too late! I am."

"Come on, it's not that big of a deal. Don't be a baby."

"I am a baby," I lament. He's still laughing. "It fucking hurt!"

"The waxing or the rash?"

"Both, but I think the rash was worse. It's gone now. I took Benadryl and it went away."

"Sorry I'm laughing."

"Apparently I'm the only one who doesn't think it's funny," I mumble and let him pull me to his lap.

"Well, it's better than being diseased. I don't have

anything either, in case you were wondering."

I nod. "That's good to know."

He gives me my phone. "You should let your friend know. She just sent some graphic pictures to show her concern."

I shake my head, but crack a smile. "I need to take that feature off so you can't read my text on screen like that. Taken out of context, things can go very wrong."

"At least you were here to clear it all up."

I reply to Erin, then take a few minutes to snuggle with Ben. I'm a little sore, but it has nothing to do with the wax or the rash and everything to do with how hard he just railed me. So it's sore in a good way, of course.

We get re-dressed to leave. I grab Ser Pounce and kiss his furry head.

"You have four bowls of water and three bowls of food. Don't eat them all at once, Fatty."

"I thought you said you didn't like that cat," Ben says and picks up my bag.

"I said I wanted a dog and got him instead. He's grown on me though, like a fungus. I do love this grump. He'll be fine though. He's so lazy and I don't think he'll even notice I'm gone." I set Ser Pounce down and put on my shoes. "Who's taking care of Harumi for you?"

"My mom," he says. "She spoils that dog. She'll be ten pounds heavier when we get back. It's her subtle way of trying to make me feel guilty I haven't given her any grandkids yet. I told her it's her fault she didn't have more kids. That's a lot of pressure to put on me."

"Yeah, very true. I have a brother and he's getting married first, so the pressure is on him, thankfully." I fish my keys out of my purse.

"I can drive," Ben says and gets his own keys.

"I can't make you do that. It's my family's party we're going to."

"I don't mind," he insists. "And you can keep your car in the garage then."

"You're sure?"

"Yeah. I kind of like driving."

I raise an eyebrow. "You're such a guy. And I kind of like that. Because I hate driving long distances."

"Perfect."

We load my stuff, I lock up the house, and then we're off.

Chapter Thirteen

Since we left several hours earlier than planned, there is plenty of daylight left when we pull into my parents' driveway. It's filled with cars already, even though the official party doesn't start until tomorrow.

"My brother is here," I say. "Be prepared to meet Bridezilla."

"She's going to talk nonstop about the wedding, isn't she?"

"I'm sure. It's a week away. Like I get it's stressful, but why freak out?" I shake my head. "Whatever. I'm all about getting drunk, getting tan, and having fun this weekend."

Ben smiles. "I think we can manage that."

"You can just park here," I tell him and point to the spot behind Jake's car. "We'll drive to our cottage later after dinner."

"We have our own cottage?" he asks.

"Yeah. I fake rented it out to make sure it would be reserved. Trust me, you don't want to be inside that house when my mom and my aunt start drinking. Or maybe you do. It's pretty entertaining. But my aunt stays in my old room, and my mom was going to set up the sleeper sofa in the basement for us." My eyes widen and I shake my head. "I'm not doing that. Besides … the privacy is nice."

Ben leans in and kisses me. "It is nice." He puts

214

the Audi in park. I grab my purse, jam my feet back into my shoes, and get out, leaving my bag in the car. "So do these cottages have electricity?"

"Yes. They're pretty much like a little house with everything you could need. Even Wi-Fi, though the connection sucks *so* bad." I can hear the waves crashing on the shore behind the house. We're a ways away from the water, but I'm able to pick up on the rush of water. My gaze goes to the lake, and I feel a piece of my heart warm. I might be a little fond of my childhood home and growing up on the lakefront.

"You can kind of see them over there," I say and motion to the side of my parents' house. "There's a boardwalk in the sand that connects everything: the house, the docks, and the cabins. But since we have bags, we can drive there and then walk in the morning."

"Sounds good to me."

We get out and walk up to the house. "I should warn you, my mom can be a little, uh, overbearing sometimes."

"She can't be any worse than mine," he says, almost under his breath.

"If she starts talking about what our children will look like, run. Well, not really. Just ignore her. She doesn't mean to come off that way. She's just totally oblivious to it."

"My mom says the same," he tells me with a smile. "She really thinks I should be married by now."

He rolls his eyes. "She wanted that five years ago too."

Thinking about the wedding doesn't bring on the same wave of pathetic sadness like it did before. I'm not going to start a Pinterest board for our future wedding—not yet at least—but having him here with me helps more than I thought it would.

I ascend the porch steps and get hit with nervousness. I told my mom I'm bringing a boyfriend, because explaining that Ben and I are casually dating and seriously fucking isn't something I can do. But Ben hasn't said he's my boyfriend, and the potential embarrassment and disappointment scare me.

I open the front door and hear laughter coming from the kitchen. Ben still holds my hand as we walk in. My mom, dad, brother, and two of my aunts are crowded around the kitchen table, all with drinks in hand.

Great, Aunt Tilly is here. She's hilariously obnoxious when she's drunk, with emphasis on the obnoxious part.

"Felicity," Mom says, looking almost startled. "I wasn't expecting you so soon. And your hair is back to brown. I like it better this way!" She sets down her wine glass and comes over to hug me.

"I got off work early," I say and give her a one-armed hug back.

"And this is—"

"Ben," I interrupt before she can question our relationship. I hate being awkward like this, and I hate that I feel like I'm lying to Ben or something. Like if he doesn't consider me his girlfriend, then I feel like a real loser for calling him my boyfriend. I'm a fucking adult. I need to get over this. I roll my eyes at myself.

"Nice to meet you," Ben says and shakes my mother's hand. She's looking him up and down like he's a mirage and might not be real ... which is better than the way Aunt Tilly is looking at him. She has one eyebrow raised and runs her finger along the lip of her wine glass, fucking Ben with her eyes.

Ben, please don't notice. Or notice but don't care. I go around with introductions and open the fridge. I get a beer for Ben and a wine cooler for myself.

"Did you get a new car?" Jake asks me, looking outside. "You can afford a brand-new Audi?"

"I can," I say, "if I don't want to eat or pay my bills. But no, it's Ben's car."

Jake turns to Ben and compliments the car, exchanging a few words about engines or something I know nothing about.

"So, Ben," my other aunt asks. My mom has two sisters, Matilda—Tilly—and Miranda, and they all look alike. "What do you do for a living?"

"I'm an artist," he says.

"Oh, interesting!" Mom comes around the table and sits next to Dad. "What kind of artist?"

Ben smiles; he's used to the questions. "I

217

primarily paint, but I've gotten into sculpting more lately."

"He has a gallery in Grand Rapids," I say. "That's how we met. I did some computer work for him."

"If you ever need models," Aunt Tilly says and dramatically flips her hair. "I can sacrifice my time for you."

Mom and Aunt Miranda laugh, then watch us, waiting for more details.

"So, what's the plan?" I ask, jumping right in and breaking up the stunned silence I'm still getting from my family. Way to make me feel good. Act like me bringing home a decent-looking guy with an expensive car is as rare as Loki handing over his scepter.

"The same as always," Dad says, finally speaking for the first time. "BBQ chicken on the grill tonight, bonfire, and watch the early fireworks over the lake. Then it's boat and booze time tomorrow with a little fishing thrown in!"

My aunts cheer. What does Ben think of us?

"The water's a little choppy for water skiing," Dad goes on. "But it's perfect for tubing."

"Tubing," I inform Ben, "is Dad's version of whipping you around the lake on an inflatable raft, laughing as you go flying off and declaring himself the winner."

"Sounds fun," Ben says with a smile.

"No one can beat me," Dad boasts proudly.

"Dad," I say, rolling my eyes yet smiling. "You can't be beaten when you don't get on the tube yourself."

"Exactly," he shoots back. "Though Felicity does hold the record for staying on the longest. Want to try and break the record this year?"

"You're on." Ben and I sit at the island counter. "Where's Danielle?" I ask Jake.

"She went with her friend to see her sister. I guess she's going through a divorce and is having a hard time. She'll be here in the morning."

"Bummer for Danielle's sister."

"It's her friend's sister," Jake corrects. "You met the friend, Zoey, at the shower."

"Oh, yeah," I say, not recalling the girl at all. "Well, that's nice of her to help her out."

Jake nods, getting that love-struck look in his eyes again. "That's just how she is. She's bringing them with her tomorrow to help cheer her friend up."

Dad stands. "Ben, do you know how to drive a boat?"

"I don't," Ben replies.

Dad flicks his eyes to me and I know exactly why he's asking. He wants to talk to Ben, make sure he's treating me well. I silently plead with my father to be nice. He gives me a wink then looks back at Ben. "Want to learn?"

"I'd love to."

"Go on, you two get changed and meet me on the

219

docks. Where are your bags?"

"In the car," I say and go through the kitchen into the small office that's crammed full of furniture and filing cabinets. I grab the keys for Cabin 18.

"That's reserved," Mom says, eyeing the numbers on the key chain.

"For Lily and James Potter," I say and shake my head.

"How do you know?" Mom asks, generally surprised.

"And you call yourself my mother." I let out a dramatic sigh. "Mom, I made the reservation."

Her lips press together then she laughs before her face gets serious. "You two together … I don't know, young lady."

I cock an eyebrow. "Really, Mom."

"Oh lighten up, Melissa," Aunt Tilly says. "She's a grown woman who lives on her own in another city. You think she never has overnight guests at her own place?"

"Fine," Mom concedes. "But that doesn't mean I have to like it."

"Love you too," I say and dash around her. "We'll meet you outside in fifteen, Dad." I take Ben's hand and pull him from the house. "Sorry," I say when we're in his car. "I told you they're a bit much."

"They're family," he says back. He starts the car, puts on his seatbelt and kisses me. "It's perfect."

I wake up wrapped in Ben's arms. We stayed outside on the sandy shore until two AM, and the flames of the bonfire dwindled to nothing. Tired and tipsy, we stumbled our way to the cabin and had lazy sex in the shower before crashing in bed for the rest of the night. It's nearing nine o'clock, and I already know we've missed whatever breakfast Mom cooked and served.

Oh well. We'll make up for it with the feast she makes for lunch.

I sneak out of Ben's arms and tip toe into the bathroom to pee, brush my teeth, and wash my face. My hair is still damp; I quickly brush it then put it in a braid to keep it from becoming a tangled mess from the lakefront breeze or the air whipping through my hair as we zip along the water in the boat.

I'm not even going to bother with makeup. I lift my arms to inspect the hair situation going on under them. Damn you, dark pit hair. I shave them dry, regret it immediately, then sneak back into bed.

Ben opens his eyes and pulls me in. "I woke up and you were gone," he mumbles. "I didn't like that."

I'm smiling as I tangle myself around his naked body. "Can I make it up to you?"

"I think so." He pulls me in, squeezing me against him, then gets up to use the bathroom and get a drink. I roll out of bed, knowing we should get up and get moving or else Mom or one of my aunts will come down here to get us.

I put on my bikini. The top has fabric clam shells stitched onto the cups, and the bottoms are sparkly green with printed scales. I pull on the straps of the bikini. Being well endowed is a blessing and a curse. I can forego support and comfort for cleavage or get something with full coverage and hide these puppies.

I went with the mermaid suit with neither in mind. Because, mermaids. It wasn't a hard choice at all. I pull on a white dress over top and slip my feet into flip-flops, then toss my phone and sunglasses into a beach bag. It's big and I have room, so I throw in another dress in case this one gets soaked and I need to change. I get cold easily on the lake.

Ben comes out of the bathroom wearing gray swim trunks and a teal T-shirt. He has his sunglasses on his head, and his hair is still a rumpled mess from sleeping. He looks adorable.

"Ready?" I ask.

"If you are."

"I am. We'll eat breakfast at the house, and I'll bring some snacks over with us tonight. I kinda forgot about it last night."

"Good thinking. I'm starving." We walk hand in hand down the boardwalk. The beach is already crowded with picnickers, and the water is dotted with boats. The sun is out in full force, with only a few clouds in sight.

It's going to be perfect.

To my surprise, Danielle and her friends haven't arrived yet. Ben and I eat warmed-over bacon and eggs—which isn't as bad as it sounds—and go down to the dock with Jake to wait for his fiancé. The boat is loaded with beach towels, food and drinks. Dad makes sure everyone has a life vest, then goes to help some of the renters with the boat they checked out for the day.

Ben and I sit in the back of the boat. He drapes his arm around me and I do my best to take a few selfies of the two of us. I look like a hot mess: frizzy hair, red spots visible on my cheeks, and puffy tired eyes.

But I look happy.

That's what matters. I like the picture and stash my phone in a cubby to keep it dry. I stretch out my legs, feeling the heat of the sun.

"Sorry if I blind you with my albino skin," I say to Ben.

"It is hurting my eyes," he says and shields his face with his hands. "You're glowing."

I elbow him. "Shut up."

He grabs my arms. "You're two different colors. Tan arms, tan face, but pale legs."

We laugh. "I know. I used to be super tan all the time living by the lake. I don't lay out or go tanning now, so this is the best I can get."

223

"Maybe you'll even out after today."

"Maybe. But probably not. Is it bad I don't care?"

"Not at all. I'm glad you don't care."

"Really?" Because I do care, just a bit. I want to look good head to toe, even though I know that's a bunch of bullshit. People don't *really* look like that.

"Really." He seals it with a kiss. "I haven't been out on the lake much," he admits. "Even though I've lived in Michigan most of my life."

"That's kind of sad," I tell him "I love the lake."

"I don't remember it being this big." He looks out at the water. "And with traveling for the military, it made family vacations hard to plan. We went to Disney World a few times, but that was kind of it."

"I'm glad you're here with me now. We can make up for it."

"This definitely helps," he says with a smile. "And my childhood wasn't bad or anything. Just different, I suppose, than most."

"It makes me feel like I took mine for granted. As many times as I wanted out of this town when I was a teen, it would have been ten times harder to start over multiple times."

He nods. "You get used to it. Well, I assume most people do."

Jake stands and waves to Danielle as she comes into view. Ben is still talking about the lake and something that has to do with his childhood, but his words go in one ear and out the other.

Danielle leads the way down the dock. She's wearing a bright-red bikini with a white scarf tied around her waist. Her sandals are jeweled and sparkle in the sun. Her hair falls in loose waves around her face. She smiles behind oversized sunglasses, looking ridiculously put together for someone in a swimsuit. Her friend Zoey, who I recognize now as the tall girl who scoffed at me during the shower, is next to her. She's too done-up too, but she's nothing compared to the tan woman walking next to her.

White wedge heels cover her feet, attached to lean legs, smooth and golden. My gaze travels up to her thin waist, tight and small with just a hint of muscle. Her bikini top is as small as her bottoms, hardly covering large, perfectly round breasts.

Her face is hard to see behind large sunglasses and a floppy hat. But I know who she is right away.

Mindy fucking Abraham.

Chapter Fourteen

I blink. I'm still drunk. Got too much sun already. I'm dreaming. No, I'm having a nightmare.

I can't stop watching Mindy walk toward us. My blood boils and my skin prickles as the devil herself nears. My heart skips a beat. Mindy is Zoey's sister. Holy fuck, the universe really does hate me, doesn't it?

My mind immediately goes into stupid compare-mode. Mindy is tall, thin, toned, and tan. Her breasts, though fake, are perky and shaped like beach-balls, holding themselves in place. Her makeup is flawless and not a strand of hair is out of place in the fishtail braid that falls over her shoulder.

Wait a second. Her hair isn't really that long. Seriously? She put in extensions just for today?

I blink again.

No. No, no, no. And why the fuck is Erin not getting here until after noon?

"Felicity?" Mindy says, literally stopping in her tracks. Our eyes have met. I should turn to stone or something, right? She flicks them to Ben. "And Ben?"

Ben turns, looking confused to see his secretary standing before us.

"You guys know each other?" Jakes asks, helping Danielle into the boat.

"She works for me," Ben says matter-of-factly

and my head shakes, still wishing I would lie and say I have no idea who the fuck this blonde bimbo is.

"What are you doing here?" Mindy asks, and I'm not sure if she's talking to me or Ben. She looks at her friends, my brother, Ben, and then me, playing the Which One of These Does Not Belong game.

Clearly, it's me.

"This is my boat," I say and blink. Jake helps Danielle and Zoey into the boat, unaware of the complete nuclear disaster that's taking place right now. Mindy takes her sunglasses off and looks at Ben.

"And you're here...?"

Ben's arm is still around me. His fingers press into my waist and he leans a little closer. "I'm here with Felicity."

Mindy squeezes her sunglasses so hard I think they are going to break. "You two are here *together*?"

"Generally, that's what 'I'm here with' means," Ben quips, and I see a side of him I haven't really seen yet: annoyed. At least I'm not the only one instantly irritated by Mindy.

"Min," Zoey starts, turning around. "Aren't you coming?"

Jake is still standing by the dock, hand out, waiting to help Mindy into the boat. She shakes herself, smiles, and climbs aboard.

"I don't get it," Mindy says as Jake works on untying us from the dock. "How..." She shakes her head and looks at each of our faces again. "How do you know them?"

"Jake is my brother," I say slowly so she can follow along. "He's getting married to Danielle, who's friends with Zoey, who apparently is your sister. And I invited Ben for the weekend."

I grab a wine cooler from the insulated bag full of alcohol and ice and twist off the cap, needing booze. A lot of booze. I'm spending the holiday with Mindy fucking Abraham.

Deep breaths. It'll be fine.

I lean back against Ben and let my head rest on his shoulder. The boat idles out past the no-wake zone and Jake pushes it ahead out to sea. Okay, out to *lake*.

Water splashes the girls up front and they shriek like the Wicked Witch of the West and dash back behind the windshields … and closer to Ben and me.

"It's so cool you and Mindy know each other!" Danielle says, much to Mindy's chagrin. I know she talked shit about me when they were up front. "Crazy how small the world is."

"Crazy," I echo.

"And Mindy knows him," she goes on, eyeing Ben. "It's like it's meant to be or something."

"That's not the words I'd use to describe this," I mumble and Ben stifles a chuckle.

"So," Danielle says carefully. "Do you have a date for the wedding? Jake says no but…" Her eyes go to Ben and Mindy snickers.

"Looks like it's the singles table for you," Mindy says softly, but we can still hear her.

"I'm her date," Ben says and puts his hand on my thigh.

"Oh, great!" Danielle says and turns away. I let out a breath and watch the lake zoom by. I know where we are going. It's a small, man-made cove off the shore that's perfect for swimming. Or just floating and drinking, in our case. It's about half an hour away from the dock. The girls chatter about wedding stuff, all the while Mindy shoots us dirty looks. Is it my imagination or is she glaring at *Ben* and not so much me? Ben tells me about some upcoming projects he's working on, and says I've been a good muse.

I take that as a huge compliment.

"Nice Ariel suit," Mindy says when the boat slows down outside the cove.

"Thanks," I say, incorrectly thinking for a split second she's actually complimenting me.

"Are those supposed to be sea shells?" She peers over the top of her sunglasses. "And where did you find that, the kids' section?" She turns to her sister, expecting her to flash me the same nasty look. Zoey looks down and I know she's torn between laughing and agreeing and not insulting her best friend's soon-to-be sister-in-law.

"They're clams," I say and look down at my breasts. "And if a store put out double-D-sized tops in a kids' section I'd be concerned." I'm not quite a double, but I do fill out a D nicely. Mindy doesn't need to know that, though.

"I like it," Ben says, leaning forward to look at my boobs. "It looks good on you."

"Thanks," I say. "Everyone wants to be a mermaid, whether they admit it or not. At least for a day."

Mindy just scoffs and turns around. Jake bitches at me to get up and help him anchor the boat, since I know how to do it. A few long minutes later, we're ready to jump into the chilly water. Ben jumps in, going under. I slowly lower myself down the ladder off the swim deck.

Legs in. No problem.

Getting my pelvis in. That's a problem. I suck in a breath and go down another step.

"Come in," Ben says, treading water. "It's not bad."

"It's cold!" I protest and slowly go down another step. I'm on the last one. Crap. Getting my nipples in the cold water is the worst. I mentally count to three then push off the small ladder. I doggie paddle over to Ben, who is holding my lifejacket. I push it under water and use it as a seat. Ben tries to wrap his arms around me and kiss me, but accidentally pushes me off my floaty seat. He catches me and we both go under. Laughing, he pulls me up.

Jake jumps in next, and Danielle sits on the swim deck and dangles her feet in the water.

"Hey, Liss," Jake says and paddles over. "I just realized … Mindy is the same Mindy who used to bully you in school, right?" I don't want to agree and let Ben know our history. The past is in the past, but it still embarrasses me. And it shouldn't. So my embarrassment shames me. Win win for everyone.

Not.

"I'm sorry. I wouldn't have let her come if I knew."

"It's fine." I brush it off. I can't look at Ben in the eye right now. I want to sink below the surface and never return. Well, I'll return in like thirty seconds. I can't hold my breath very long.

Jake gives me a lopsided smile and I know he genuinely feels bad. Though he's younger than me, he took his role of brother seriously when we were growing up and stood up for me as much as he annoyed me. He turns and works on coaxing Danielle into the water. I grab Ben's hand and pull him into the cove. The shore is rocky and covered in weeds, making it undesirable for beach goers. Which is desirable for us boaters, who like the calmness of the water without the hassle of dealing with the boat getting tossed into a swimmer.

"Your tits really do look fucking fantastic in that," Ben says as we get away from the boat. "They look fucking fantastic on their own too. You can ditch the top anytime."

"Tonight, baby. They're all yours."

231

"And sorry if saying I was your date imposed," he says.

"No, not at all." We try to embrace but end up bumping legs as we both tread water to stay afloat. "I wanted to ask you, but wasn't sure if you'd even want to go. I know weddings can be kinda lame."

He nods, agreeing. "Being with you isn't lame."

"Thanks," I say and let my arms fall, giving up on swimming and kissing. I float on my back, spreading my arms and legs out to keep myself up. "I was seriously dreading being stuck at the singles table again since they're not doing the head table with the whole bridal party. Or be put with my parents like a loser."

Ben laughs softly. "You're not a loser now."

"You don't mind going?" I ask, unable to hide my insecurities. "I know you have a lot going on."

"Do you want me to go?"

"Yes. I really do."

"Then no, I don't mind at all. I want to make you happy," he tells me. "And I don't want you to feel like a loser."

I laugh. "That's very considerate of you. And now I'm actually looking forward to the wedding." A weight I didn't know was on my shoulders lifts. Not only do I have a date to my brother's wedding, but it's the best possible date ever.

Ben stacks our lifejackets together and sits on them, then pulls me into his lap. With a little paddling, we are able to keep our bodies locked and stay above the surface.

"It's nice here," Ben says, moving his head down to kiss me. "Did you come out here a lot when you lived here?"

"We did. I feel like this is our little spot of the lake. I get pissed when I see other people here, like those guys over there." I narrow my eyes at the other boats, who no doubt feel the same about us. "The seaweed is pretty bad so a lot of boaters don't bother. That's why the boat's way out there and we have to swim here. And the shore isn't good for laying out or playing or anything. The water is calm and it's quiet. I like it."

"I do too. I imagine the lake isn't always this crowded either."

"Not at all. Weekends are pretty full, but not as bad as a holiday. I like coming out during the week at the beginning and end of summer, when the kids are still in school."

"More privacy," Ben says and kisses my neck.

"What about you?" I ask. "What did you spend your summers doing?"

"Typical, boring stuff," he laughs. "I played sports and hung out with friends. I did camps when I was younger. And by younger, I mean I went until I was fifteen."

"They still let fifteen year olds in camps?" I tease.

"They let you go even longer. We lived in the

233

same place for all of my high school years, so I had friends to hang out with then. Summers were boring, but winters were more fun. I like to snowboard."

"I didn't know that."

"I'd say I'm better than average at it, but I'm no pro. It's fun. I still go every winter with friends. And ride snowmobiles."

"I much prefer warm weather activities."

He chuckles. "I like warm weather too. I told you, when it's bad I won't even go into work. But it's different when you're doing something fun like snowboarding and skiing, or riding a snowmobile. You get all geared up and stay warm."

I wrinkle my nose. "I don't like feeling all bundled."

His eyes drop to my tits. "I don't think I'll like you being all bundled."

I shiver, despite the sun beating down on us. He reaches down into the water and rubs my core, wiggling his eyebrows and making me giggle. I think he's joking until I feel his cock start to harden underneath me. I raise my eyebrows in question.

"You're turning me on," he says and pulls me closer. I crane my neck to keep it above the water. "That's a problem."

"It is," I say and look behind me, seeing Zoey and Mindy finally join Danielle and Jake in the water. They make their way over, to the cove. "But I think I have a solution."

"You're sunburned already," Ben says as we head back to the dock for lunch.

I look down at my shoulders and grimace. "I was going to put sunscreen on and forgot."

"It's not too late," he says.

"I'll get it when we get back."

Mindy laughs, holding her hat with one hand to keep from blowing off. "You are really pale. No wonder you burned easily. I tan. I never burn."

"Anyone with skin can burn if they're out long enough," I say dryly.

"You don't even have a base tan." She rolls her eyes and I feel like the lame-o in high school I once was, not allowed to go to the tanning bed due to my mother's fear of me getting skin cancer. I'm thankful now, but that was just another thing added to the list of why I never sat at the cool table.

"I don't care," I tell her bluntly.

"I can tell," she scoffs.

Ben watches the exchange but doesn't say anything. Maybe he feels awkward since Mindy is an employee? Whatever. I'm not going to let Mindy fucking Abraham get under my skin. Not today. Not ever again.

The boat slows when the dock comes into view.

We have our own slip and it's never an issue getting in, but the loading ramp near the dock causes the water to get a bit congested. Jake idles the boat and we wait for some of the other watercrafts to clear out of the way.

"Ew," Mindy says, elbowing her sister. I follow her gaze, expecting to see a dead fish floating in the water. Instead, she's clearing pointing to a girl who can't be any older than eighteen. I don't understand what's wrong. The girl is on the shore, chasing a toddler who may or may not be her own child. She's wearing a tankini, and part of her stomach is showing. She turns around to scoop up the kid, who just face planted in the sand.

Mindy and Zoey laugh. My blood boils.

"She should *not* be wearing that in public," Mindy says and shakes her head like she just witnessed a legit crime. "Why they make swim suits in that size is beyond me."

A line lay before me and I knew I needed to pick one side to stand on. I can turn my head, think of something else, and let it go, or I could push Mindy fucking Abraham off the boat, rub my hands together, and laugh like I'd just taken over the Death Star and can carry out my mission to destroy an inhabited planet. Metaphorically, at least.

I cast my eyes down and realize that I'm not just standing up to Mindy, I'm standing up to every entitled, bitchy, thunder cunt in the world who thinks self-worth is defined by your waist size. The words bubble inside of me and I know I have to say something. Mindy points and laughs again, making fun of the girl's stomach. I look down at myself. I'm not overweight, but I'm not fit with flat abs. My words die in my throat.

I turn my head and look at Ben, who has his feet up, shades on, looking sexy as hell. I can still feel him between my legs as he thrust that big beautiful cock in and out of me, fucking in the boat as fast as we could before we got caught. I set down my wine cooler.

I have a motherfucking spaceship to take over.

"Seriously?" I say and push my shoulders back. Mindy, Zoey, and Danielle turn to me. "Just because you're insecure about how you look doesn't mean you have to make fun of someone else. Tearing her down doesn't build you up. Pointing out her cellulite doesn't make yours disappear. It's because of women like you that body shaming is an issue. Why belittle and bully other women when you can empower them? Grow the fuck up and focus your energy on something that actually matters."

Ben, who I think had been oblivious to Mindy's comments, sits up and looks at me like he wants to lay me down and fuck me again. Jake turns around from the wheel, eyes wide as he tries not to smile. Danielle will not look at any of us and Mindy just stares blankly in my direction.

"Well ... if she didn't want people to talk about

her then she shouldn't have worn that in public," she finally responds.

"Oh my god," I say slowly. "I just can't with you." I blink and turn away, fearing that her stupidity might be contagious. I snap my mouth shut, knowing I won't be able to stop once I get started. I could argue until I was blue in the face and it wouldn't change Mindy's mind. She's right and the rest of the world is wrong. I'm not wasting my time.

We dock the boat and climb out. Ben and I are the last out. He takes my hand, helping me onto the pier.

"That was pretty fucking awesome," he says. "And I agree with you. It's all petty bullshit that's annoying to listen to."

I nod and reach into my bag, seeing if Erin has texted me she's on her way yet. She hasn't.

"Are we eating now?" Ben asks, linking his fingers with mine as we walk toward the beach. The little section that stretches along my parents' cabins is a private beach, and shouldn't be this packed with people. But my parents don't really care, as long as people aren't getting crazy. It's a holiday, after all. The whole point of holidays is to celebrate something and not be a dick, right?

"We can eat all day if we want to hang around here," I say. "I'm sure my mom has everything out now. The party officially starts at three, but most my relatives show up before then. My dad will start grilling soon too."

"I like this," Ben says and we step off the wooden dock into hot sand. "It's very American." He chuckles. "This is how you should spend the Fourth."

"It's how I always did. What did you guys do?"

"Picnic and fireworks, but not to this extent."

"Halloween gets my vote for best holiday because of the costumes, but this is a close second just because of the food and the water."

"I agree. Halloween isn't as fun as when I was a kid, but I do like watching the Halloween movies on TV," he admits with a smile. "And Christmas is ... too much."

Oh my fucking God he's my soulmate. I push my heart back into my chest. "Yes! It's just too long and too commercial, though I do like presents."

"Who doesn't?"

We hurry through the sand, our bare feet not able to take it much longer, and climb up the steps to my parents' deck. It's just as hot. Feet: 0. Sun: 1. Shoes are going back on. I slip my dress over my head and lead Ben inside to fill our plates. We take a reprieve from the heat and sit in the living room, enjoying the wonderful modern amenities of ceiling fans and air-conditioning.

I come back with my second hot dog and sit close to Ben. The back door slides open and Jake, Danielle, and her lovely friends come inside to escape the heat for a bit as well. Mindy only eats fruit. I grit my teeth.

It's not worth it ... it's not worth it.

"I hope you like our little family tradition," I say to Danielle.

"I do," she says and I know she means it. She links her arm through Jake's. "This is so cute and I just *love* the beach. Plus it's nice having access right outside the house."

"I always felt bad for the people who had to park and walk, carrying coolers and kids, and all the other crap you bring with you."

"I hadn't even thought of that! But you are right."

"We liked it growing up," I say. "Had a few parties, lots of good memories."

"You had parties?" Mindy says to me, raising her eyebrows. "I never heard about them."

I slowly inhale. "Yeah, I did. It was a lot of fun."

Jake quickly changes the subject to sports, talking to Ben about how he's looking forward to football starting up again already. They talk about teams and someone getting banned—things I know nothing about—and I relax against Ben now that my skin isn't hot to the touch anymore. He puts his arm around me without even thinking, hand resting on the curve of my hip. My phone buzzes; Erin just let me know she's on her way. Dave was slow, as usual.

I warn her about Mindy fucking Abraham. Erin was shy and quiet. She still is, really. She was able to fade into the background during school and was never the subject of direct bullying.

Unlike me.

She stuck up for me when she could, even though social confrontation was right up there with facing an entire army of Daleks without the Doctor by your side. She really is a good friend, and I can't wait for her to meet Ben. I set the phone down and rest my head against Ben's muscular shoulder. I'm not that tired, but a full belly plus a morning spent in the sun makes me want a nap.

"So, Felicity," Mindy starts. I open my eyes and find her perched on the edge of the couch next to her sister. She's so fucking pretty it kills me. Then the maliciousness comes out and I can see her true face. "Do you still do that nerdy costume stuff?"

"You mean Cosplay?" I ask and sit up. "Yes, I still do that nerdy costume stuff and really enjoy it. Ben's a fan of my nerdy costumes, aren't you, Ben?"

Mindy's face scrunches up like someone just ripped a stinky fart. "Ben likes wearing costumes?"

"He doesn't wear them," I clarify. "I said he's a fan of *my* costumes." Well, just one costume, but I'm sure he'll like others.

"Ben, really?"

He smiles. "I feel like I shouldn't say anything because your brother is in the room and he won't want to know."

"Huh?" Jake says. Then it clicks. "Oh, ew. Yeah, no details please. I don't even want to—nope. Just stop."

Everyone else laughs. Everyone but Mindy. I know the woman hated me in high school for some unknown reason, but why be a bitter bitch now?

"Don't you feel a little old to be dressing up in costumes?" Mindy asks.

I've been asked that before, many times, actually. "No. There's not an age limit at Comic-Con, and Cosplaying in my spare time doesn't hinder my adulting. Well, not that much. I still go to work and pay my bills and all that. I don't see how it's any different than any other hobby. Some people jog and knit and do other … uh, things. I like to sew costumes."

Mindy raises her eyebrows. "Yeah, sure. I think it's weird."

"Just because it's weird to you, doesn't make it weird," Ben cuts in. "Felicity is right, again. I say to each his—or her—own. As long as your hobby doesn't involve chickens, Vaseline, and a dark shed, what does it matter?"

"All I'm saying is there's a reason hardly anyone is into that stuff." Mindy purses her lips and leans back. Danielle is beginning to look mortified, which makes me like her a little more, even if she's friends with Mindy and her sister.

"Do you know how many people attend Comic Cons?" I ask. "A lot. And I like that it's not mainstream."

"Life is too short to worry about the opinions of

others," Ben says pointedly. "Not a lot of people are brave enough to do what they love without fear of judgment." His eyes meet mine. "It's just one of the things I like about you."

I'm smiling, and the background fades until it's just Ben and me left in the room. My heart flutters and Ben's fingers press into my skin.

"Want to go outside?" Ben asks. "I want to look at the water. It's inspiring."

He takes my plate, sets it in the kitchen, and we go out the front door.

"You should fire Mindy," I say and look down the driveway for Erin's car.

"I've thought about it," Ben confesses. "But she's actually good at selling stuff, and I hate interviewing people."

"Meh, I guess." I take Ben's hand and make a mental promise to myself. No matter what, Mindy is not ruining the rest of the day. I'm not going to talk about her or bring her up. I'll save her from drowning if need be, though I'll wait until she goes under and ruins her hair and makeup before diving in. Other than that, I'm ignoring her.

Today is all about fun and friends, and she's neither of those.

Chapter Fifteen

"He is seriously perfect," Erin whispers. "I can tell he really likes you."

"I hope so," I say back. "Because I really like him. It's been so intense since day one. I can't even with the passion. Like it's just so much." I shake my head and smile. "I just hope that he doesn't feel this way about anyone else."

"I don't think he's seeing anyone else," Erin says and leans on the sink. "Not with what you've told me, and not with the way he looks at you."

I wobble when I stand, turning to flush the toilet. We ran inside before the fireworks started to use the bathroom and gossip. "But we never had a relationship talk. He said he dates other women."

"When did he say that?"

"Uh, before we hooked up the first time."

"Things can change," Erin slurs. I've lost count of how many alcoholic beverages I've had. I still got my wits about me—okay half my wits—but I would say I'm drunk. Erin is probably just as drunk and she's had two wine coolers. Such a lightweight.

I wash my hands and run them through my messy hair while Erin uses the bathroom. I give up on my hair. I need something more substantial than my fingers, and loosen the ties on my bikini top. I kept it tight to hold the girls up, but my neck is starting to hurt. The struggle is real when it comes to these puppies. But it's a love-to-hate problem.

Ben gets along great with everyone, and everyone likes him. I've never been ashamed of anyone I've brought home with me, but I've never exactly been proud of them either. And I'm not talking about his incredible good looks. I'm talking about Ben. Who he is. What he does. He's just an all-around great guy.

The sun is almost set and I get hit with a blast of hot, humid air when we leave the house and step out onto the deck. My entire family is crowded on it, all sitting in a circle around a fire pit that is probably dangerously close to the house. But in our family, we drink and roast marshmallows wherever the fuck we want. Even if it's against a fire code.

"I love nights like this," Mom says. "When it's still hot after the sun sets."

I put my hand on Ben's and pick up a red plastic cup from the deck floor. It might be mine. It might not be. I'm just drunk enough to not care. As long as alcohol gets in my mouth, I'm fine.

"I love summer," one of my cousins chimes in. "It always goes by so fast after the Fourth."

"Especially for us teachers," Danielle says, and another cousin agrees. He teaches math at the high school here in town.

"I can't wait for fall," Mindy says. "I live for pumpkin spice, leggings, and Ugg boots."

I cannot hide the horror on my face. Not only is

245

Mindy an insult to the female race, she's the most basic one at that. I stare at her like she just got caught not washing her hands after taking a shit, then shake myself. I don't care, remember?

We continue talking and drinking, then turn our chairs when the fireworks start. We "ooo" and "aww" for nearly an hour, eat some more, talk, laugh, and continue drinking. The party breaks up around midnight. I walk Erin to her car, give her a hug goodbye, and promise to call once Ben and I get back into Grand Rapids.

Zoey and Mindy leave without saying bye, which is fine by me. Jake, Danielle, Ben, and I help my mom and aunts clean up most of the mess until the others are too tired to keep going on. Danielle kisses Jake goodnight, saying she'll see him in the morning. I see the question in Ben's eyes, so I'm not surprised when he asks me about it once we slip outside.

"They say they are waiting for marriage," I explain and collect red Solo cups from the deck, pitching them into a recycling bin.

"Waiting to have sex?" Ben asks like he can't believe it.

"I haven't asked for details, like if just slipping the tip in counts or not, but yeah, they say they haven't slept together yet."

Ben's nostril flare. "People still do that?"

I laugh. "Some people, yeah, I guess. Hmm … maybe I should go cold turkey and save myself too."

"Hell no," Ben says. "I love fucking you."

The smile is back on my face. "I assumed so. And I love fucking you too."

"You better."

I shake my head and run my eyes over him. He's still shirtless, somehow not sunburned, and just ... amazing. I'm floating above the sand, looking down at the shore. Is this real life?

Fireworks continue to go off, reflecting on the lake. We end up on the edge of the dock, swinging our feet above the water, arms around each other. We talk about everything and anything, and the next thing I know, the sun is creeping up, and storm clouds are rolling in on the horizon. Exhaustion hits me when I stand (and probably dehydration; it's hot and I drank a lot) and I hold onto Ben to keep from faltering. We walk down the boardwalk hand in hand, and thunder rumbles distantly over the lake.

"Good timing," Ben says slowly. He yawns and pulls me in. I twist and wrap my arms around him. The wind picks up and he kisses me. Time stands still. My heart races and everything is finally perfect in my world.

It's been just over a month but I think I'm in love with him.

Fuck. Me. This shouldn't be happening so soon. He pushes his tongue into my mouth and I'm hot and wet in an instant and ready to throw him down in the sand. Actually, who cares what "should" be. I've

247

never been one for rules anyway. We tangle closer together, stumbling over the sun-warped wooden boards until we get to the cabin. I rummage through my purse for the key.

We strip out of the little clothes we have on. I yank down Ben's swim shorts and he pulls my dress over my head, then slowly pulls the strings on my clamshell bikini top. My breasts are still damp from the material, and feel cold under Ben's warm hands. Sand sprinkles on the floor and rubs my skin. He unties my bottoms and we head to the bathroom and into the shower.

The water is still cold when we step in, but we're so wrapped up in each other neither of us cares. Ben kisses me, then trails his lips down my neck and onto my breast. He pulls back, makes a face, and spits.

"You're all sandy," he says with a laugh.

I'm laughing too as I step away from him to let the water rush over me. "Better?"

"I think so." He picks up where he left off, and I cast my eyes down to watch his big, beautiful cock rise to action. I take it in my hand, slowly pumping up and down while he kisses me all over.

Then he drops to his knees and keeps his hands on my waist. I lean back against the shower wall, holding onto the little plastic bar in the middle for support. Carefully, he props one of my legs up over his shoulder.

And I slip.

He catches me, uprights me, and puts his head between my legs. The water isn't just warm now. It's hot, as hot as I'm feeling for Ben right now. I'm holding on for dear life. I don't want to slip again and risk him stopping.

His tongue lashes against me and my other hand goes to his strong shoulder, pushing myself against the shower wall to keep from sliding. He parts me with his fingers, hot tongue on my clit, and slips two fingers inside, working along with the rhythm of his mouth. He pushes against my g-spot, holds his fingers there for a second, then releases, all the while he's licking and sucking and—holy fuck—using his teeth just enough to drive me absolutely wild.

I'm screaming his name in just minutes, coming so hard he has to hold me up to keep me from falling. I'm tingly all over from the orgasm, panting and heart racing. He hooks his arms under mine and pulls me to him.

"Felicity," he says and looks into my eyes. "I ... I think I—"

Thunder booms above us. The storm is coming in fast. It's probably going to be bad. There's something unsafe about being in the shower during a storm, right? I can't think straight, and I honestly don't care.

I wrap my arms around Ben and take a breath, steadying myself before I bend my still shaking legs. I take a second to appreciate the girth of his dick before opening my mouth and welcoming it in. I take my time, enjoying feeling Ben squirm from pleasure, hearing him pant and groan until he's so close he pulls back and lifts me up.

He spins me around and I bend over, my ass against his front. He enters from behind, reaching around to stroke me while he thrusts in and out, fast then slow, until we are both coming at the same time. I've never had that—orgasming together at the same exact moment—but I've always wanted to.

We're out of breath, panting, and not at all clean, when I shut the water off and grab towels. Rain and wind slap the small cabin, and the lights flicker.

"Storms come fast and hard off the lake," I comment as I dry myself off.

"Kind of like you," Ben says with a grin.

I shake my head and smile, legs still unsteady. I move over in front of the mirror, flip my head upside down, and wrap my dripping hair in the towel. Hastily, I rub lotion over my sunburned skin, then wind my way into the bedroom and collapse into bed. Ben joins me, pulling the blankets over our naked bodies.

I yank the towel off my head and drop it on the floor, wiggling closer to Ben. He envelopes me in his muscular arms, and we drift to sleep, snuggled safe inside together, listening to the storm rage around us.

∽❦∽

It's still going strong when we wake at nine.

"This is good sleeping weather," Ben mumbles and rolls over, lazily throwing his arm around me. "And I think I can sleep all day."

"Me too," I say and adjust my pillow. It's only a matter of minutes until the rain and the wind lull me back to sleep. We don't get up again until close to noon. Ben is sprawled out when I slip out of bed. A day filled with stuffing my face and drinking leaves my stomach not so happy.

I hurry to the bathroom, needing a few minutes alone before Ben gets up. I close the door. Turning on the fan is too obvious. Well, I *do* need to shower. I nod, thinking that yes, this shall work. The water goes on and I'm about to sit down when the bathroom door opens.

"Showering without me?" Ben asks, giving me that I'm-going-to-fuck-you-*again* look. When I don't return it, he raises his eyebrows. "It's fine if you want to."

"It's not that," I blurt.

"Then what is it?"

I try to come up with a lie but shake my head. I hate how women aren't supposed to admit they go to the bathroom yet everybody has to take a poo every now and then. "I was using the shower to cover up the fact that I really need to poop."

Ben bursts out laughing. "Yeah, don't want to be

251

in here for that."

My cheeks heat up just a bit. I refuse to be embarrassed by a totally normal body function. "Raincheck?"

"Maybe in a while, once the air clears. Should I pack my stuff?"

"Yeah, we can do that then go to breakfast, well, lunch."

Ben still has a look of amusement on his face. "I'll work on that while you take care of business."

I press my lips together but end up laughing. "Deal." I do take a shower too, since there is still sand in my hair that needs to be washed out. I get out, towel my hair, and get dressed while Ben hops in for a quick shower.

Since it's raining and we need to leave soon anyway, we drive to my parents' house and I get my dad to open the garage door so we can run in and stay dry. We eat leftovers from last night, say our goodbyes, and head home.

An hour into our drive, Ben tells me he has two events to go to this week. He doesn't even mention bringing me with. After a weekend like we just had, I don't know how much more it will take for him to want me to be his girlfriend and be worthy of going to fancy art shit with him.

I think about it for too long, and I use the excuse of being tired when Ben asks why I'm not talking. I force myself to put on a smile the rest of the way.

"I'm starving," Ben says when we pull into my driveway.

"Come in and I'll make you something," I say. "Mac and cheese sounds good."

"It does, actually. I haven't had that in a while."

I raise an eyebrow. I thought all single people lived off of a diet that consisted of at least 50% mac and cheese. He brings in my suitcase, sets it in my room, and joins me in the kitchen. I'm feeling better and not so insecure when we take our bowls into the living room.

"I don't want to go to work tomorrow," I say and take a bite of food. Ben just nods, his mouth too full to answer. "Even though it was just a weekend thing, I feel like I need a day to recover."

"Me too," he agrees once he's swallowed. "I probably will take tomorrow off. Perks of being my own boss."

"That is so not fair."

"You went into the wrong profession."

"Apparently." I take another few bites. "I have a feeling you're going to have an awkward reunion with your secretary when you do go back too."

He raises his eyebrows. "You can say that. And I'm sorry she gave you shit."

"Why are you sorry?" I finish my mac and cheese and set the bowl down on the floor for Ser Pounce. He likes to lick the leftover cheese sauce.

"Ah, fuck. I forgot you didn't know."

253

My throat goes dry. That's never a good thing to hear. "Didn't know what?"

"I know you guys had a bad history in high school or whatever, but Mindy was extra bitchy because she's jealous of you."

There's only one reason she'd be jealous of me, and that involves Ben. "She likes you?"

He nods. "I don't think she ever got over—"

"Got over? Wait. You two had a … a…" I couldn't bring myself to say it.

"Yeah, we dated when she first started working for me."

My heart stops beating. Ben, perfect, amazing Ben, dated Mindy fucking Abraham. I blink, then turn away.

"It wasn't anything serious," Ben says and it's like his voice is echoing in my head. "We went out and hooked up a few times, that's it."

Now my stomach is twisting. Hooked up. He hooked up with Mindy. I can't hide the abhorrence on my face.

"Felicity?"

"You … you and Mindy?" You and Undesirable No. 1, more like it. "Hooked up?"

"Yeah, but it's over and it never meant anything to me."

All I hear is how what we have might not mean anything to him as well. "I just…"

"It's not a big deal," he says slowly. "I've hooked

up with other people in the past, and I'm sure you have. Actually I know you have because you're quite good at more than a few things, and I'm thankful for that."

"It is a big deal," I say and I know the words are coming out of my mouth on their own accord and there is no stopping once I get started. "You put your dick in her, and then in me, so it's basically like I had sex with her."

"It doesn't quite work like that," he says. "You're mad, but I'm not really sure why. I didn't do anything wrong, Felicity." He's getting defensive.

I blink. Somewhere, deep down in the hallow pit that is now my heart, I know he's right. But another part of me, the part that I try to ignore, the part that houses all my insecurities, tells me this makes sense.

It makes sense that Ben would date someone like Mindy. It makes sense now why he wouldn't take me to a fancy art event when he could take someone like Mindy instead. She might be a cum-guzzling thunder cunt, but she doesn't *look* like one. Well, as long as she keeps those fake tits under control and her stupid mouth shut.

No, Mindy is perfect on the outside. Perfect hair, perfect skin. Her nails are always polished and not chipping. She'd never wear miss-matched socks or forget deodorant or have frizzy hair when it rains or even when it doesn't.

She might not be a nice person, but you can't tell

by looking at her.

And my Ben—my sweet, wonderful, passionate Ben, who I'm pretty sure I'm fucking in love with—dated her. But it's more than that. He dated the type of woman that I hate. The type that brings others down to make herself feel better, who doesn't give a shit about what's right or wrong as long as it benefits her.

Suddenly I'm a teenager again watching Mindy shove her tongue down the throat of my crush.

"Hey," he says. "Come on." He nudges my arm. "Let it go."

"I need time to process this, to process that you literally slept with the enemy."

"I thought you said you were over that."

"I am! But still … she's fucking married and has a kid! You slept with a married woman!"

"She's getting a divorce, and she doesn't have any kids I'm aware of, just a niece. She told me they were separated at the time and not living together. I believed her and didn't check into the facts. I never would have hooked up with her if I knew she was still living with her husband, I promise. I'm not like that. And it wasn't anything serious. Just a fling that meant nothing to me."

A fling with Mindy fucking Abraham is right up there with a lunch date with Hitler. It's nothing to be taken lightly. He puts his hand on my arm and I flinch away.

"Felicity, don't be stupid."

A nerve is struck and my anger and self-doubt boil over, bubbling together into a deadly combination that sends me into rage mode. "I'm not being stupid! I guess I just finally see this."

"See what?"

"What this is, who I am to you."

"What the hell are you talking about?"

"This!"

His eyes widen and he shakes his head. "You're not making sense. Calm down and let's talk about this like adults. If I knew it would cause such an issue, I never would have brought it up."

"Well, I'm glad you did because now I know the truth on where we stand." I must be a fling too. Nothing serious. Maybe I mean nothing to him too. The thought breaks my heart and instead of feeling sad, I'm pissed. The anger will fade and the hurt will be setting in, but not yet. I'm mad now. I need to hold onto that anger while I can to protect myself.

No, I don't think rationally when I'm in an emotional crisis like this. "It makes sense now. You never took me to one of your fancy art shows. You're still seeing other people, bringing them to your house … I saw the women's shoes there, by the way … and I can't—" my voice breaks with emotion and my mind continues to whirl.

"Maybe it's my fault and I gave you the wrong impression because I slept with you on the first date.

I don't do that. It's not who I am, but there was something special about you, something I couldn't ignore and you made me get carried away. It meant something to me, but I guess it meant nothing to you."

I stand and turn around, wiping away tears before Ben can see. Push him away before he pushes me. It's a subconscious defense mechanism and if I calmed down, I'd realize what I'm doing.

But I don't. I can't. Ben means too much to me that logic isn't going to apply right now.

He doesn't move. He doesn't speak. My heart pounds in my ears and each second that goes by makes me realize that my words are true. If they weren't, he'd protest, tell me I'm wrong, say he was sorry for messing with my head. The silence is killing me, and my mouth opens despite my better reasoning, saying I should shut the hell up because I say things out of anger that I regret later. I know I do. Always have, always will.

"Then the office booty call … The signs were in front of me. But I guess that's how you are with everyone, right?"

Still, all I get is silence from him.

"If I mean so little, then just go. Call up one of the other girls you're seeing or even Mindy."

I get nothing. Come on, Ben. At least be angry. Shout, yell. Tell me I'm right and that you don't care. Tell me I'm wrong and I'm stupid.

Just.

Say.

Something.

"That's what you think of me?" he finally says and his voice is broken.

"Yeah. It's obvious now."

He sharply inhales. "Felicity, that—no," he cuts off, shaking his head. "I thought *you* were different, but I guess I was wrong. I should go."

I whirl around, not expecting that. And I'm not expecting the hurt on his face.

Oh, fuck.

"Ben," I start but he's already on his way out. His hand is on the doorknob. He turns, eyebrows pushed together.

"I never asked you to go to my fancy art events because I always take my mom. It's her shoes you saw at my house by the way. She stays with me when she's not staying with my dad, who has memory problems after so many head injuries fighting in the war and needs round-the-clock care. You could have just asked me about it. I don't bring it up because it's not exactly fun to talk about, and most people here don't understand the culture on my mother's side, and see living with their parents as a burden. But I thought *you* would." He turns his head and our eyes meet for what I'm sure will be the last time. "I thought I loved you. I was wrong."

Then he leaves.

And it hits me all at once: I did the very thing to Ben I hate that people do to me.

I judged him. I made assumptions and filled in the blanks with misinformation. I let my own insecurities get the best of me, and I let Mindy fucking Abraham ruin my life, nearly ten years after high school.

You've won, Mindy. Again.

My chest rapidly rises and falls and I suck back a sob. I blink and shake myself, then sprint to the door. But I'm too late. Ben is already pulling out of the driveway, driving down the street. I watch, tears filling my eyes, as the tail lights of his Audi disappear.

Suddenly I can't breath and it takes everything I have to go inside and close the door behind me. I fall onto the couch and cry. I messed up. Big time. I was so worried about getting hurt that I ended up hurting myself.

I am my own self-fulfilling prophecy.

Chapter Sixteen

I don't know what to do. I wipe my eyes, sit up, and swallow a sob. My phone is in my purse, by the couch. I pick it up, madly rummage through for my phone, and call Ben. I get his voicemail. I wait a few seconds then call again. It rings once then goes to voicemail.

He hung up on me.

I close my eyes, barricading more tears, and try not to hyperventilate. He's mad right now. Just like I was. He needs time to calm down, and he's not even home yet. I fall back onto the couch and wait.

One minute goes by.

Then one more.

I want to call him again. Now. But it hasn't been enough time. My heart is still pounding, and I feel sick. I fucked up. I said things out of anger and fear, things that make no sense and that I don't really believe.

He said he thought he loved me.

And now I know that I really do love him. I fell for him even though I didn't want to, even though I was sure he would hurt me.

I hurt him.

I hate myself for it.

And I have no idea how to make it better. I can't take back what I said. I can't delete this glitch, reprogram the day and start over. I bite my trembling lip and know the only thing I can do is tell Ben I'm sorry and wait for him to calm down enough to hear me out.

I call him again. Two rings then voicemail, and take a breath. The words die in my mouth and I'm hanging up without saying a word. I fall onto the couch, tears running down my face. I'm suddenly exhausted, and it feels like it takes an incredible amount of energy to put our dishes in the sink, grab a bottle of wine from the fridge, and go into my bedroom. I sink into bed and start drinking. I gulp it down, letting emotion be my guide, and soon I'm feeling sick before my mind hazes over. But I don't stop now. I keep drinking until I literally can't and pass the fuck out.

I want to wake up and have everything be better.

But that doesn't happen. Instead, I wake up hours later feeling like roadkill warmed over, with a dry mouth and a full, angry bladder. I check my phone—no missed calls—and get up to pee. I shower because that just seems to make sense. Warm water pours over me and then I'm crying again, sinking down to the shower floor.

I messed up. Again. I let my insecurities get the better of me. Two times in my life I've thrown something amazing away. The first time it was because I didn't want my shitty-ass boyfriend to leave me, and now it was because I didn't want to get hurt.

So I hurt Ben instead.

I crawl out of the shower, dry off, and collapse into bed. I set my alarm for work in the morning and let sorrow and sleep pull me into darkness.

"Rough weekend?" Mariah asks when I sit at my desk the next day. My eyes are puffy from crying. Ben never called me back, and he never answered my calls. Things were over between us, and I wanted to be mad at him for not even trying.

But I'm not.

"You can say that," I mumble. "Drank too much. Have a headache." I don't want to be short, but I think that gets my point across so she'll leave me alone. I don't want to talk to anyone. I don't want to explain what happened or even think about it for a second more than I have to. Because if I do, I'll start crying again.

Ben is the best thing that's ever happened to me. He is everything I want, and everything I need. And I didn't just let him slip away, I opened the door and kicked him in the ass, forcing him out of my life.

I turn to my computer, not even sure what I should be doing. It takes me a few minutes to get my mind to focus, and I put everything into this new assignment. And as if the universe didn't hate me enough, the site I'm designing is for a local wedding dress shop.

Not only is my heart broken, but I have no date for my brother's wedding. Ben won't be there with me, talking and dancing and secretly laughing at how Danielle freaked out over details when none of that really matters. I'll be alone, like I'm sure I'll be the rest of my life.

Because you don't meet someone like Ben Hartford more than once in a lifetime.

For the first time ever, I find myself dreading the end of the day. Work goes by slowly, but it's at least a distraction. I kept my phone on my desk all day, just in case Ben called or texted me.

He doesn't.

And I'm not sure if I should call again. I did more than once yesterday and got nothing. I've been trying to convince myself he's still just mad and this will all blow over, but when I walk to my car that evening and still haven't heard from him, I know it's more than that.

I want to be mad at him and say he's being dramatic. But really I know that he must really have meant it when he said he loved me, because only people you care for deeply can hurt you that badly.

The more you love someone, the deeper the wound. I don't like making anyone feel bad about anything. Knowing I said things that hurt Ben's heart kills me and makes me feel no better than Mindy fucking Abraham.

I get into my car and put my head in my hands. It's hot in here, and I can hardly breathe. I need to turn the air on, open the windows … something. But I'm a glutton for punishment right now, punishment I deserve.

My phone rings and you'd think I had three seconds left to cut the wire on a bomb for how fast I dig that sucker out of my purse. It's not Ben. It's Erin, and I don't want to answer. It's not that I don't want to talk to her, but I don't want to tell her about Ben and start crying again. Because I know I will.

I feel guilty as I ignore the call. I start the car and tell myself I'll call her when I get home, where I can ugly cry my heart out in the privacy of my own home. I keep my phone on my lap in case Ben decides to get a hold of me.

He doesn't.

Not on the way home, not throughout dinner, not even during the four hours I marathon watched *Doctor Who,* eating ice cream and feeling sorry for myself. I'm holding onto hope, but that hope is slipping away.

By the time I should get ready for bed, I call Erin.

"Hey, lady," she says, upbeat as usual. "Just wanted to make sure you got home and everything okay. You didn't log on to any of your accounts last night."

I close my eyes. "I know. I did make it home."

"Uh, but everything isn't okay?"

"No, it's not." Then I start crying, and tell her about the stupid fight and how I said things I shouldn't have because I have no filter and don't know how to stop myself when I get started. "I ruined everything," I sob, wiping my eyes. I tuck my legs underneath myself and lean back on the couch. Ser Pouch sits next to me, offering me what little comfort his asshole self can.

"No, you didn't," Erin assures me. "You got in a fight. It happens. Do you know how many time Dave and I got into fights? If you do, tell me, because I lost track a long time ago. People fight, Lissy, it happens. What happens next determines your fate. Tell him you're sorry and explain that the word vomit is a result of being insecure. I think he'll understand."

My eyes are puffy from crying. I blink a few times and take a shaky breath. "I don't think Ben knows how insecure I am, and I think once he does he won't feel the same, well the same like he did before the fight. I will apologize the first chance I get but I have a feeling explaining why I said what I did won't help."

"I disagree. He said he loved you. I'm sure he still does. You don't just stop loving someone. Falling out of love isn't really a decision. It just happens, and it usually happens gradually. Call him. Go to him, just talk to him."

"I'll call," I say and feel nervous about it already. "I just want things to go back to how they are."

"People fight. People make up. Then they come

out stronger in the end."

"You make it sound so easy."

"It's not easy, hun," she tells me. "Nothing about relationships are easy, really. They take work. Hang up and call him."

"Okay. I will."

"Good. Love you, Lissy. Call me if you need me, anytime."

"I know. And thanks, Erin." We hang up and I decide I need to clear my head and mentally go over what I'm going to say to Ben. I get in the shower, make my lunch for tomorrow, and settle into bed. I have 2% left on my phone. Heaving a sigh, I get out of bed to retrieve my charger, then plug in my phone before laying back down, intending on getting up in a half hour or so to call him.

I end up dozing off, my thoughts on the good times I had with Ben over the weekend. I don't want to wake up and step out of my dreamy mind. When I wake up, it's one AM and too late to call. I'm relieved, actually. It's one more day that I can hold onto the false hope.

I'm calling Ben after work today. I have to. I didn't yesterday, and there is no more putting it off. Tuesday actually goes by fast, as the dread of being hung up on or told to get lost haunts me. I run through everything and decide the best is him saying it's okay, he forgives my stupid mouth, and wants to see me tonight. We have mind-blowing sex and things are fine.

The worst. Well, I can't really decide. The worst involves him telling me he never wants to see me again in some sense. The words that surround it will determine how much wine I need to buy on the way home.

I feel bad but avoid Cameron. He has to know something is up because I've been quiet, and didn't sneak any extra donuts throughout the day. I pretend like I leave for lunch but really take my egg salad sandwich and apple slices into my car and eat while listening to upbeat music to keep my mood in check.

I get back to my desk and go over an email sent to me from the owners of the wedding dress shop. They want customer photos included, and I glower at the happy faces and kissing couples.

Ah, fuck. I need to tell my brother I don't have a date to the wedding, though by now they've turned in the number to the caterer. Erin is already invited and RSVP'd for herself and David, so I can't take her as my plus one. Danielle is so anal about everything I'm sure I'll get an earful about the wasted plate later. Hell, if it's that big of a deal, I'll eat two meals.

I take my time finishing up for the day, giving time for the parking lot to mostly clear. I parked in the back, facing the street so if I break down, it's possible no one will see me before I make my getaway.

My heart is racing as I walk out. Clouds rolled over the bright sun and the air is humid. I drop my keys I'm shaking so badly. I pick them up, close my eyes, and take a breath. I can do this. I can do it for Ben. For us.

I toss my purse into the back and sit in the driver's seat. I crank the AC, turn the radio off, and get out my phone. My fingers tremble as I pull up Ben's number. Without giving myself a second to hesitate, I press on his name.

I put the phone to my ear and swallow the lump in my throat. The phone rings and rings. He's not going to answer. I get his voicemail, and hearing his voice, even though it's recorded, hits me in the face and I miss him so much.

"Ben," I say. "It's me, Felicity. Ben I'm ... I'm sorry. I didn't mean what I said. I'm not the girl who's used to having someone amazing like you like me, and I panicked. I convinced myself you were going to leave me, that you really didn't like me to protect myself and I'm such an idiot. Ben, please know I'm so so sorry. It might not make sense, I know, but I pushed you away to keep myself safe and in the end I hurt us both."

I'm rambling and repeating myself and need to stop before I dig a second grave. I take a second to breathe. "Ben, I don't just think I love you. I know I do."

I close my eyes and tears stream down my face. I end the call and let the phone fall to my lap. I put both hands on the steering wheel and pitch forward, allowing myself to cry for a moment before starting the engine and driving home. I finish my one bottle of wine that I had left before dinner and regret not going to the store to get more on my way home from work.

Oh well. I'll get it tomorrow. I keep my phone on me, ringer up as loud as it can, and work on my Comic Con costume until 1 AM.

Ben never calls.

After saying what I said on the message, I don't know what else to do, how else to prove to him I'm sorry and that I want to be with him. I'm exhausted when I get out of the shower and get under the covers. I lie awake for an hour, a sick feeling of regret replacing any and all hope that I had left in me.

I fucked up. And I'm going to have to live with that.

Chapter Seventeen

"You did your final fitting, right?" my mom asks me as I walk out of work Thursday. The wedding is only days away and everyone is running around like chickens with their heads cut off. And according to Dad, who swears he's seen it, chickens really do run around after you take an ax to their neck. I don't believe him.

"I did," I lie. I haven't even tried the damn thing on since I picked it up. Years of making costumes has left me a rather good seamstress. I need to go home and do that ASAP. It's going to be a long night. "It looks great. And I have my shoes and the jewelry Danielle wants us to wear."

"Just making sure," Mom says. "I'm excited to see you all dressed up! And to see your boyfriend again. Who knows, maybe wedding bells are in your future too!"

I internally wince. I never heard from Ben. I got a big fat nothing after I poured my heart out in that message. No calls, no texts. He hadn't even updated his Instagram since last week.

"Maybe," I say and force myself to inhale slowly. I spent all of yesterday trying to pull myself out of the self-pity puddle I'd melted into. I'm dripping, but at least I'm standing and not drowning now. "I need to go. See you tomorrow. Love you, bye!"

I hang up before Mom can go on even more. I'll see her in the afternoon tomorrow. I'm working a half day then going back to her house, where I'll stay for the weekend. Where I'll have to tell her why Ben isn't with me.

I don't want to do that. I don't want to deal with anyone's pity, and I don't want to be reminded how utterly alone I am at my little brother's wedding. I'm not conventional by any means, but knowing he's younger than me and getting married first stings. Just a bit.

I stop at the store on the way home. My period started in the middle of the night Tuesday and I'm down to my last tampon … and it needs to be changed. Now. I was worried all day something would travel down the crack canal and leave a not-so-fun stain on the back of my pants. I'm pretty sure the universe really does hate me. I sigh. At least Aunt Flo should pack up and leave by Saturday. I really need to get on some sort of birth control. This inconsistent uterine bleeding ruined my second favorite pair of PJ pants.

I accidentally looked into the eye of the Target symbol and was bespelled, and my basket is half full of stuff I don't really need by the time I reach the feminine hygiene aisle.

"Hey, Felicity."

Oh for the love of all things good in this world. Why does it have to be her? I press my lips together.

272

"Mindy, hi," I say flatly. I look past her for the brand of tamps I want. She pulls a pink box of panty liners down and puts it in her cart.

"What's wrong with Ben?" she asks, cutting to the chase.

"I don't know," I mutter and grab a variety box.

"I'm sure you do. He left work Tuesday morning and didn't come back until today. He's been quiet and in and out all day and doesn't want to talk about 'it,' whatever that means. I'm pretty sure he was at the nursing home. Did his dad die?"

My heart stops in my chest. He mentioned it just once, while we were fighting. His father has memory issues and needs constant care. Oh fuck.

"He'll talk about it when he's ready," I say and keep walking. "Bye."

She doesn't say "see you this weekend at the wedding," thank God. Though, she still might show up. Who knows. I get what I need, pay for it, run to the ladies' room, and high-tail it home. I have some research to do.

Within an hour, I know that Ben's father lives at Meadow View Centers in downtown Grand Rapids. I hacked into the admission records, but drew the line at digging into medical records. I'm no criminal anymore.

His father was admitted a month before Ben moved here from New York.

It all makes sense now, and it hurts my heart even more. Ben left his dream job, left a potential for national recognition and fame as an artist for his family. He really wasn't anything like the player I thought he was, that I knew he really isn't. I was so scared of what *could* be, I let what actually is fly right by.

I close my laptop and bite my lip, trying to decide what to do. I pick up the phone and punch in the number for Meadow View. It rings for a long minute before someone answers.

"Hi, is James Hartford available?" I ask the nurse.

"He's in the dining room eating dinner," she says and relief floods through me. "Can I take a message?"

"No," I say, relieved even more. I didn't actually want to talk to him. "I'll call back. Thanks, bye." I hang up before I'm questioned and hope they don't check the caller ID.

Ben's dad is alive at least, though I know that didn't mean he was "okay" by any means.

I sigh. Now what? Should I call Ben again? Give it just one more shot? I don't want to come across as desperate, but that's exactly what I am.

And people do desperate things for the ones they love.

I call Ben, hands shaking as the phone rings. He

doesn't hang up, but he doesn't answer.

"Ben," I say to his voicemail. "It's me. I'm sorry, and I miss you. Can we please talk in person? I … I just need to know."

I hang up and close my eyes, wondering how long it will take before I'm back to my old self. I was happy. A little lonely, yeah, but I was doing all right. Living and loving life and just being me.

I want that again, but not as much as I want Ben.

I didn't get the dress altered in time before I passed out on the floor of my guest room. I woke up at 4 AM, crawled into bed, and slept for two more hours until my alarm blared. Then I called into work and said I was sick.

I'm feeling guilty now as I sit behind the sewing machine. Cameron is concerned; he said he noticed how quiet I've been over the last few days and wants me to take it easy so I can get better and be back to my old self Monday morning.

I let out a breath and cut a thread. Almost done. I like making costumes, but altering this dress made out of horribly flowy material … not so much. It didn't take much work. I had to shorten the hem and let it out around the boobs. I pull out the pins, snip any extra hanging threads, and try it on.

Perfect fit.

Finally. I wrinkled the dress when I altered it, so I take it into the bathroom, hang it on the shower curtain, and get my steamer. I never realized how helpful being into costuming would be. Not everyone has a vast array of thread colors or steamers available in their homes.

I clean up and start packing my bag. I need something fancy to wear to the rehearsal dinner tonight, since the Boba Fett dress probably won't go over well with my parents. I settle for a plain black dress and my Harry Potter heels. I gather everything I'll need for tomorrow and load up the car. I lose myself in League of Legends for a while, until it's ready to say bye to Ser Pounce and make the long drive home alone.

The house is empty when I arrive. I assume everyone is at Jake's or the hotel where family is staying. I use the time alone to take everything up to my room. I had planned on staying in one of the available cabins with Ben, but that's not really necessary anymore.

I take my computer downstairs, find the leftover booze from last weekend's party, and pour myself a glass of red moscato. Then I settle on the couch and make it through one-and-a-half episodes of *Supernatural* before my parents come home.

"Oh good, you're here!" Mom says as soon as she walks through the door. She's wearing those temporary Styrofoam flip-flops they put on you when you get a pedicure. Dammit. I knew there was something I was supposed to do. I bend my legs and hide my feet under my body. There is nail polish in the upstairs bathroom. Left over from my childhood, but if I shake it enough it'll be okay. Right? I hope so.

I cannot get my shit together to save my life.

"Where else would I be?" I ask her.

"I called you and you didn't answer!"

"Oh, yeah, left my phone upstairs." I pause the episode, leaving Dean in an awkward position with Castiel. I snicker to myself.

"Did you remember your dress?"

"Yes."

"And your shoes?"

"Yes, Mom."

"And the necklace Danielle got you?"

I tap my neck. "I'm wearing it."

Mom sets her purse down and comes into the living room. "Good." She inhales and closes her eyes for a second before exhaling. "I'm so nervous. I'm having heart palpitations."

"Calm down, Mom. The last thing we need is you passing out."

"I'm not going to pass out. Why, do I look like I'm going to pass out? I'm not pale, am I? I skipped the sunscreen a few times this summer to get a glow." She spits that all out rather quickly.

"No, Mom, you look gorgeous. The tan is very

youthful. Just relax. Danielle has that fancy wedding planner, and everything else is all set. It's going to be perfect."

Mom smiles at me. "Yes, it is. And I'll worry more at your wedding, anyway. At least I'm not paying for this one."

I roll my eyes.

"Speaking of," she stars. "Where is your hunky boyfriend, Ben?"

I clench my jaw, locking eyes with my mother. I want so badly to tell her everything, to cry and blame myself for losing him, and to have my mommy hug me and tell me it's going to be okay. Life sucks for a while for everyone, but then things get better. They always do. They have to.

But I don't tell her.

She's already stressed and this weekend is all about Jake. I don't want to take that away from him, and I don't want my mom to worry any more than she already is.

"He had this big art event he couldn't turn down. Something about investors in New York," I say, unable to look at Mom as I lie. I go back to my computer, trying to seem uninterested. "He'll try to come tomorrow."

"Oh, what a shame. But I understand. And your cousin Randy will gladly fill in for him if he can't make it."

"Ew, Mom, that's super creepy."

278

She waves her hand in the air. "No, he just looks up to you."

"Mom. He has a picture of me hanging in his room. And his locker at school."

"He graduated high school this past year. So just one picture of you."

I wrinkle my nose. "The one in the room is the creepiest. It's right above the lotion and tissues."

"Why would he—oh, don't go there, Felicity."

"You're the one who brought it up."

She presses a smile and shakes her head. "I'm going to get everything ready for tomorrow. Do you want me to pack you snacks?"

I raise my eyebrows. "Do you have to ask?"

"That's my girl. There is chicken salad in the fridge. Eat something before we leave. We're going to the venue after the rehearsal so dinner won't be until later. Danielle wants everyone there in case the planner needs help."

I roll my eyes. "What's the point of hiring a planner if we have to help her? Jake told me what that lady cost."

Mom purses her lips. "It's her day. Just go with it and then you won't have to see her until Thanksgiving."

"Fine." I won't go into why it's not just Danielle's day, but Jake's too. I finish my episode of *Supernatural*, eat, then go upstairs to do my hair and change. I'm ready before Mom, and join my dad on the couch.

"You don't seem like yourself, kiddo," he says, even though he's only seen me in passing since I got here.

I force a smile. "Just tired, that's all."

Dad nods, not convinced. I turn back to the show he's watching. As much as I'd like to think I could totally survive the zombie apocalypse, I know I wouldn't last two days on *Naked and Afraid*. I shudder at the thought of bugs in my coochie.

Mom's running late, and is getting bitchy at Dad like it's his fault. He shakes his head. This happens a lot, and he's used to it. We pile into the car and drive to the church. Dark clouds are gathering overhead. None of us say anything, but I know we're all thinking it: Danielle is going to lose her shit if it rains.

Though Danielle isn't originally from Mistwood, the small, beach community is picture perfect for her wedding. Any wedding, really. I've driven past this old place of worship many times but haven't been inside. It's white with a tall steeple that has a bell tower and flowering bushes around the church front.

It looks like something straight out of a Lifetime Movie Channel wedding special. I'm not expecting this ball of emotion to roll around like lead in my stomach, choking me up and bringing tears to my eyes. I blink and turn away from my parents, inhale then press forward and walk into the church behind them. I'm so happy for Jake, proud he manned up over the years and is ready to settle down and be a husband.

And I'm so pissed at myself for hurting Ben. For throwing away my chance at maybe—just maybe—being a wife someday. Another deep breath. Hold it. Let it out slow. Okay. I'm feeling a bit better.

Danielle is sitting on a stool near the altar, with her bridesmaids gathered around her. I would have been totally fine *not* being one. I'm only included because I'm Jake's sister, not because Danielle and I have any sort of friendship going.

Zoey turns and gives me the side eye. Great. I'd nearly forgotten about her. I channel my inner Hermione once again, reminding myself that what is right isn't always easy—thanks, Dumbledore for that one—and fake a smile. I go to the rest of the bridesmaids and tell Danielle she looks so pretty.

Ten awkward minutes tick by as we wait for the last to arrive, then start the rehearsal. It's a standard church ceremony: we walk in, take our places at the altar, wait for the bride … blah, blah, blah … and then we get to sit for the church part of the wedding. Danielle is already crying as she walks down the aisle, carrying a bouquet of ribbons and bows. Then I see the way Jake is looking at her and, fuck, I'm a goner too. I hold in my tears, crying on the inside like a winner.

We run through the procession five times. Five. Anyone who's seen a wedding movie knows how to do this. Even the priest looks bored when Danielle wants to go over it one more time.

Finally, we're done practicing the lineup. My stomach grumbles and I think we're going to go to the venue but nope, the photographer is here to take pictures. Is that a thing now? I'm glad I did my hair and makeup.

Forty-five minutes later, we run through the parking lot, dodging raindrops, and load into the cars. The venue is about half an hour away, and the rain slows things a bit. The hall is rather new, having opened two years ago, and is gorgeous.

I stop when I go through the entrance, stepping into a two-story foyer. The ballroom is directly ahead of us, and the large, double doors are closed tight with a sign on the door telling staff not to enter. A curved staircase sweeps around, the balcony running the length of the building. Deep-red, velvet carpet lines the stairs, and everything has a rich, country club feel to it.

The wedding planner beams and tells Danielle and Jake to close their eyes. The photographer snaps pictures while her assistant records the reveal. Even I'm feeling the anticipation when the planner slowly opens the doors. Danielle squeals with excitement and the bridesmaids start gushing on and on about how pretty things are. I hang back with my parents, letting the others go in first, then follow.

The lighting is low and everything is set perfectly. Okay, yeah ... this is pretty fucking impressive. My mind wanders to how much each large centerpiece costs as I admire the satin bows tied to each chair. This looks like something out of a magazine, and I start to get a little bit more excited for tomorrow.

There is an open bar, after all.

Danielle goes through things with the planner and has nothing to change. I'd be surprised if she did since everything is so beautifully put together. I might not be able to ever afford this planner, but I want her business card just in case.

It's raining even harder when we leave the venue and head to the restaurant. Mom is sure the sky will get the rain "out of its system" by tomorrow, but when Dad pulls up the radar, it doesn't look like Mother Nature agrees.

I'm quiet throughout dinner, and Dad takes notice again. I brush it off as being tired, and check my phone between sips of wine. Ben still hasn't updated his Instagram. There is nothing new on his gallery's website either. I'm stopped with ways to stalk him. Well, legally stalk him via social media that is, and I'm not crossing that line anymore.

Mom goes to bed early when we get home. Jake, who's spending his last single night away from Danielle, stays up for a bit with Dad and me, watching TV and trying to relax. Two hours later, he gets up and says he's going to bed.

"You should too, kiddo," Dad says and pushes himself out of the recliner.

"I'm not tired yet," I say, knowing I won't be able to sleep.

Dad waits until Jake goes upstairs to continue. "You've been saying you're tired all day and now you're not. What's wrong, Felicity? You're not your normal self."

I sigh. "I'm fine, Dad. I will be, I mean."

"Women don't use the 'fine' word and ever mean it." He sits next to me on the couch. "What's wrong?"

I shake my head. "I got into a stupid fight with Ben, said things I don't mean, and probably ruined everything."

"You, say things out of anger? No way." Dad gives me a smile. "Did you apologize?"

"I did, but not right away. And that makes it worse, I know." I let out a breath. "But it's fine. I'm sad, I admit that. I really *really* liked him, but I'll get over it. I promise."

"You know your mother and I met in college."

"I do."

"But I don't think I ever told you or your brother about our first date. I took your mother to a frat party. I was so nervous I got drunk and then puked in her car on the way home. I was so embarrassed I never called her back, never asked her out for a second date. Then she called me."

"To ask you out again?"

Dad chuckles. "No, to make me pay the cleaning bill for her car. But when I saw her again, I thought

I'd give it one more shot and ask her out. She turned me down right then and there, but when I got home, there was a message on my machine from her. I took her out that weekend and the rest is history. My point is, people forgive mistakes. If Ben isn't willing to forgive you for something as small as a 'stupid argument' then he's not the right man for you."

I let Dad's words sink in and know he's right. This won't be the last time I say or do something stupid to piss Ben off either. "You're right. Thanks, Dad. I actually feel better now."

"Good." He gives me a one-armed hug. "Now go upstairs and get some rest. It's going to be a long day tomorrow."

Chapter Eighteen

"How are you?" Erin asks softly.

"I'm okay, really," I say, smiling to prove it. I just arrived at the venue, and snuck away to find Erin. She and her sisters just delivered the cake. Everything at the ceremony was beautiful, and the rain held off long enough for us to get a million pictures outside the church and in the garden.

Erin raises an eyebrow.

I sigh and wish the bar would open up already. "Okay, I'm sad. I miss Ben and I'm mad at myself. And there's nothing like the uniting of two people to remind you how freaking alone you are, either."

"If not Ben, you'll find somebody else. Hey, maybe somebody here!"

"Maybe," I say to appease her positive attitude. I'm still in that "there is no one in the world but Ben" phase. I decided to give myself a full week to feel sad, then force myself out of it. So, basically, I have until tomorrow. Might as well live it up, right? "I should probably go out there, huh?"

"Yeah," Erin says, checking the time. "Your introductions will start soon."

I wrinkle my nose. I walked in with Jake's friend Teddy, who apparently has had a crush on me for years. I just found out today when he got drunk in the limo and spilled his guts as well as tried to cop a feel of my boobs.

"Hang in there," she says. "And I'll meet you at the bar as soon as it's open." She winks and links her arm though mine. I stay in the fancy lobby while she goes inside the hall to sit next to David. I'm the last bridesmaid to get in line, and Danielle gives me the stink-eye. It's not like I made them late or anything.

Everyone wants to dance on their way in, and I awkwardly shake it just to fit in. Being the only one not dancing sticks out more, ya know. Thankfully, we get food first, then the speeches start. I just have to make it through the cake cutting and the first dance. Everything is so perfect and I'm really happy for my brother. Knowing Danielle puts up with his lazy ass and makes him so happy changes my mind about her a little more. I want to like her. After all, someday she'll give birth to my nieces or nephews.

Once I can, I get up and go to the bar to order the "signature drink." It's something sweet and purple, and hardly tastes like alcohol.

This can be bad.

Erin and I talk for a while, then she and David hit the dance floor. I get a refill of my cocktail and look out at the happy couples holding each other close as they dance to Ed Sheeran's *Thinking Out Loud*. The alcohol makes me vulnerable, so what do I do? Keep drinking. Because I'm a champion like that. When my eyes mist over and I'm missing Ben so badly it hurts, I slip outside, walking past the smokers crowding around the door who are quickly inhaling their toxic fumes before someone from the venue sees them. This place is all non-smoking.

I walk to the edge of the covered vestibule and sit on a bench. It's raining, and dark. The lights in the parking lot are motion censored and no one has come or gone, probably due to the rain. Wind blows little misted droplets of water over my skin. I shiver and wrap my arms around myself and close my eyes.

I hate feeling sad. I hate feeling sorry for myself. But it's a phase, right? Something everyone goes through after a breakup. I'll get over it, I'll move on, and I'll find someone right for me. Maybe I should really look into online dating...

The rain comes down harder, falling in sheets and flooding the pavement. Thunder rolls over and lightning flashes in the distance. I shiver again and am about to stand and get up when a light turns on in the back of the parking lot. I stare at it, thinking it's odd that I didn't hear a car drive up. My mind flashes to *Supernatural* and *Doctor Who*, and I wish my life was exciting like that. No time for love or broken hearts. Just rocketing through life at a hundred miles an hour saving people, hunting things ... You get the idea.

I sigh and shake my head at myself. I need to be my own hero. Take matters into my own hands and find my own damn happiness. I had before. I can do it again. I turn to leave and a dark shadow catches my eye.

Okay, I really didn't mean what I just thought. I have no weapons to battle demons or Weeping Angels right now. Then I realize it's none of those. My mouth goes dry and my heart hammers. It's worse than fictional characters. Worse, because I have no idea what's going to happen.

My eyes are wide and time stands still as he walks through the parking lot, umbrella held close to his body but doing little good to keep the blowing rain away. He's just feet from me and I start to shake.

"Felicity," Ben says, air leaving his lungs in a whoosh. The umbrella goes slack in his hands when our eyes lock. He slows like he's shocked to see me, like he's not expecting to face the reality just yet either. He's yards away and suddenly I can't take it.

I run to him, rain rolling down my skin, heels splashing in puddles. He drops the umbrella and pulls me in, lips crushing against mine. He holds onto me like I'm the last woman in the world, like I'm the only one who can keep him together.

And I hold him even tighter.

"Ben," I whisper, cupping my hands around his face. "What … why…" I stumble over my words. "You're here."

"I'm so sorry," he says.

"No, don't be. I'm sorry. I didn't mean anything I said and I—"

He cuts me off with another kiss. He lifts me up and cradles my head into his face, kissing me as hard as he can. We break apart and move under the awning.

"I tried to call you," he says, taking both my hands in his.

"My phone," I start and realize I'm not even sure where it is. In the bridal sweet, I think.

"It's okay," he says. "I didn't expect you to answer."

I look at his handsome face, tears in my eyes. Was he really here? Did I imagine this, or maybe drink too much and pass out?

"Let's talk," Ben says and takes his jacket off, draping it around my shoulders. I pull it closed, scared talking might lead to a final goodbye. "I shouldn't have left like that and—"

"And I shouldn't have said those things," I interrupt. "I'm sorry, Ben. I'm so, so sorry."

"I know," he says and wraps an arm around me.

"I don't really think you're a man whore."

He chuckles. "Good. And I never got the wrong impression about you. I can't say I've never slept with someone after one date, but I've never felt so much passion for anyone before. You're all I wanted, all I could think about."

Past tense. Am I overanalyzing again? I close my eyes, pushing back tears. "That's how I feel about you, and it scared me. Because I didn't know why you'd feel the same about me. I'm not fancy or put together or on time for anything. I'm just a nerd. I'm not the kind of woman you deserve."

"I don't look at you and see a nerd or anything else. I look at you and see Felicity, a beautiful woman who isn't afraid to let others dictate her life." He puts his hand on the side of my cheek and tips my head up to him. "I don't understand why you think you're nothing special. I've never met anyone like you, and I don't think I ever will again. I don't want to lose you. I don't want a day to go by that I'm not kissing you, fucking you, waking up next to you and telling you I love you."

"You really do love me?"

"I do."

He kisses me, and warmth flows through my entire body. Everything disappears and it's just us, wind, rain, and storm swirling in the distance.

"Why?" I ask, needing to know.

Ben gives me his famous grin. "Isn't it obvious?"

I shake my head. "Not to me."

"You don't let anything stop you from doing what you love, from being who you are. You're unlike anyone I've ever met. There's so much to you, and it's complex and complicated in the best way possible. And isn't that what life is about? Coloring outside the lines. Pushing boundaries and testing limits. Not letting anything hold you back. That's exactly what you are, what you've made me do. You are my outside the lines. And I love you."

Tears prick the corners of my eyes. "I love you

291

too."

"I'm sorry I didn't call you back," he begins. "I listened to your message, and was going to, then Tuesday my dad fell."

"Fell?"

"He forgets he needs helps walking and gets up out of his wheelchair. He fell and hit his head on the corner of his nightstand. He was rushed to the hospital, and had to stay at the hospital until Wednesday night. I was there until he got let out, and the cell service in the hospital is horrible. I should have taken a minute to call you, I know. But then too much time passed and I thought I blew my chance."

"Your dad's okay?"

"He will be. He's bruised and sore, and has a few stitches. My mom was—well, still is—a mess though. The whole time I just wanted you there, even though I was pissed. Seeing my parents together, seeing my mom take care of my dad after all these years…it made me think. A lot. I know it's not easy taking care of him. I know my mom's life has been reduced to days and nights spend sitting in a chair in a nursing home next to a man who doesn't always remember her name. She doesn't have to do it, but she wants to."

I look into Ben's dark eyes, and he takes my hands. "That's what I want," he confesses. "Ultimately, that's what life is about, right? Finding someone who will take care you of, who will still love you, no matter how bad it gets. And I know we haven't been together that long, but I want that person to be you."

He brushes my wet hair out of my face. "I went to your house Thursday evening because I was scared if I called, you wouldn't answer. Because I didn't answer, like an asshole, and I'm sorry. I convinced myself it was over, but when I woke up today, I knew I couldn't let things end."

"I'm glad you didn't. I don't want them to end either."

"I don't know what the future holds for us, but I do know I don't want to think about it if you're not by my side."

He holds me against him, and I listen to his heart beating. Lightning flashes above us and we stay tangled together on the bench.

The wind and rain intensify and Ben holds me closer, then leans over to kiss me, not stopping until we both need air.

"Can we pretend this didn't happen?" I ask as I play with a button on Ben's shirt.

"That's fine with me," he says with a smile. "And to be clear, do you want to officially be my girlfriend?"

I'm smiling back. "Of course."

He brushes my hair back. "Good." He kisses me once more. "So is your sister-in-law going to freak out that you're dripping wet?"

"Nah, we already took the pictures. As far as I know, my job here is done."

"That's good to hear." He slides his hand down and grabs my ass. "Because I want to dance with you."

"That means I have to go back in looking like this."

"No it doesn't." He takes a step back, putting one hand on my waist. "You can hear the music."

"All I hear is rain."

He twirls me around. "That is the music. Dance with me, Felicity?"

My wet hair sticks to my face as I turn my head up. "Of course."

"I could get used to this view," Ben says, lazily pushing off the large porch swing on the back deck of one of my parent's cabins.

I sip my coffee, watching the sun come up over Lake Michigan. "It's easy to get used to. And even easier to miss."

We stayed at the wedding for a while after Ben showed up, then left so I could go home and change. It was cold being soaked with rain and in the air-conditioning. Plus, Ben and I had some passionate make-up sex to follow through with.

"Did you plan to come back here?"

I take another drink of coffee. After the sex, we stayed up talking, smoothing things out until we both felt better. What happened was the first fight, and we both agreed it wouldn't be our last. I don't want it to be our last. Because people fight, people get mad over stupid things, and people even say stupid things they don't mean.

But they make up.

Because that's what you do when you love someone.

"I don't really know," I confess. "I like Grand Rapids, and it's not so far I can't come back here. And I like to travel around. I guess when I imagine myself settling down to pop out a few babies, this town would be nice to call home. Maybe. I don't know. It's so far away."

I rest my head against Ben's muscular shoulder. The swing slows and Ben pushes his foot on the deck again, keeping us in motion.

"But then again, this is all I know as far as childhood," I say. "If that makes sense."

"It does," he says. "And I moved around so much it's hard imagining what it would be like to have stayed in one place."

I nod, thinking how difficult that would have been for me. "We got a few years before either of us need to worry," I say, then feel embarrassed. "And a few years before we decide if that worry is together or

295

not," I backpedal.

"Right," he says. "Not worried yet." We swing in silence, and I finish my coffee. I set the cup down and twist so I can wrap my arms around Ben. "Tired?" he asks.

"Yes. Want to go inside and lay down?"

"I do, but I don't want to move."

I softly laugh. "Same here."

A few minutes later, we get up and move inside and in bed. Ben's wearing boxers and nothing else, and I have on his T-shirt and undies. We snuggle close together, hearts beating in sync. I close my eyes, listening to his heart beating.

Everything is right in my world again.

I have what matters. Love. Someone who sees me for exactly who I am and accepts me fully. It hits me then, that this is what life is all about. Not letting anyone confine you, not limiting yourself to fit in. Being you, and being happy.

Living outside the lines.

Epilogue

Ben

A year later

Sunlight streams through the large windows in the kitchen, the ones that give a magnificent view of the water behind the house. There's hardly a cloud in the sky, and the day is already hot. It's going to be perfect for boating, perfect for going out to that little alcove, the spot that's become ours. I take my eyes away from the water and pick up my fork, stomach grumbling with hunger but nerves making it hard to eat.

"If you don't want the rest of your bacon, I'll eat it," Felicity says, eyeballing my plate.

I can't help but smile at her, moving my gaze to her face. We've been staying in Cabin 18 again, oversleeping and arriving late for breakfast at her parents again, like usual. Her hair is in a messy braid, her cheeks are slightly sunburned, and her sundress shows off her large tits that are hardly covered in a red and blue bikini top.

She's beautiful. She's the best thing that's ever happened to me, and today, I'm going to propose and make her mine for the rest of our lives.

If she says yes, that is.

I don't know why she wouldn't. We've talked about weddings and getting married and having kids.

297

We've even walked through jewelry stores, looking at rings so I would know what she likes. I combined a few of her favorites and came up with the design myself.

I hope she likes it.

"When have I ever not finished bacon?" I ask, raising and eyebrow.

"Hey, there's a first for everything," she says and cuts into her pancakes. "Still tired?" she asks, lowering her voice. "I mean, I know I wore you out and all last night…"

"I wore you out," I shoot back. "How many times did you come?"

She kicks me under the table. "Shush! My mom's right over there!"

I laugh and look behind me. Her mom is busy washing dishes, unable to hear us talking. Besides, I think I can say anything right now and she wouldn't care. Being old fashioned, I asked her parents' permission for their daughter's hand in marriage.

They gave me their blessing and her mom has been on the verge of ruining the surprise all weekend. And now I'm on the verge of asking her over pancakes, because I want to see that ring on her finger, I want her to know that she's the one, that I'm never going to let one day go by without her in my life.

I want her to know that I love her more than anything in the entire world.

And yeah, I want to make sure she says yes and feels the same. There's always a chance when it comes to her. Felicity is full of surprises, which is one of the many things I fucking love about her.

"Ready to get wet?" I ask when we finish eating. She gives me another shut-the-hell-up glare then wiggles her eyebrows and nods. Over a year of being together and the passionate sex hasn't slowed down. I hope it never does.

"On the water. What did you think I mean? You have such a dirty mind."

"Oh please, and you don't."

We put our dishes in the dishwasher, spend a few minutes talking with her mom. I cringe at how obvious she is, and feel relief when just the two of us finally go outside. The morning is spent riding the jet skis around on the water, not stopping until we're hungry and ready for lunch.

We've gone a few miles from the house, and dock the watercrafts at a lakeside restaurant and eat outside along the water. Then we ride around for another hour before going back to her parent's house to shower, change, and nap.

We spend the rest of the day on the beach, being lazy and just enjoying each other's company. Dinner is served late on purpose, and Felicity's mom asks her to stay inside and help clean up, giving me time to set stuff up by the water.

I move about frantically, getting the bonfire

299

started, and setting up the blankets, wine, and candles. When it's finally how I want it, I panic and realize I left the ring in my bag back in Cabin 18. I run like a lunatic up the boardwalk, grab it, and run back down before Felicity comes out. I'm panting and out of breath, but not from the short run.

My phone buzzes in my pocket. It's Felicity's mom, letting me know Felicity is on her way.

I swallow my pounding heart and wait, watching her dark figure draw closer and closer, until firelight flickers off her beautiful face. She slows as she draws near, taking everything in. She's smiling and looks slightly terrified at the same time. Not terrified of what's to come, but terrified she's getting it wrong.

"Ben?" she asks, voice shaking. "What is all this?"

I go to her, taking her hands and leading her closer to the water. I kiss her, drinking her in and pulling her to me. I can't help but get turned on the moment our lips touch and I feel her body against mine. I never want to let her go.

"Felicity," I start, keeping my hands on her. "From the moment I spilled coffee down your shirt, to us standing here right now, I knew we were meant to be. There is no one else I can imagine spending the rest of my life with—you forgave me for mixing up Star Wars and Star Trek, after all—and you've made me the happiest man in the world."

She has tears in her eyes and one hand over her mouth. I reach around and pull the box from my back pocket, dropping down to one knee.

"Will you marry me?"

Her head moves up and down, unable to speak. "Yes," she says softly as tears roll down her cheeks. I take her left hand and slip the ring on her finger. It's a perfect fit, thanks to Erin finding out her ring size. Speaking of, she should be arriving at the house soon. Everyone closest to Felicity was in on this in some way, and they are all coming to celebrate.

I stand and pull her to me, kissing her for a few minutes until she pulls away to look at her ring.

"It's beautiful!" she whispers, turning her hand so the firelight catches off the diamonds.

"I'm glad you think so. I came up with the design."

She looks at it a minute longer than kisses me again. "So it's beautiful and one of a kind."

"It is. Just like you."

About the Author

Emily Goodwin is the author of the twice banned dark romance, STAY, as well as over a dozen other titles. Emily writes all types of romance, from love stories set in the zombie apocalypse to contemporary romances taking place on a western horse ranch. Emily lives in Indiana with her husband, children, and many pets, including a German Shepherd named Vader. When she isn't writing, Emily can be found riding her horses, designing and making costumes, and sitting outside with a good book.

STALK ME

www.emilygoodwinbooks.com

www.facebook.com/emilygoodwinbooks

Instagram: authoremilygoodwin

Email: authoremilygoodwin@gmail.com

Made in the USA
Charleston, SC
28 August 2016